HUNDRED WATERS

By David Gregor:

Hundred Waters Volume Two in the "Mare's Nest Trilogy"

Variations On All The Perfect Things - Poems

In Different Times Volume One in the "Mare's Nest Trilogy."

In "X-Ray Magazine" Number Six, variant excerpt from *Hundred Waters*

HUNDRED WATERS

A Dangerous Journey
into the Heart of a Man

*With an introduction,
by James Tepiyac: A Participant*

~~David Gregor~~

[signature]

Puget Sound Press, Seattle
2001

HUNDRED WATERS

David Gregor

Published By:
Puget Sound Press
6523 California Ave., S.W.
PMB 292
Seattle, WA 98136-1833
http://www. pugetsoundpress.com
email: psp@pugetsoundpress.com

Copyright, 2001 by David Gregor

All rights reserved. Except for use in review, no part of this publication may be reproduced, stored or transmitted in any form, or by any means mechanical or electronic, photocopying, recording or otherwise, without the prior written permission of the author and publisher.

A portion of this book first appeared in slightly different form in *X-Ray Magazine*, Number Six.

ISBN: 0-9660092-9-0
Library of Congress Card Number: 00-108503

Cover design by: Dean Ingram
Cover Illustration: Kathy Wilburn
Original Illustration Concept: Andrea Freccia

Printed in the United States of America

1 2 3 4 5 6 7 8 9

For Victoria. Simply the best.

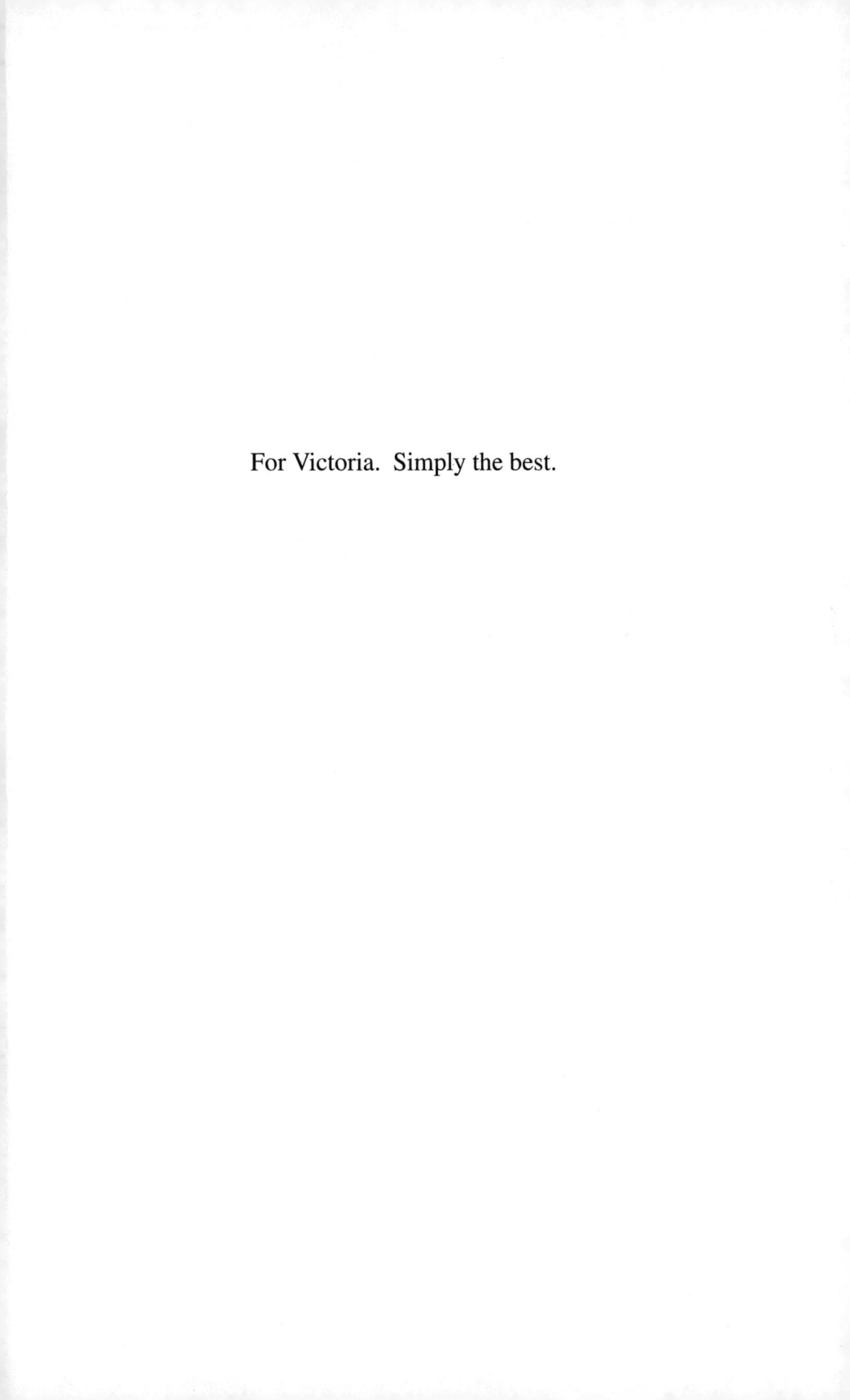

"If every generation is driven by an overriding attitude, then ours is the fear of not living."

Eddie Carr

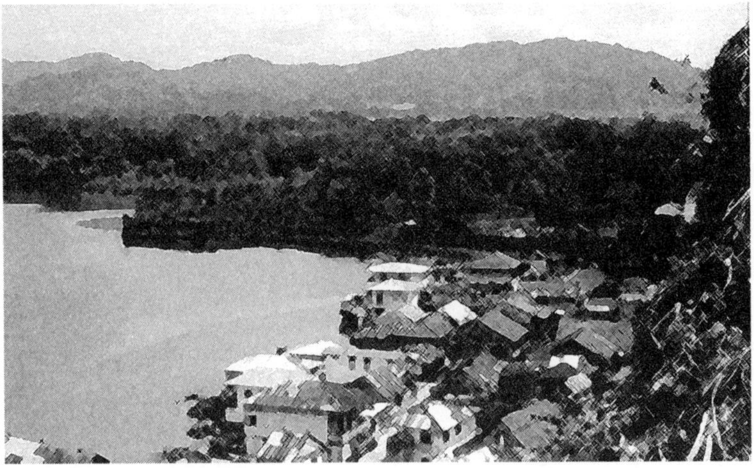

Introduction

In the fall of 1967 I, along with eight other fresh graduates of the Army Security Training Center at Fort Devins, Massachusetts, including my friend Eddie Carr, were assigned to the army listening post in the Canal Zone as our first duty assignment. We were in the army's information-gathering business, and our tour of duty in Panama was for eighteen months. Eddie and I were Morse code interceptors; others in our group were cryptographers, linguists and analysts. For most, Panama was considered lush duty compared to the Aleutians, Turkey or Southeast Asia, where hundred of U.S. soldiers were dying every week, including some in intelligence. But for my friend Eddie Carr, the assignment was from the outset both a disappointment and a turning point in his life.

Eddie never accepted the fact that he wasn't sent to the war. I, on the other hand, was not one to complain. Panama for me was a good assignment. I spoke Spanish and so did the Panamanians. I liked the warm climate, having grown up in south Texas, and was very happy I had not been shipped to Vietnam. I had no desire to spend time in a war zone. All I wanted to do was serve my four years in as safe

DAVID GREGOR

an environment as possible and get back home in one piece and get on with my real life. I had a beautiful fianceé (now my wife of twenty-eight years) waiting for me in San Antonio, and I was just looking for an uncomplicated stint in the army. My stay in Panama turned out to be anything but uncomplicated.

I was discharged from the army in 1971 and immediately returned to my hometown and married my high school sweetheart. After twice attempting college, I took a job with the Allied Universal Life Insurance Company and have been with the company ever since.

When I first met Eddie Carr, I still wanted to be a writer. First I wrote songs, which we used to sing around our bunks, then a few stories for magazines. Now I write insurance policies. I still write an occasional poem, but after my first daughter was born, I all but lost my drive to create with words. For twenty-eight years I had happily gone about my work and my quiet, though fulfilling, life in San Antonio. Then one afternoon in November 1998, I received a phone call from David Gregor who introduced himself as an old friend of Eddie Carr. He told me he was compiling a book based on Eddie's writings. He said he had been given access to a trunk full of documents that belonged to Eddie, and there were documents in it that referenced me. Mr. Gregor had located me from the return address on several letters I had written Eddie, and now he wanted to show me the material and get my recollections of the events described. I agreed to speak with him, and three weeks later David Gregor flew to San Antonio.

We spent three days going over my memories of Panama and several events that occurred during our tour in the Canal Zone. He helped jog my memory with some of the material in the footlocker he had gotten access to from Eddie's family. The locker, I was told, had suddenly arrived at Eddie's parents' home. There were still remnants of red sealing tape with the words *NSA SECURED* printed on it in bold, black print. But more prominent was the yellow tape that read: *DECLASSIFIED*.

The contents of the locker included short handwritten notes, a journal, reams of typed and handwritten pages, some of which appeared to be in crayon, and declassified military documents. There were also a lot of personal items: yellowed newspaper clippings, a passport, a Canal Zone driver's license, copies of army orders, a coaster from the Amigos Bar, notice of expired auto insurance, a matchbook from the Tivoli Guest House, a swizzle stick from the Red Coat Inn, a 1-inch roach and a color photo I remembered being taped inside of Eddie's locker of a pretty, young, blonde woman holding a small child. Eddie said he was engaged to the woman but never spoke of her or the child again, and I only asked once. There were various-sized black and white photographs of faces I had known and places we had been. Several items were stamped *CONFIDENTIAL*.

I had long ago forgotten smuggling paper in and out of the Fort Clayton Hospital for Eddie during those weeks after we returned from our search in the jungle for Harry Miles. Something or someone had really gotten to Eddie out there. He was under armed guard in the hospital and subjected to daily interrogations from our security officers. He kept asking for more paper, and I kept bringing it. Then Eddie would slip me fold sheets and tell me to put them in his footlocker.

While casually examining the material before me, a flood of memories about Panama, its jungles, the people and the hospital washed over me. I tried to put the writings into some kind of chronological order and then began to methodically read through the material. I was struck with how many things I never knew about Eddie, even though we were the best of friends, and how many more things I had never learned about that fateful trek we took into the jungle.

While this is not my story, I am involved and to some degree responsible for several events by virtue of my participation. Some of the critical events began before we ever arrived in Panama or I ever knew Eddie Carr or Harry Miles. But they came to fruition some fifteen months after our arrival, when Eddie and I tried to save Harry Miles from himself. Our success or failure in that endeavor is a matter of debate, even though the official army record is closed. To this day I am not perfectly clear myself as to the results. One truth is the National Security Agency did confiscate Eddie's blue metal footlocker and impound it for over twenty-five years. What is also certain is that I, Eddie Carr and a Panamanian national we knew as Bobdog went into the interior of Panama in search of a friend; when he was found, he was in a world that was not our own.

There is a note at the end of Eddie's account, which reads: *I have no recollection of ever writing these entries and cannot swear to their veracity, even though they appear to have been written in my hand. E.C.*

Nevertheless this account is real, and nothing has been made-up. I, for one, am not clever enough to fabricate a more fantastic story. As Eddie wrote on the back of a photograph of himself and Harry Miles: "*There is no need to lie or exaggerate. The truth is strong enough. Only memory need be feared.*"

After more than a quarter century, I have been forced back to a place of very strong memories—a place of change. Forced to remember Panama...to see it again, to feel once more

HUNDRED WATERS

something of the life we had there and to know for myself that parts of it were not just a dream or a wild imagining. It is important to know that it was real.

James Tepiyac
San Antonio, Texas
December 1999

HUNDRED WATERS

Editor's Note

What follows reflects what I have done with the contents of Eddie Carr's blue metal footlocker. I examined the notes, the sometimes-cryptic journal entries, army documents and newspaper clippings, as well as the extended narrative of events that Eddie had written. And with the help of James Tepiyac, I have tried to shape them into an accurate recording of the events. I was also given access to Eddie's letters to his parents which they had saved for nearly thirty years. I have added nothing to the text, nor have I rewritten any parts of Eddie's account. The headings of the different formats in which the material appeared have been regularized for clarity and continuity. The spelling and punctuation has been standardized. Dates of composition have been included, when noted, as well as the places composed when that information was provided. All ellipses are Eddie Carr's. The end result is a narrative of pieces, reflecting one man's encounter with the power of place and the uncertainties of self.

David Gregor
Seattle, Washington

North
W
E
S
Caribbean Sea
Porto Bello
Nombre de Dios
GOLD ROAD (Porto Bello Branch)
GOLD ROAD
Bay of the Mines
COLON
San Lorenzo (RUINS)
Chagres
New Chagres (NO TRACE)
Monkey Hill (Mount Hope Cemetery)
R. Chagres
R. Quebrancha
Sta. Rita
R. Grande
R. Claro
R. Gatun
R. Aguasuria
R. Boqueron
R. Pequeni
R. Chagres
CORDILLERA DE PACORA
Venta de Chagre
Gatun
Tiger Hill
Lion Hill
Buena Vista
Frijoles
Barbacoas
San Pablo
GORGONA TRAIL
R. Chilibre
Cruces
R. Obispo
GORGONA FORK
R. Pedro Miguel
Gorgona
Matachin
Obispo
Empire
R. Trinidad
R. Lagarto
R. Salud
R. Indios
R. Caño
Arraijan
Rio Grande
PANAMA
Chorrera
Pacora
Taboga
I. TABOGA
I. TABOGUILLA
I. CHAME
Capira
Chame
PLAYA CHAME
Bay of Panama

Part I

The Enchanted Circus

Prologue

[Handwritten Narrative. Composed in blue ink on unlined paper. Place of composition for this piece is noted as Seattle, and dated January, 1971.
(Note: Other pieces of the narrative, hereafter referred to as MANUSCRIPT, have been typewritten with different places of composition and earlier dates.)]

    My name is Eddie Carr, and this story begins with me. I arrived in Panama in November of 1967 from Fort Devins, Massachusetts where I had spent six months learning to translate the dits and dots of the Morse code into letters, numbers and international characters.
    I had an attitude about Panama from the start. I didn't want to be there. I wanted to be some place where something important was happening so I could do something important. I had spent my first nineteen years doing nothing important, and I wanted to change that. I wanted to do something big, something so big that the people back home would look at me differently. I wanted to be remembered, to standout, to find myself in something bigger than I had ever known. I was a soldier now, and the army, at least for the next three years, was my world—not the civilian life I had voluntarily left nine months before. If I were to experience "something

important" anytime soon, it would be in the realm of my military service. I had succeeded in avoiding the infantry, but by the time I passed my code exams and was ready to ship out, my perspective had changed. Part of that change came during a weekend pass in Boston in the summer of 1967.

It was a Saturday evening, about dusk, and I was walking alone in the section of downtown Boston called "the combat zone." At a street corner I stopped behind a girl—eighteen or nineteen—with long straight dark hair and tight-fitting bell-bottom pants, and waited for the light to change. Suddenly the girl turned and looked me over like she was sizing me for new clothes. I was flattered by her attention and got optimistic about my weekend.

"You in the army?" she asked, coolly.

She was cute with hair like Cher's. I smiled. "Yes, ma'am."

She leaned her head back and blew a mouthful of spit into my face. "You pig!" she said. "You baby killin' pig!"

I stood there shocked and dumbfounded. I had never killed anyone in my life. Her spittle quickly cooled on my face. Several older women walked by staring at me, like I had three eyes. I was mad and embarrassed. I immediately felt the meaning of "enemy country." Right then I wanted to get as far away from my country as possible. When it came time to request my first duty assignment in the fall of 1967, I was psychologically ready for deep change and made my three choices without reservations: The War, The War, The War.

* * *

This remembrance begins long before I arrived in Panama. It begins before I volunteered for the war, before I considered running away to Canada to avoid the draft, and long before I lost the one woman who had truly loved me. That tropical country was to be my incubator, the Panamanians my nourishment and the Panamanian jungles my nest. Out of them all I would either become or dissolve. But this account also begins long before me. It originates in history, which is the mother of us all, and from which none of us is very far removed. This story begins specifically in the history of Spanish exploration with those who came to this place, long before me, looking for their own land of desire.

* * *

[MANUSCRIPT section, titled "Historical Spine." Holographic text in Eddie Carr's hand. Ink. Dated August, 1969.]

During the Spanish conquest of the Americas, the Conquistadors built a trail across the isthmus of Panama out of ballast stones from sunken ships. The sole purpose of the stone road was to provide a route by which the gold and treasure found in the Americas could be transported from the Pacific terminus in Panama City through fifty miles of jungle to the village of Nombre de Dios on the Atlantic coast. There the gold was loaded onto galleons anchored in the sheltered bay and shipped to Spain. To transport this wealth through the jungle, slaves were brought in from Africa and the islands of the Antilles. The gold cargo was heavy, and there was extreme heat and disease. Those who faltered or collapsed were put to the whip or killed outright. Some slaves, still chained to one another, tried to escape into the jungle under the veil of night to reclaim their life in the wild. Most failed; a few succeeded. But for the Spanish there were always more slaves to replace those who escaped.

DAVID GREGOR

In May 1538, during one of many shipments, a group of slaves miles deep into the jungle refused to go on without rest and water. A confrontation ensued, followed by an insurrection during which a large group of shackled slaves escaped into the jungle. For delaying the convoy, the Spaniards took revenge on the others with whips, broadswords and lances until, according to one Spanish account, the stone trail was "awash with the blood of the dark ones." Too few slaves survived to continue the caravan, so army runners were sent back to Panama City for additional slaves, but the runners never made it out of the jungle alive. Neither did the contingent guarding that shipment of gold. Their bodies were later found either hacked to pieces, hanging from trees, or in piles of burnt flesh heaped over once large fires. That blooded place deep in the jungle along the Camino del Oro was thereafter in native lore called "The Place of Hundred Waters," the place of cleansing, because it was said that it would take the water of a hundred rivers to wash clean the blood of the slaves from the trail stones.

The Spaniards knew who was responsible for the massacre. The escaped slaves were thereafter called *Los Cimarrones*—the Untamed. The *Cimarrones* quickly started raiding mule trains, killing men and women, and carrying off children. The Viceroy of Panama eventually dispatched a special regiment to dispose of the *Cimarrones*. These soldiers were specially trained in jungle warfare tactics and wore the regimental insignia of a lizard on their helmets and breastplates. For several months the special regiment trampled through the jungle with only an occasional Indian prisoner for reward. Then one night while camped near a small Indian village on the Chagres River, the Spaniards were surrounded and attacked by a large party of *Cimarrones*. The Spanish jungle fighters were nearly decimated under the *Cimarrone*

HUNDRED WATERS

cry of *"Ahorca lagarto!"*—Hang the lizard! The expedition was abandoned, and the few soldiers who made it out of the jungle alive were sent back to Spain. Word quickly spread through the jungle and the Spanish settlements of the *Cimarrone* leader who adopted the name, and some accounts say the appearance, of the lizard etched into the breastplates of the defeated Spaniards. The village site of that battle was named Ahorca Lagarto and still carries the name today.

For the *Cimarrones*, the unmapped "Place of Hundred Waters" has remained to this day a sacred place of cleansing and great power. It is also said that to divulge its whereabouts or disclose the identity of any *Cimarrone* is punishable by death...or worse. There are those today who testify to the power and veracity of that threat. I am just one of many.

Edward Carr

Carr, MANUSCRIPT in author's hand. Titled "One year in country Anniversary. A remembrance."

    The blue Panamanian land crabs were more plentiful that year, and no one knew why. On that sweltering November morning in 1967, thousands of bright-blue crabs crawled up out of their holes in the immense mud flats that skirt the mouth of the Panama Canal, and within an hour the muddy shoals shimmered blue with the sea of crabs marching shoreward. The crabs moved en masse across the dirt road that served the waterfront, and they were crushed by the hundreds under trucks and heavy equipment. The dirt road for weeks was stained blue until the rains came, and the crushed shells disappeared in the mud. The road is still said to emanate a blue glow on exceptionally warm nights.
    There were also fewer golden frogs reported seen and even fewer captured, and no one from the *Compania Postal Nacionale* could find the square tree they had made famous in an old postcard. Shark sightings were at an all time high with two bathers still missing from a beach west of Rio Hato. There was also an increase in the number of political abductions and murders throughout the countryside, though many

DAVID GREGOR

of them were not reported in *La Prensa*. I knew that because at work we intercepted information like that on a nightly basis. It's what we did for the army.

November 1968 marked our anniversary. James Tepiyac, Harry Miles and I had been in country for one year with just six months to go. There was revolution in the air. You could smell the fear in the sweat of the whores in town.

* * *

Tepi and I were two of one hundred manual Morse interceptors who worked thirty positions in three eight-hour shifts. Each position was equipped with a radio receiver, a set of earphones, a typewriter, and an interceptor who monitored Morse code transmissions and translated the dits and dots into numbers and letters. Our mission was simple: TO KNOW! That included everything from civilian weather traffic to diplomatic messages from Cuba to Tierra del Fuego.

The man I had replaced the previous November, Tom Conklin, was the first American outside Bolivia to officially hear of Che Guevara's capture. Conklin had intercepted an unscheduled message from a small detachment of the Bolivian 8th Army in a remote part of northern Bolivia, and as usual, the information was immediately forwarded to the National Security Agency. Two days later this news item, which is still framed in our S-2 office for all new arrivals to see, appeared in the *Miami Herald*. It reads:

Miami, FL. Oct 9— On October 7, 1967, Cuban revolutionary Ernesto "Che" Guevara while leading a band of Communist guerrillas in Bolivia for almost a year was finally surrounded in the hills around Churo Ravine and captured by Bolivian militia. During a sporadic but intense skirmish, Guevara's small band of guerrillas reportedly separated into

HUNDRED WATERS

two groups, with Guevara remaining in the hills above Churo Ravine. Later that afternoon, Guevara and two other guerrillas were captured by the Bolivian militia. Guevara's rifle was reported to have been rendered useless by a bullet lodged in the barrel. Guevara and his two men were escorted under heavy guard to the small village of Higuera, two miles from Churo Ravine.

Yesterday, at approximately 1:45 P.M., one day after his capture, Che Guevara was pronounced dead from multiple gunshot wounds to the heart. The special militia unit of the Bolivian 8th Army was trained by the CIA at Fort Gulick in the Panama Canal Zone. The whereabouts of the second group of guerrillas, said to be led by one Inti Perez, was unknown by the Bolivian militia.

* * *

Tom Conklin had been lucky that way. He had kept several copies of the newspaper clipping so he would have something of history to show his kids. But his luck did not last. Tom Conklin died three weeks later on a picnic near Diablo Heights. He went into an uncontrollable fit, his female companion said, passed out and never woke up. The official cause of death was that his brain fried from overexposure to the sun. The rumor mill reported that when the autopsy was performed, the army medical examiner removed the head of a large iguana lizard from Conklin's throat. His female companion was never seen again. Another rumor claimed she was a Catholic Cardinal in Colon.

When I replaced Tom Conklin, I inherited his intercept "position" at work. I felt special—like I had been singled out by fate for important duty. But I later learned the position's specialness and availability was due to the fact that no one

DAVID GREGOR

else would take it, despite the fact that it had new equipment. The first night I reported for work, there was a piece of cardboard folded like a tent on Conklin's typewriter. It read: "CHE'S DEAD! TOM'S FRIED! AND YOU'RE NEXT, CHERRY. WELCOME TO THE ZONE!"

* * *

Carr, *JOURNAL*. Written in pencil. Dated March 20, 1969. There is a small drawing of a liquor bottle in the middle of a water ring at the bottom of the page with the word "rum" written on the bottle.

I was sent here with Army Security to listen, to eavesdrop, to report and compile, to electronically monitor the affairs of friend and foe. I found both. For fifteen months I was a denizen of dim light and dark flesh, and I've grown to need the smell of cheap perfume and 80-proof rum to endure long bouts of emptiness. The brick streets and plaster walls, covered with political posters like so many paper Band-aides, simmer with the heat of bodies past and present. Nothing leaves this place, everything stays if only as another. A French sailor's blue eyes now seen in a dirt-stained girl clutching the dress of her Chiriqui mother, brown and flat-nosed. A cobbled street near the fish market made of the ballast stones from an ancient Spanish galleon that died of a broken back. Footbridge mortar, old as the Spanish memories that laid it, powders to the touch at the jungle's edge and with it falls to the ground a moment's work in 1561.
    To breathe in deeply here is to risk becoming a host to history by filling your lungs with the past: the dusty remnants of a pirate's boot, the flakes of viscount bone scuffed up from the dirt. There is no escape from what has come

before. *Events happened and people lived and the shadows of both remain. Some of them you can see and touch. The smells of decay have not changed because they are constant here, only more so with the heat. They are reminders of all that is farther back, though not so far away. They are reminders of life. And so it is today.*

* * *

Carr, TAPE RECORDING. Sony 90-minute cassette. Seattle. Dated: January 1971.

I still have the pictures. I also have the photographs, and I look at them often to revisit old friends and to remember my fortune.

If it is true that we are shaped by the places where we've done time, then it is certain that Panama, with that dark-skinned woman, its sweet Jamaican rum, and its low threshold of joy, has embraced me as a blood relative.

Like the photographs, my old foldout army map is always there...worn at the folds and sweat-stained. Every time I look at it and recall each of the places marked with my penciled "X", I am taken back to those last turbulent months when everything changed—when the riots came, and Harry and I were lost to different callings.

* * *

Carr, MANUSCRIPT. Panama. 1969.

The first time I ever heard the name "*Los Cimarrones*" was about two weeks before I made the Homestead courier run that brought me back into the riots that changed our lives.

DAVID GREGOR

I had stayed in town all night, finally falling asleep in a place called La Mar Cantina in the old-town section of Panama. It was a workingman's bar, and that morning two sleeping whores anchored down either end of the long bar like a pair of fleshy bookends. Only one stirred when I was startled awake by a woman's scream from the street outside. It was early, a chill in the air, but there was a warm golden glow outside the bar. The woman's scream was followed by a rumbling of voices that sounded like a brawl. The bar owner drug his broom over to the swinging doors, and I awkwardly stepped past him out into the early morning light. I was quickly overwhelmed by the smell of dead fish, salt air and drying kelp. Already there was a large crowd gathered in the middle of the narrow cobbled street. Many of the older men were backing out of the growing crowd, their mouths covered with their hands, talking in loud whispers. Younger men pushed and pulled, trying to get inside the crowd where men and women and small boys were looking down at a dark object in the street. It was there, in the middle of the narrow street outside La Mar Cantina, that I first heard the name *"Cimarrones."* It was whispered just under the breath of the fishermen as though it were some secret password. At first I thought they were saying *"camarones,"* talking about a load of shrimp. I eased my way between several men in white t-shirts who smelled of fish and sweat, and immediately saw the upper half of a prostrate man. He was pretty good-sized, larger than the wiry fishermen hovering over him, and the name "shrimp" didn't fit. I moved in closer, admiring his tan linen suit, and then I saw his face. You never forget that look—the empty eyes. The man in his mid-forties was on his back, his left hand clutching his throat and his wide-open eyes so white, staring straight up to the sky, frozen still with their last image. His face had lost its color and there was a fat-bellied iguana lizard, about a foot long, stuffed lengthwise into his mouth. The lizard was also dead.

Later that night at work in the Operations Building, I read a news item in *La Prensa* with a photo of the man I had seen in the street. His name was given as Cardinal Paloma, a Panamanian Intelligence Minister known as a tough opponent of Indian anarchists in the interior. The preliminary cause of Paloma's death was called "suspiciously mysterious." The story did not mention any visible wounds, the lizard, or make any reference to *Los Cimarrones*, and I would not make a connection between the *Cimarrones* and my own life until that day in Ramon's jungle cabin when I saw Harry Miles covered in blood with a lizard hanging over his head.

But this is where it began, that sunny morning in old town, outside La Mar Cantina, with a dead man and a lizard stuck in his mouth. It's where every adventure begins—when things start going wrong.

* * *

I first met Harry Miles six months into my tour, the night I ran into Adolf Hitler on the airwaves. Harry was a Spanish linguist and cryptographer assigned to our shift straight out of school in Monterey. He and the other linguists worked in a large room down the hall from us behind a soundproof, fireproof door. All information behind those doors was handled on a "need-to-know" basis. If you didn't need the information for your job, you didn't know it. And for my first six months, I didn't even know Harry was on our shift.

Every Morse position had assigned missions: a military group, a diplomatic frequency, an outpost in Chile or a naval detachment. Each target and its frequency was laid out through your shift by the time they came on the air. On any given shift you might have twenty to thirty scheduled transmissions to monitor. After a while you got so you recognized the operators on the other end by the way they keyed their code: their speed, their delivery—either smooth or jerky—and even something of an electronic voice. In the dark world of radio waves, even the simplest electronic emissions took on an identity that crept into the lives of all but the dead.

The day shift was the busiest, graveyard the slowest. Weekends were quieter than weekdays and holidays near dead. That Sunday evening after I had finished copying a scheduled transmission, with an hour to kill before my next, I began searching the airwaves for unscheduled or new transmissions as we were instructed. Around 2:30 in the morning I rolled onto a faint, unknown signal. I listened for a moment to make sure it wasn't just weather traffic or junk shipping news. Once I felt sure it was good copy, I entered the time and frequency and began taking down the code. It was in plain-text Spanish, and while the transmission was badly garbled and broken up with static, I clearly got noticeable Spanish words intermixed with numbers that were not falling into any clear pattern. I quickly called for a linguist when I typed out the words "Hitler" and "submarine." Further on there were the word groups "heading north" and "coast of Venezuela."

Harry Miles arrived a few moments later clutching what before long I would affectionately refer to as his "Holmes" pipe, and he immediately tried piecing together the hodge-podge of broken text. Though I would find out later we were the same age, that night he had the unpretentious, unforced air of someone of much broader experience.

Harry Miles called for a DF shot once he saw enough text, but the signal began drifting before our "shooter" got a lock on it. A small group of co-workers gathered around my position to see what the fuss was all about but were quickly dispersed by our trick chief. Finally it was just me and Harry Miles, and I began sweating nervously. And instead of just focusing on the signals coming through the receiver and typing down what I heard, I started looking down at the words as I typed them and quickly lost my concentration. It was like I suddenly started watching my feet while walking and then abruptly found myself face down on the cement. I started getting only isolated words with the signal fading in and out. Then I lost the signal completely before we got its location. I tried finding the signal again, but it was gone. I looked up at Harry Miles as he stared at the broken text.

"Sorry," I said. "I've lost him."

"Just sign off with the time of last transmission which would be...zero two thirty-seven."

"What do you think it means?" I asked him.

"Hard to say," he replied, calmly drawing on his pipe.

"It did say 'Hitler' and something about a submarine, right?"

"Those words are certainly here in the text."

"So it could mean something then? Maybe something important."

"Like what?" he said.

"Like maybe he's still alive. Maybe he escaped. Maybe he's moving around on a submarine. Hell, I don't know. You're the guy from crypto."

Harry didn't say anything.

"Well?" I said.

"Well, what?" Harry calmly replied.

"Well, what do you think?"

Harry stepped in front of me, blocking my position from view of my trick sergeant at the head of the room. "You know," he said in a whisper, "if my superior saw me talking to you about this, he'd ask me if you had a 'need to know.'

And when it was determined that you didn't, they would write us both up. And neither of us wants the boys in S-2 poking around do we..." he looked at my name tag..."Carr?"

I reluctantly shook my head. Harry tore the script of the transmission from my typewriter and walked away.

I never heard anything more that night about the message after I turned it over to Harry and cryptography. It killed me not knowing what had ever come of that message or if there had been others like it before. I spent the rest of the night thinking about what Harry had said about superiors and S-2, and while I realized he was right, I wasn't sure if he was a smart-ass or honestly being protective.

Several nights later I ran into Harry at the coffee machine where I reintroduced myself and apologized for asking too many questions. He complimented me on my mustache which looked a lot like his, and he invited me to a private party he was having at a little place some friends had just rented back in the old part of Panama City. He started to walk away then came back and picked up a donut. "And off the record," he whispered, "that was the second message I've seen in six months naming Mister H."

Harry's declaration made me feel good inside, like I had just been made privy to something incredibly important. It had happened so matter-of-factly that within a few days the entire event seemed like a dream, like something that had happened to someone else. But as weeks passed, thanks to Harry, I retained a lingering sensation that I just may have wandered unexpectedly into some unknown crease in history.

* * *

HUNDRED WATERS

Carr, *JOURNAL*. February 16, 1969.

 After fifteen months in country, the one thing that remains predictable is the weather. Always there is the heat. Blistering heat in the dry season and when it isn't just hot, it is sweltry and wet. In the rainy season water either pours down in blinding sheets that quickly turn street gutters into small, rushing rivers or it drips on you like a heavy mist. For three months the rains come here everyday like clockwork between 1:00 and 2:00 p.m., so that even without a watch you know the time of day by the rains.
 The landscape tones are green on green into green so green that it's black like the faces of the ancients who have been here since the traders brought their ancestors here as cargo, to carry the wealth of the Spaniards across the green and shadowed trail called the Gold Road.
 Hot reflective heat of a thousand fires burns down on this elbow of primitive land with no sense of relief unless you're chest-deep in the Bay of Panama, the surf at Rio Hato or sitting on the sandy bottom off Taboga Island where Gauguin the painter once cooled himself while looking for his own paradise.
 The dusty green mold that powders everything not kept dry and warm can settle in your lungs and rot you from the inside out. Such a simple death. The moisture here creeps into everything save the most arid hearts of those who work the strip of bars that skirt the Zone.
 Fall and spring do not exist in this land of extremes. There is the rainy season and the dry. The wet and the hot. No gentle shift of mood to ease you through change. Change here is abrupt, often fatal. Hills rise straight up and drop straight down. In these tropics no life remains unchanged; even the slow moving four-foot iguanas, their dull green hide,

leather-hard and scaled, turn on one another when crowded, razor-sharp teeth locked in a mortal grip. There is no such thing as "harmless" here; everything has a cost, and everyone pays.

I remember that...I honestly do remember that....

* * *

Carr, MANUSCRIPT. March, 1969.

...I was sitting out a rainstorm in the Moza Cantina off Avenida Ramon, three days deep in rum and Coke. Something in the way the rain fell and blew in through the open window, misting my arm, reminded me of back home and the rain I swore I would never miss. I remember recalling something my father had said to me on the eve of my departure for the army.

It was over two years ago, February of 1967 to be exact. A foggy Northwest morning, frost on the grass, and my father—who was not a very talkative man—led me out into our small backyard where he had his miniature four-hole golf course. It's where he went to get away from us. He handed me the five-iron he kept just inside the fence gate. The steel head was rusted. "You shoot," he said, his breath turning to steam. I shot and hooked my ball off into the dead raspberry stalks. We played around the remaining three holes without much discussion, and when we finished the fourth hole, my father turned to me and said, "Whatever you do, don't volunteer. Do what you're told, keep your nose clean but never volunteer."

I remember that now...remember clearly....

...that I acknowledged his advice only out of courtesy, since I had already broken his cardinal rule by enlisting for four

HUNDRED WATERS

years in the Army Security Agency. I did that to avoid the infantry and getting shot at. As it turned out, I never did follow his advice. In boot camp I volunteered to be one of two company drummers for marching. I saw it as a way of standing apart from the mass of olive-drab boots with the collective name of Company H. I was no longer a number or just a face with a name. I was the pulse of the company. I also knew the bass drum was a much lighter load than my rifle and fifty-pound pack. As it turned out, I ended up carrying the bass drum in addition to my field gear. It got even worse whenever we were given the order to double-time, which happened frequently. On our first march out to the firing range overlooking the Pacific, our drill sergeant ordered us to double-time the last half mile through the Monterrey scrub. I almost immediately stepped in a chuck hole and rolled head over heels like a human wheel with that bass drum strapped tightly against my chest and my rifle and heavy pack slapping the back of my head like the fists of some vicious thug. I was too embarrassed then to remember my father's words.

But I remember them now....

Six months later after completing my training as a spy, I volunteered again, this time for my first duty assignment. For all three choices I wrote THE WAR. I was now inside what I had feared as a civilian, and I was no longer afraid. The time and duty would be the same wherever I was sent. I wanted the extra money from the Hazardous Duty Pay and to be a part of the Big Show. Incredible things happened in war zones, and there were important things to know there, things I wanted to know about myself. But in November of 1967, the army sent me to Panama for eighteen months.

I've been remembering that.....just remembering....and now....

DAVID GREGOR

...for fifteen Panamanian months I have waited for THE WAR, but the bastards did it to me again. Next stop—Thailand. I remember...

Never volunteer...I remember that....

...that was the last time I officially volunteered for anything. The next time I wanted something that strongly I just went off into the jungle after him. Instead of the WAR, I got what a Frenchman named Darnand called "a strange exodus into vicious disorder."

* * *

Five weeks after I arrived in country, I lost my soul. It was on my third night out in Panama City. I went with two guys on my trick to an off-limits whorehouse in the Las Minas suburb. It was my first visit to such a place, and I was both excited and wary. The building was divided into two large rooms. The front bar, which was open to the public, was filled mostly with pimps, cab drivers waiting for their fares, and old fishermen playing dominoes. The rear bar was off-limits to American servicemen. It was accessed through a door then a maze-like chamber that made three 90-degree turns and opened out into a barn-like room with tables, chairs and a loud jukebox. A wide, open, wooden staircase led to a dozen small rooms on the second floor.

Dozens of young women, mostly undressed, moved around the smoke-filled room bouncing from table to table and man to man. A few had on tight-fitting, short dresses that exposed their bare butts when they bent over, but most of the women roamed the room braless wearing only their panties.

When I walked through the maze entryway, designed to impede the MPs, and I saw bare-breasted young women walking nonchalantly around the large open room, I felt I

HUNDRED WATERS

had just stepped into my wildest erotic dream. Bare-skinned women were everywhere, sitting on guys' laps, descending naked in pairs down the staircase, crawling under tables, and being fondled openly at the bar. It was a room charged with fantasy and lust, and it seemed as if I had just been dropped inside Dante's skull midway into a wet dream. The only thing missing was fire, though the place was as hot and stuffy as an August bus with closed windows.

The three of us went to the bar and ordered beer. Immediately several half-naked young women approached us, smiling and asking for drinks. A woman with a patch over her left eye approached me and stuck her hand between my legs.

"I love American boys...I very horny," she said in one breath.

I turned to my friends and nervously laughed at her boldness. "Why aren't girls back home like this?"

"Then it wouldn't be back home."

The bare-breasted woman with the eye patch rubbed the inside of my leg and spoke to me like we had known each other for months. I pulled her hand away and shook my head. She was persistent. She lifted her dress, reached inside her panties, rubbed herself slowly and then extended her open hand and flexed it twice to indicate ten dollars. When I declined, she removed her false teeth, sucked her lips in and out and said, "Five dollars." I shook my head and drank. She laughed hard and loud, and slapped my shoulder. "You young boy," she said, laughing. "I have good thing for young boys." She flipped up the black patch over her left eye exposing a deeply indented cavity of badly scarred flesh and said, "You young boy...have this for three dollars!" I was too grossed out and then embarrassed to do anything but back away and shake my head. Even at the age of twenty, my small town life in the Northwest had not prepared me for this. But the sweet rum and the golden smoke combined with the sea of bare, brown flesh swirling through that off-limits back bar eventually got to me. And so did the one-eyed woman. That night I crossed a line and it would take over a year for me to get back. From that night on, all offers of affection were considered...with far too many sought and so little in return. But that night in Las Minas was satisfying, like I had just emerged from days in the desert without water and suddenly found myself at an oasis. I quickly found that level of life where the future is now and tomorrow doesn't exist, and it felt like home.

* * *

Carr, *JOURNAL*. October 19, 1968.

James Tepiyac is my closest friend. We've been friends since our code school days at Fort Devins. He quizzed me day and night, which is the only reason I passed my speed exams. He also taught me to play enough guitar to make him look better. He's from San Antonio, the home of the Alamo. That's all I know about his hometown. He says the river that runs through town is beautiful. I showed him a color postcard of Puget Sound winding around rugged islands and wooded peninsulas. He's engaged to a good-looking girl who manages a big restaurant. He gets new pictures of her all the time, and I'm dumbstruck with how pretty she is. I have one photograph of Sara and her baby, taped to the inside of my locker, that I show him. Sara looks very happy. I lied to Tepi and told him we're engaged. The truth is she's been married and widowed since that picture, but deep inside I believe I'll see her again. Tepi must think I'm a creep for spending so much time with whores if I'm engaged to Sara and there is a child involved. I want to tell Tepi that I wished her husband dead. He was shipped to the war just before I went off to Fort Devins. When Sara told me in a letter she had gotten married and where her husband was, I prayed that a VC bullet would find him. I wished it out of anger and the pain of having turned my back on Sara when we still loved each other. I'm not certain that I meant my prayer, but the next letter I got from her brought me the sad news of his death from enemy fire. Deep inside, I believe I'll be with Sara again. The honest truth is... everything here is a lie.

Part II

The Descent

Whoever fights monsters should see to it that in the process he does not become a monster. And when you look long into the abyss, the abyss also looks into you.

Fredrich Nietzche

Carr, *JOURNAL*. January 5, 1969. Hotel Chiva, Panama City.

Even now this room is ovenly hot from the morning's heat. A chicken carcass lies dormant on this table. His bony back flush against the Herald, his chest arched in silent prayer. But it's too late, too late for so many things...including me. This God-forsaken place has taken my scrawny ass, stretched me out across its urine-washed streets and eaten at my soul. God this place is lonely, like the heart of a whore. I need someone to talk to. A woman. I need to talk with a woman about anything but money. I need the comfort of a woman's voice to right me. I work...I sleep...I prowl, like a cat...day in and day out. I'm getting a bit worried. There are nights that I love it. Nights like tonight. I walk the dark streets alone looking for something of myself, and I always find someone else. Sometimes a memory. I loved a woman once, but I loved her too late or too little. I was unsure. There are so many things I want to be sure of now. This scrawny chicken barely eased my hunger, and I have not even moistened my taste buds on this cesspool I now love too much. Jesus...what has happened to me?

* * *

DAVID GREGOR

Carr, MANUSCRIPT. Typewritten. Panama, 1969.

My first night of night school at Canal Zone College turned out to be my last attempt in Panama to join the American institution. It was the second time I had started the bookkeeping class, trying to learn something that might be useful in the future, and I was determined to finish it this time. I was obsessed with doing something constructive with my last months in Panama. And nothing seemed more constructive or more sensible than understanding the recording of money transactions. The world would always need people who could keep track of money, and I wanted to be needed.

I was sitting in the back of the class when attendance was finally called, and one by one people responded when they heard their name. The instructor took a head count, checked his roster number, then after a moment scanning the faces in the room, he approached a young Panamanian woman two rows directly across from me. She wore a short black dress and a red sweater. I had noticed her when I came in. Her shiny black hair was pulled back and her skin was the color of rich cocoa. She had what looked like some sort of scar on the left side of her neck. When she looked over in my direction, she caught me staring at her, and I remember she was not smiling,

The instructor asked her to follow him outside, and when he returned a moment later, he came back alone. There were some speculative comments made around the room about the removed woman's livelihood and also her nationality, which some thought was the reason she was ejected from the class. The college was for U.S. citizens only, and I heard from those around me that almost every class had at least one illegal trying to sneak in.

HUNDRED WATERS

After class that night I asked the instructor about the young woman.

"It happens every quarter," he said. "Panamanian nationals try sneaking into classes by answering to the names of people who have signed up but are absent the first night. I feel badly for some of them. They really want to learn and get ahead, but our policy says 'no.' Hell, I'd feel slighted if I didn't have at least one per class."

Bookkeeping lost all of its attraction for me when I learned the Panamanian woman who did not smile would not be returning. Two weeks later I officially dropped the class. Accounting was clearly not the answer. I needed more than numbers in my life, so I forgot about accounting and turned my efforts toward *discovery*.

* * *

I finally made the last payment on a Pentax camera with a telephoto lens that I had been buying on layaway. Again I was determined to do something constructive. Almost immediately I set out to capture the ghosts I felt pulling me through each day. Tepi and I took day trips around the city and the Canal Zone, shooting black and white film like it was free. And when Tepi couldn't go out, I went alone.

I took pictures of Panama City from every conceivable vantage point, from high atop Ancon Hill, through Chiva bus windows and walking down narrow streets. I went out to Old Panama and photographed the ruins that Morgan the Pirate stomped through after sacking the city. When that didn't provide me any answers, I turned to infrared film for exotic help in penetrating the lush rolling landscape.

Infrared film was primarily used in surveillance to locate hot spots where live targets might be hidden from sight but detectable on this film because of the heat they produced. I was compelled to find whatever was out there for me to know, even if I couldn't see it. The film turned dark tree trunks and dark clumps of leaves into bright white poles with bright white bushy tops. It looked extremely wild, like a surreal dreamscape, with everything turned inside out and reversed. I paid close attention to those pictures, once they were developed, looking for what I was sure was an unseen answer to why I was here and not in the war, and even why I was forced to try to find this out with the help of a camera. I shot pictures of ships passing through the Pedro Miguel locks morning, noon and at night using long, timed exposures resulting in strange images of elongated, wavering streams of light cutting across the black night. I stared at those pictures like a scientist, in search of a direction, a connection, an answer to a question I could not clearly pose. But no matter how many pictures of buildings or ancient streets I took and no matter how many faces I captured in the film of chemical emulsion, there was still something concrete missing from the images. I took hundreds of photographs, and they still left me wanting. I could not find in them what I felt pulling me through my days, and I was desperate for a key.

    I gave the situation with the Panamanian woman in class no further attention until almost a month later when I woke up in the corner of a small, wood-slatted room after I tempted the gods of the dark streets.

INTELLIGENCE REPORT. USASA SOCOM. Fort Clayton.
REF: Spec. 4 Edward Carr
SUBJECT: Hundred Waters
SOURCE: Bicycle (prostitute)
TAPE RECORDING made May 17, 1969. Sony Cassette. Transcribed by Spec. 5th class Anthony Wise

QUESTION: [An 8x10 b & w photograph of Specialist Edward Carr is shown to the interviewee] Is this the American you know as Eddie Carr?
BICYCLE: Oh sure...How I know him. I know him three, maybe four times.
QUESTION: And the woman called Bobdog?
BICYCLE: Sure. I know her too. Four months maybe.
QUESTION: What do you know about Bobdog and Eddie Carr?
BICYCLE: They lovers.
QUESTION: What else?
BICYCLE: He did not always pay money, so do not you think that. Not like in the beginning when someone comes to bar and wants someone and he pays the bar and then pays the girl so he can have her. Sure he paid Bobdog money, at

beginning. He paid everybody. Even me. (Laughter) At beginning she need his money. Just business. Who knows if they have love for someone later, so you get money and when you find something about love later it's okay. No more money like when you pay in the bar. With Bobdog, she had affection for this one Eddie.

QUESTION: Did they talk?
BICYCLE: Sure. They talk all the time.
QUESTION: Did you ever hear them talk about the army or any military subjects?
BICYCLE: Eddie said he need more money. (Laughter) No money in army for good time. (More laughter)
QUESTION: When and where did you first see Bobdog and Eddie Carr together?
BICYCLE: I will think. (Long pause) It was the Red Coat Bar where I first see *"bigotito."* That is the name I have for Eddie when I see him. He have mustaches, like this around his mouth, like a bandito. I don't like *bigotes*. Tickle my leg. (Laughter) Bobdog like his mustaches quickly. I think maybe he is like the men back in her village, only Anglo.
QUESTION: So that's where they first met. In the Red C o a t ?
BICYCLE: *Si*. Bobdog she new to Panama City, only four...maybe five months from Colon and Nombre de Dios. Eddie, he quiet, you know...not loud like the others. No smile so much. Bobdog quiet too. It was not so easy for her to go with strangers. I think she scared that first time with Eddie. But I remember

HUNDRED WATERS

	what owner of the Bar Red Coat tell me, so I tell Bobdog. I tell Bobdog smile much and cross your legs many times. I tell Bobdog her legs are "aces" and I say to her, cross them slowly many times and smile. So she smiled much.
QUESTION:	So did you ever hear Eddie talk about army matters with Bobdog?
BICYCLE:	No.
QUESTION:	Are you sure. They never discussed Eddie's work?
BICYCLE:	G.I.'s come to Red Coat to relax...have good time. They come to ride Bicycle. (Laughter)
QUESTION:	Is it safe to say you heard *every* conversation Eddie Carr and the woman called Bobdog may have had in the Red Coat?
BICYCLE:	I don't understand.
QUESTION:	Did you hear *everything* Eddie and the prostitute Bobdog may have said in the bar?
BICYCLE:	No...no...never!
QUESTION:	So it is possible Eddie Carr may have discussed military subjects with this Bobdog woman in the Red Coat Bar even when you were in the bar?
BICYCLE:	(A short hesitation) *Si. Es posible.*
QUESTION:	So is your statement that you cannot be certain that Eddie Carr never discussed his work or anything to do with military affairs with the prostitute called Bobdog?
BICYCLE:	*Si, señor.* I am not certain.
QUESTION:	And this is your sworn statement before God?
BICYCLE:	*Si señor.* I swear on the *Christo Negro.*

(End of Interview)

Carr, *NOTE*. Holographic text written on both sides of a brown paper bag in ink. Ellipses are the author's. Dated "Wednesday Morning—Late."

This can't be the end. This can't be all there is to it. I sense there is more. There must be more, I can feel it. To die in this humid cesspool so far from home...so far from anyone I truly care about...to die here...like this...would be a sin. And for what? The night. The late night when you are closer to your own thoughts and your deepest fears. Why is it that the night oppresses? It's the darkness of the night. The darkness and the light tropic air filled with the smell of sour citrus...of lemons...of oranges, the smell of gray water baking off the narrow night street. The smell of coconut milk and urine, the reek of wet dog hair after a squall. The dark brings them all out and brings them closer...closer to the narrow streets. These streets where the buildings crowd up next to the wet pavement littered with waste, buildings that rise high enough to shade the sidewalk at noon but at night those buildings with their wrought-iron balconies bring life closer to the street. The whores hang over the iron railings and watch and laugh and giggle. Some even call down:

"Hey G.I. You want woman? Hey you, pretty boy, you want some...?" When you look up she lifts her skirt and

spreads her secrets before you. But it is dark, and your head is full of rum, that devil sweet rum again, and only your numb head responds. You can always buy that, you tell yourself. Anytime, anywhere. It's the power of money, the power of the night. What you really want is somewhere else out there in the dark. But it's as empty as these late night streets. As empty as the Locos Bar, where Bicycle can usually be found...early in the morning...in the far corner of the white-tiled barroom. But even she is gone. And when Bicycle is gone the world is a darker place. That's how late it is. So late that the young boy who sells meat-on-a-stick from his brazier on the street outside the Buffalo Cantina is gone. When it's this late and the air is filled with only the remnants of promise, you want to fill yourself and the meat-on-a-stick fills your stomach for awhile, but the boy is not there in the street. A peek in through the swinging doors of the Buffalo Cantina offers one plump whore with a nasty mouth, in a red-sequined dress; she turns...waves...and her smile exposes a dark gap in her teeth. Your heart wasn't in it anyway.

I'm in love, I tell myself. In love with a memory. I'm in love with what should be inside me. I can still remember when I loved a woman and when she loved me, and I can still remember its fullness. I'm in love inside; in memory love lingers. For love to linger still only serves to tell me that this is not all there is. There is something more...something deeper...something more important than this darkness. But why is the dark so feared? Perhaps it is feared because everything exists in the dark. Yes, perhaps.

Carr, MANUSCRIPT. Dated: Panama, 1969. Titled "The Night and All That Crawls In It."

    The end did truly begin that sunny morning in old town, outside La Mar Cantina, when things started going wrong. Cardinal Paloma lay dead in the street with an iguana stuffed in his mouth, and the day before I had learned for the second time I was not going to the war. My next assignment was Thailand, and I felt betrayed. I had been in country over a year, with four months to go, and I was in no shape to stay longer. While every bar held unlimited opportunities, right then La Mar Cantina was my only hope. I went back inside the cantina and bought another drink.

    The two whores, who had been asleep on the bar before the ruckus outside, stumbled back inside rubbing the sun out of their eyes. One of them chattered on and on about the body while the other nodded and fanned herself with a newspaper. For the second time I had asked for the war, and twice I was denied. All I had to show for my request was a lie. The whole damn thing was a lie. They didn't want volunteers. They wanted the reluctant, the fearful, those who wanted no part of the war. I didn't really want the war; I wanted the experience that it brought. I wanted the force of life that only the threat of death could provide. Some fat cat must've figured out that anybody who volunteered for the war was in it for themselves, not the team effort, and he was probably right. Everything boils down to the self; everything about us grows out of our self. I had no self and I knew I needed one badly. But the lies were stacking up on themselves, and people were getting buried under them. The more time I spent thinking about missing out, the more I hated the lie and everything that went with it.

* * *

That morning in old town life suddenly got more intense...or maybe fragile is the word. Perhaps it was just me, and had nothing to do with a virus at all. Maybe it was desperation that hit me, the way the chills struck me on my way to work the following night. Maybe I had lost more than I thought on those streets. The army had warned us when we first arrived about getting too close to local nationals. We had TOP SECRET clearances, worked with sensitive material, and there were people who wanted to know what we knew. Hell, after fourteen months in that sweat hole, they could have had what I knew—whoever *they* were. I was so far removed from the decencies of life that I was becoming dangerously attached to the night and all that crawls in it. I clearly preferred the night to daylight. The night is where possibility lived in Panama, but what I saw that morning outside La Mar Cantina altered things. I was desperate to get a grip on myself. Three nights later I fell out of love with the night.

* * *

It was one of our few nights off, and I had been drinking with Tepi in the Buffalo Cantina for hours, playing stud poker with several of the whores who were having a slow night. Public gambling for money was illegal, so we played for cigarettes. But not even the gaming helped. The cheap rum was watered, and I was sure the girl called Daisy was cheating, but I didn't care enough to cause a scene. Tepi finally called it quits about midnight, but I stayed in town because I loved the Buffalo at night. You could spit on the sawdust floor and the jukebox had Deep Purple. The women who came there late at night were some of the least attractive in the city, but the later it got and the more you drank, the better looking they got and the less you cared. Besides they were always friendly to me. And sometimes when I got lucky, usually toward the end of the month, somebody would take me home with them, through the dark streets, just for company and a bowl of chicken and rice.

But you could get lost in the Buffalo or the Amigos, the Tropics or the Red Coat, and I often did. For me the Buffalo was a good place to disappear. The girls loved it when you were something else, someone bigger than life. Big Jim, Spike, Bones, Suavecito. The girls in the Buffalo loved big things: big stories, big lies, big fights, big bodies in the dark. It made me wonder about the rest of their lives. So on a good Buffalo night, if the girls found someone big, so much larger than anything real, they were very happy. If not...well, that's the way it was, the night I fell out of love with the night. The rum failed me, so did the cards, the jokes and the grab-assing. The women did not care, the bartender probably spit on my nationality every night after I left, and my kidneys hurt. It had been over a year since I had spoken to a woman socially where the subject of money wasn't being negotiated. I realized in the middle of a winning hand that night that all I had in my life was what I had walked through the swinging doors with, and it didn't seem enough. After fifteen months there was not enough of me left to make anyone's life better, including my own. I had run out of joy. The last thing I remember of the Buffalo that night was leaving the girls and the poker game without a word and walking out into the night streets alone. I walked past an open cafe where skinny men sat at counter stools eating *menudo*, the smell almost nauseating me. I passed a store with several radios playing, moving farther into the city with fewer lights, fewer people on the streets, fewer sounds and stronger smells. I had no idea where I was, but I didn't really care—the cool, night air felt good on my face and it got cooler the farther into the night I walked.

    I walked deep into the dark night until there were no more bars or bright lights or people passing me on the street. Then I passed what appeared to be a walkway off the main street, and I could hear sounds way back off the street and see flickering light. Something about the shadows, slowly moving in the hazy light, drew me in. I crept down the narrow walkway and there were small balconies up above on either side. Faint voices echoed overhead. Up ahead, above the street level, I could see yellow-lighted windows like eyes in the night, occasionally darkened by figures moving behind them. Look for yourself.

***

Exhibit 5. PHOTOGRAPH. 8 x 10. b&w Pencil caption in Carr's hand on reverse side, "B.J. Alley, with sound," followed by holographic text. Dated: February 25, 1969.

*   Dark, narrow walkway between two wood-frame buildings. The alley leads back into a courtyard surrounded*

by balconies overhead. A cul-de-sac, black and dark with faint glimmers of yellow light through gauzy windows. There are dark figures standing, undulating and dark figures kneeling...swaying time...before them...large shadows sway against the lighted walls, human forms cross the yellow lights, like tree limbs moving before a lighted window. Large figures. There are painful sounds. Ugly cries. A head cocks at the sound of the new visitor. Silhouettes quickly fill the empty doorways...feminine voices call out from the shadows, and the stink of foul water fills my nose. These are the mothers of other men...the daughters of good mothers...good sisters lost in the dark. Suddenly the rancid smell of life worn thin is feathered by the raucous howls of struggling flesh. A man yells out like a burned child. Someone is gasping like they are chasing their last breath. A dark figure emerges from the shadows and calls my name..."Hey G.I..." The touch of a firm hand moves along my arm...up my thigh...then clutches my groin firmly like a bunch of grapes. The shadow guides me farther into the dark, and in that dim place shadows dance above me as if to mock my very existence.

***

Carr MANUSCRIPT. Typewritten.

When I woke up, I was wrapped in a patchwork blanket on the floor in the corner of a bare room with wood-slat walls. The sun streaked across the floor. Harry Miles was sitting bare-chested at a table reading a newspaper. Water was running in another room. The place smelled of Harry's pipe smoke...like cherries.

"How do you feel?" he asked.

"Where are we?" I said, standing then sitting down on the bed.

"Above Delgado Street."

"Your place?"

"Belongs to a friend. Do you know where I found you last night?"

"I remember an alley...."

"You were wandering around a pretty dangerous neighborhood."

"And you brought me here?"

"Let's just say, some friends came across you before harm did."

I laid down on the bed and out of the corner of my eye I saw the naked body of a dark-haired woman walk across the room. The picture made no sense, and I felt like dying.

Exhibit 6. A Large Color POSTCARD of the Panama Canal at Night. Size 5 x 9. Written in Carr's hand in pencil is "TOCUMEN AIRPORT, PANAMA," followed by :

"Every life is a series of deaths." I read that somewhere. Maybe I just thought someone else said that. I didn't read that anywhere. Why not "Every death is a series of lives." I didn't read that anywhere either. If there is one thought that could act as the spine of my life here, it might be "Every life is a series of lives." What life am I living today?

* * *

Carr, *JOURNAL*. May 7, 1969. Small drawing at top of page of a skull open at top with words flying out.

How is it possible to bring order out of memory? There are a hundred places to start because there are a hundred names and a hundred places and a hundred smells and faces to remember because each one of them is a clue. The high heels in the Zona Rosa, the wiggle of the whore named Bicycle, the Pedro Miguel Locks at midnight, the beauty of Taboga Island, the shimmering sea of blue crabs, gutter stench, the bloody hue of the Chagres River, the whiteness of the Amigos Bar, the civility of the Tivoli Guest House, Harry

DAVID GREGOR

Miles, Nombre de Dios and a hundred others locked into my memory. They are not just random people or places. They are connective tissue...points of departure. They have given and they have taken. But where does one begin?

Choose ONE to begin with—not because it is more significant than any of the others, but because it is now facing me from this notebook, the place where all this is logged. This is just as good a place to begin as any. I am, after all, no painter. Painters create. This is memory. A return. And the easiest way to pry open the doors of memory is with a name. A name like...Bobdog.

Carr, MANUSCRIPT. Handwritten in both pen and pencil. There are two moisture rings on the first page and what appears to be an ash burn near the lower right hand corner. There is the title, "A New Stage Under Favorable Signs" written boldly across the top of the first page. Next to the title is a drawing of what appears to be a crudely sketched skeleton on a cross.

   That afternoon after I lost my love of the night, I woke up again later in that small bare room, this time under the wood-frame bed. The first thing I saw was the cream-colored spine of a book. The U.S. Government AREA HANDBOOK FOR PANAMA. I pulled myself out from under the bed dragging along the handbook and sat upright again in the corner of the empty room. I tried unsuccessfully to rub some clarity into my aching eyes. There were dry, red flakes on my right hand along with a soreness and a scabbed-over wound on the inside of my thumb. I had no memory of my hand getting hurt or how I ended up under the bed. There were sounds of muffled voices next door and car horns down below on the street. I couldn't bring myself to look outside or even open the window for air; I had seen enough of Panama City for one day, and my head would not stop hurting. I noticed immediately that

Harry Miles was no longer sitting at the small wooden table. There was no smell of pipe tobacco. Perhaps I had just imagined him. I glanced quickly at my watch. It was 11:20 A.M. I laid my head in my hands and pressed my fingers against my throbbing eyes. It relieved the pain just long enough for me to fall asleep where I sat...in the corner of the room.

When I woke up I was in bed, covered with a sheet, and I smelled coffee brewing. A door off of the main room was closed, and I could hear a shower running. The room was bright with sunlight but the flat gray walls still looked as depressing as they did when I had crawled out from under the bed. The bed felt good, though. I pulled the sheet up over my face. I did not want to move. The handbook I had opened my eyes to underneath the bed was now laying under the covers next to my leg. It was worn and stained, and I could see that several pages were dog-eared. I lay there under the sun-brightened sheet wondering to myself what had gone wrong, why I was in that shabby room feeling so empty inside.

I remembered my walk into the late night, stumbling into the alley with all those shadowed bodies and the sounds that came out of the dark, and just remembering sent a shiver through me.

The water shut off behind the door, and a few moments later a woman came into the room wearing only a pair of white panties. Her breasts bounced like small cups of Jello as she toweled her hair.

"So you live now," she said. Her face was familiar. I tried to picture the bar I knew her from, but nothing registered, yet I knew I knew that face. There was an intensity in her eyes that was not common among most Panamanians I had seen. It was as though she had seen more than her eyes could hide.

"Harry had to go," she said.

"Who are you?" I asked.

HUNDRED WATERS

She stepped in front of the small wall mirror and brushed her hair. "I am called Bobbie. And you are Eddie, no?"

"Are we engaged?"

"Engaged?" she said.

"A joke. I was making a joke."

"Harry said you are a good man, so I trust you with my room."

"Well...I trust you with mine," I said. "Are you going somewhere?"

"To Colon."

"What time is it?"

"Late," she said. "I will be back tomorrow. You can stay, but you must do me some favor."

She was still standing at the mirror wearing only her white panties.

"What is the favor?"

She handed me an envelope with money in it. "Give this to the señora when she arrives. It is due this day."

I pinched the envelope until I saw a thick wad of paper money then laid it on the night table. I propped my head against the wall.

"Don't try funny business with my money," she said. "I know who you are, and I have a knife."

"And good morning to you too. You some kind of tough cop?

"Huh!" she said.

"Tell me, how do you know Harry?"

"Harry is friend of some friends." Bobbie finished buttoning her blouse and tucked it inside her pleated skirt. She looked like she was going to school or off to a job at a bank.

"He said he found you outside the Alley. Harry is good friend. It is not so safe to be alone in the Alley." She reached over and turned off her hot plate. "This coffee is finished. Fix for yourself. I can't miss my train."

She knelt across the bed and grabbed her garter belt and nylons and slipped them on from the end of the bed.

"You lucky," she said. "Some times dead bodies are found near the Alley."

"Sometimes they are found in the streets of the old part of town."

She had her hair pulled up on top of her head with a rubber band, and from where I sat, I saw dark markings on the side of her neck that looked like ink lines. I moved closer to get a better look, and Bobbie quickly whirled around and slid off the end of the bed.

"No monkey business," she said.

"I was just looking at those marks on your neck."

"It's nothing." She pulled off the rubber band, and her hair dropped down around her neck. "Do not forget the envelope for the señora. I work at the Red Coat. Maybe you come and buy me a drink sometime."

"Do you go to school?" I asked.

"Don't be silly." With that she slipped out the door and pulled it closed behind her.

I reached across the night stand for a cigarette, and before I got it lit the door opened and Bobbie stood staring down at me.

"I go to work in two days, so don't come in sooner." She winked and closed the door.

The sudden quiet was relaxing. I stared around the wood-slatted room and wondered how I ended up in the room of a skinny whore I didn't know who trusted me with about $100 of her money. I picked up the envelope again, checked the wad of bills then laid it down on the night stand. I lit the cigarette and grabbed the area handbook from the bed. The

HUNDRED WATERS

name "J. Murdock, USAF June 67" was inked across the front cover. The spine of the book was broken so that when I opened the book, it fell open almost in half at a section of glossy photographs and reproductions of old maps. I pulled open the fold-out map attached to the right-hand page and gently smoothed it out.

I loved maps. I loved the lines, the names, the connections rivers had with places, the altitudes of mountains. I especially liked the legend explaining which symbols represented which natural formations. I liked to study the symbols: lines with crosses for railways, dark dots for major towns, small dots for villages, upright crosses for churches and so on. I scanned the length and width of the country, the coastal island groups—the Pearl Islands and the San Blas Archipelago—the southern Darien jungle Balboa had crossed, and the patchwork design of the narrow isthmus that followed the canal. I was following the dot/dash line of the Canal Zone border and the Panamanian Railroad line which nearly paralleled each other when my eyes caught a broken diagonal line that headed off into the great unmarked area away from the populated Canal Zone. I checked the legend to see what a single, broken line of dashes represented and found out it marked a trail. I turned the map sideways, looking for an identifying name, and found "Las Cruces Trail."

I crawled out of bed carrying the open book to the hot plate, and I poured myself a cup of coffee. I draped the bed sheet around me and sat down at the table where I had seen Harry reading the newspaper and picked up on the trail. I followed the trail due north across the lower end of Madden Lake then even farther north, deeper into what was clearly uninhabited jungle, until the broken line split off like a "Y" in two directions: the left arm went to a place on the Caribbean marked "Porto Bello" while the right arm traveled north to the coast and a place marked "Nombre de Dios." I went back to where I first caught sight of the trail and followed the broken line south until I found a place on the southern bank of the Chagres River called "Las Cruces." Next to the name was a small "X." I turned to the legend at the bottom of the map: "X..........ruins." I sat up straight in the chair like I had pinched a nerve. The word "ruins" had a magical look to it. Someplace important had been remembered on a contemporary map, and someone knew enough about the place to note it was in ruin but apparently still visible. The word "ruins" spelled mystery, and I wanted to know more. I got up and poured myself another cup of coffee, and with the area handbook laid out before me, I spent the rest of the morning reading up on the mystery surrounding the village and the trail called "Las Cruces."

Carr, *JOURNAL*. May 8, 1969. A b&w 3x5 photograph of a young woman naked to the waist is stapled to the page. The staple has rusted, leaving a brown metallic stain.

Her bar name was Bobbie but I loved her longer as "Bobdog." She was medium height—about an inch shorter than me—and skinny with shoulder-length dark hair that bounced like a spring when she moved. Her face was cute like a little girl's, with a small nose, soft-looking eyes, rounded cheeks. Her cocoa brown skin was mottled with faint splotches of discoloration that made her look older than twenty. The first time I saw the discoloration from a distance it just looked like a variation in skin pigmentation, but up close the splotches were a series of small round scars, like she had been infected with some childhood skin disease. I later found out they were tribal tattoos she had received as a young girl. The childhood tattoos had long lost their initial designs and now just looked like tiny raised scars. In the early morning light following our first night together, I caught myself staring at the marks before Bobdog was awake, wondering what they meant. I tried to find the original design in them without asking her, but nothing I saw made any sense. A snake...headless woman...broken cross. My imagination was stronger than the images were clear. Even that made perfect sense.

Carr, MANUSCRIPT. Typewritten. The margins are filled with pencil sketches of a woman. The title: "There was a Loneliness" is written in red ink across the top of the first page.

By the time I met Bobdog, I had wrung my insides dry for the last remnants of female affection known to me. Now I was empty. I had dipped into the well for the last time and pulled up dust. There was a loneliness that came from the absence of a woman in my life, and it grew deeper and more overpowering the longer I was without someone. No amount of rum or gold smoke filled the hole, and when the effects wore off, I was still alone and empty. All I wanted was someone to love, the way you loved a woman back home, without a passing thought of buying her. But I found out that in Panama I didn't have enough money for my needs—I could no longer afford love.

* * *

Exhibit 6. PHOTOGRAPH, 5x7. b&w Photo subject is that of the Panamanian national known as Bobdog. Ink text written on back of photograph is in Carr's hand.

DAVID GREGOR

I am thinking back on that evening in the Red Coat Inn when I first saw Bobdog at work. She was sitting off in the corner and her red dress blended in with the red felt wallpaper. I remember the yellow table light. She was alone and the dark shadows that played over her face did not make her particularly inviting, at least from my distance. I had lost much of my interest in bar life and honestly didn't pay that close attention to her.

* * *

Carr, MANUSCRIPT.

"She is new," the bartender said. I had gotten to know him over the months I had been going there. "Perhaps you should speak with her."

"I've had my fill of bar women." It had gotten so that the mere thought of a whore made me count to myself the 151 days I had left in Panama. But all that did was remind me just how much longer I had to go.

I kept glancing at her in the mirror behind the bar, watching her sit there at her table quietly, waiting, and repeatedly crossing her long, slender legs. They looked familiar but I apparently had blocked out everything else about her. She occasionally spoke to a passing GI but never propositioned. She didn't strike me as all that aggressive, and I guess that's why she didn't register as the same woman whose room I had woken up in. I got the immediate impression that working the bars wasn't her real line of work. She didn't seem at all comfortable.

"Señor Eddie," the bartender said. "I think that one is for you."

For me, I thought. The only thing for me in this country is 151 days.

HUNDRED WATERS

"I can't afford someone for me," I said.

"I am sure she is clean, Señor Eddie."

"It's not her health I'm worried about. Fill this up," I said and slid my glass across the bar. "The cost of companionship is too high."

Carr, MANUSCRIPT. Handwritten with the title, "Where the Red Door Peels." There are four drawings of doors above the title: three are closed and one is open.

The first time I paid to take Bobdog out of a bar was almost two weeks after I woke up under her bed following my visit to the Alley. I stopped at the Red Coat Inn for a quick drink before heading for the cheap bars back in the barrio when I saw her sitting alone. She looked up at me with marginal interest, then looked again when she remembered my face. It took me a moment to recognize her also, but once my eyes adjusted to the dim red lighting, I saw the striking profile I had seen that morning in her room. It was also a profile I had seen somewhere else, but I couldn't put my finger on where or when. When my drink arrived I walked down the bar and stood next to Bobdog.

"Hello Mr. Eddie with the large mustache."

"You remember," I said.

"I trusted you with my money. I remember."

"I suppose I should be impressed."

"I saw you here a week ago. You looked at my legs, but you did nothing. Something wrong with my legs?"

"Can I buy you a drink?"

"Not necessary," she whispered. "It's only tea."

I ordered another drink for myself. "How was your trip to Colon?"

She looked at me like I had just spoken Chinese.

"When I first met you," I said, "you were on your way to Colon."

"You remember that?"

"I also remember you walking around your room half naked."

"You did not look so good to remember anything. You look better tonight."

"I don't know about better."

"Oh yes, I think better." She lowered her eyes and then looked up at me with a smile. "I will drink now."

Later that night, she took me up to her room above Delgado Street. Although I had been there once before, I barely recognized it. There were no numbers or letters on the doors. Bobdog's door was covered with flat red paint peeling from all the edges. All the other doors on the floor were painted different colors—yellow, blue, magenta. There was something unusually appealing about a color address, like there were no preconceived limits with numbers and letters. Anything was possible, and in Bobdog's case, everything was likely.

The room behind the red door was small and claustrophobic with gray unfinished wood-slat walls. A bare light bulb hung down from the ceiling on a long black cord and the naked light it produced made the room at night feel ugly...exposed, and much too harsh on the emotions. There were no pictures to take you elsewhere or drapes covering the gaps in the window casing. A stained yellow shade muted the flashing red neon sign outside the one window that faced over the street. The only other color came from the six or seven dresses that hung on hangers from wall nails, like so many ghostly figures detached from life. Her metal bed creaked and squealed at the slightest movement. My pillow

HUNDRED WATERS

smelled of Vitalis and spicy sweat. The walls were paper thin, and nothing we would say or do that night would ever be a secret.

Across from the metal bed was a wood nightstand with a mirror, water stained from the humidity. Next to the window there was a small round table with two worn chairs. Near the door a sink hung on the wall above a chipped white and blue enamel douche pot. The small bathroom, with the pull-chain toilet, was just off the large main room.

She told me she took the name Bobbie from a photograph of a young American girl she saw in a *Life* magazine. She had seen the magazine when she first came to Panama City from her small village on the Atlantic side. The girl in the magazine picture was pretty, she said, and the name Bobbie was similar to her own family name—Bobadilla. The night I first heard her real name, I had been drinking and heard it as Bobdog, and that's what I called her from then on. I loved that name, and I would come to love her more than she would ever know.

The two most personal objects I noticed that first night in her room hung above the bed: a large cross made out of bound thatched grass and right next to it, a plaster of Paris coat of arms. The plaster was nicked, and the gold paint covering most of the emblem was worn and chipped. When I asked Bobdog about the plaster coat of arms, she said she was royal.

I didn't exactly laugh; it was more of an internal chuckle. "You mean royalty?"

"Yes, royal," she said proudly, as if that were enough.

"You mean like royalty royal?"

"Yes, but old," she said.

"Now it's old royalty. Like from the House of Whores?" I burst out laughing.

"You pay me now."

"Now wait," I said. "I want to know if I'm really sleeping with royalty."

She unhooked her bra and threw it over the back of a chair. Her small brown breasts, the size of halved coconuts, stood erect. "What you look at?" she said.

"Royalty I'm told. Maybe *old* royalty."

"*Correcto!*"

I smiled and shook my head. "Like maybe the Duchess of Whoredom?"

I laughed again.

"Don't be stupid," she said. "You pay me now before we play."

I took a ten and a fiver from my wallet and handed them to her. She slipped the money into her purse, then peeled off her panties.

"Old like what?" I asked.

"Spanish old," she said.

"Like old Spanish royalty?"

"The Spanish who came here for gold. Old Spanish."

"That old. So how do you know...you're royalty? I mean coming from a small village like you do."

"It is known in my family. In my name. My family name Bobadilla comes from a white woman."

"Now you're white royalty. This is getting interesting."

"Her husband was very, very important when the Spanish came here."

"You and a white woman are related? A white woman of royalty?"

"Her name was Doña Isabel de Bobadilla. My family name Bobadilla is from her."

"So how does this Spanish woman's name make you royal?"

Bobdog stood naked before me, her hands on her hips.

HUNDRED WATERS

"Names are power, and my people had no names here."

I propped myself up on my elbow. "What do you mean your people had no names? What people?"

"People brought here by the Spanish. Those with no names...those who carried the Spanish gold."

"Now we've got nameless people and white women of royalty and a girl from the jungle."

"My people were slaves. When they escaped, they had no names. So they took names that have strength so they could be strong and survive."

"And you are from these nameless people?"

"Bobadilla is a strong name, with much power. And I have that name."

"And who are these people of yours?"

Bobdog stood defiantly at the edge of the bed. "Those without masters."

"Like revolutionaries?"

"No, those who live apart."

"On the edge."

"I don't know. Maybe."

"You're kind of out there yourself," I said. "I like that. I like a whore who'll stand before you buck naked and swear she's a queen. That takes some pretty hard bark. I christen you Bobdog, queen of the wild frontier."

She did not laugh. She nonchalantly dipped two fingers into a jar of Vaseline she pulled from under the bed, lubricated herself, then slipped under the sheet. I slid in next to her, still smiling. As I started touching her, she leaned up onto her elbow and stared at me. The young girl in her was more visible at that close a distance, and I leaned forward to kiss her but she pressed her hand against my chest.

"Tell me...Mr. Eddie mustache...what is this wild frontier?"

Carr, *JOURNAL*. Hotel Chiva, Delgado Street. Dated: January 3, 1969.

I feel better today...not sure why. I spent another night with Bobdog, and she can lift my spirits. She told me things about her past. Maybe that's the answer. The past...or maybe just hearing something new. I asked her about her name again, and she said it was an English bastardization. What isn't around here? This whole place is a bastardization. She said her family name was Bobadilla, named after the first Spanish woman in the Americas. I thought if only that woman could see her namesake now. I asked again about the lizard tattoo on her shoulder, but again nothing. There's something she's hiding about it. Makes me even more curious. I want to know what she wants to hide. There is great power in secrets...great power in the past. I sense I am on a collision course with both. I'll need all the strength I can get.

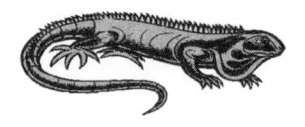

PHOTOGRAPH. 8x10, b&w An affixed label carries the I.D. number EC-0145 along with "Fort Clayton Photo Lab" stamped on the back side. "Approaching Taboga Island" is also written on the back in ink, in Carr's hand. Attached to the photograph are two sheets of lined paper, each folded once in half, holographic text on both sides.

I remember very well taking this picture. The three of them are standing against the rail of the Taboga ferry that ran the twelve miles between Panama City and Taboga Island. In the picture, Harry Miles is flanked by Tepi on one side and Bobdog on the other. Harry looks like a scholar with his pipe and mustache. But he also has the rugged handsomeness that would have allowed him to work as a wilderness outfitter. Bobdog is smiling through thick strands of black hair frozen across her face. Both Harry and Bobdog are so at ease, they look like they could be a couple with a dark past. Just looking at her and the mystery in her eyes reminds me why I was attracted to her and how much I came to care for her. It also reminds me how strongly I kept her out of my life. I remember too clearly the sweaty nights in her room in the Hotel Chiva and the scent of the coconut oil she rubbed on her skin. Just thinking about those smells together makes me thirsty for rum. It is the power of this silver image to rekindle both love and pain. Even now I wonder about Bobdog and what became of her small boy she so badly wanted me to be a father for. There is also a place in me that will not allow me to dwell on that question. Knowing why makes it even harder to pierce the emotional membrane that has grown over that truth, like so much scar tissue.

Tepi is looking straight-faced into the camera like some frightened immigrant fresh off the boat from the old world. His large ears prominent. His eyes always were his strength; they carried his morality like badges pinned to his face. I can see now why I needed Tepi in my life. His allegiance to an ideal was enviable. He honored his fiancée back home and the pledge they had made before he left the country. He was for me what a cane is for a blind man. But the day this picture was taken, like so many days, I rested the direction of my life on the fickle whims of the anonymous.

Just over Bobdog's left shoulder, about 25 yards out, there is a dark object cutting a narrow froth line in the water. A moment after the picture was taken, someone on our side of the ferry cried "shark," which was followed by a series of gasps and shrieks that can only be elicited by that creature's name.

This is one of my favorite pictures. It is an image of apparent carefree happiness. None of us could have ever imagined that bright sunny day on the ferry to Taboga just how desperate that trip would turn. God, we were so very young that day.

TOURIST BROCHURE. Single sheet, 8 1/2 x 11, folded once lengthwise. Six color photographs with text and captions.

Taboga Island. The garden spot of Panama lies just twelve miles offshore from downtown Panama City. It is a major weekend destination for local residents and tourists alike because of its cleanliness, white sandy beaches and its simple beauty. The water is clear and warm and full of colorful sea life which is perfect for snorkeling. There are comfortable accommodations with all the modern conveniences. Ask one of the island's professional guides for a trip to the Caves of Wonder and the Shark Museum.

* * *

Selected transcript of follow-up interview with James Tepiyac, Specialist 4th Class. Tape recording with title notation "Sworn Statement, recorded May 9, 1969 at SOUTHCOM HEADQUARTERS, Fort Clayton, Canal Zone. Subject: Personality Profile. RE: Edward Carr, Specialist 4th Class."

It was a Tuesday I believe. The three of us guys were on a one day break, and we decided to go out to Taboga Island. By going on a weekday, we missed the weekend crowd of tourists and pretty much had the beaches to ourselves. We stayed in the hotel just off the beach there at Taboga Bay that had once been the old Panama Canal Commission Sanitarium. The room was small, basic and inexpensive. But just fine for us.

That afternoon the three of us and Bobdog [*the female Panamanian national (transcriber's note)*] were stretched out on the beach, drinking...umm...rum. You know, since we were off duty...and listening to Harry Miles' portable radio when Eddie suddenly got up and walked out into the water. Harry, Bobdog and I paid little attention. We were just trying to relax in the sun.

The tide was coming in, but the sand causeway connecting Taboga Island and the small rocky island just off shore was still passable, so you could walk from the beach out across the narrow channel. It's fun to follow the dips and mounds of the sandy bottom to the smaller island. Some places dip and rise a couple of feet, in others it's more. Makes the trek out and back interesting.

So Eddie walked quite a ways out onto the flooded sandbar. When I looked up and saw him, one minute he was dipping down to his trunks then the next he was climbing up so that just his feet were covered by water. He continued out along the sandy ridge for about another five yards in what was only about two feet of water. You can look on either side of the narrow sandbar and see where the bottom drops away. The bar is three to five feet wide, and standing on it some thirty feet out from the beach gave the illusion that Eddie was walking on water.

Then out of the blue, in the middle of the sand spit, Eddie suddenly just sat down. He had his back to us, and he was just staring out into the ocean. It looked like he was just sitting on top of the water.

I asked Bobdog, "Is there anything wrong with Eddie?"

HUNDRED WATERS

She shook her head and said she didn't think so.

Harry Miles said, "Maybe he just feels like sitting in the ocean."

* * *

Excerpt of a LETTER from Eddie Carr to his father Joseph. Written in Eddie's hand in ink on US ARMY SECURITY AGENCY letterhead and dated December 1968.

...There was something very appealing about sitting out in the ocean so removed from the world around me. I tried to imagine myself living there forever, but I couldn't think what I would do. But the water felt good like bathtub water, and the air smelled fresh and clean. Very different from the streets of Panama City. For a moment I felt too alive. Then the sand under my butt squirmed and I jumped straight up. An eight-inch crab came up out of the sand and squirted out between my legs. Scared me half to death. I hate those creatures. They're so primitive looking. About a year ago we had a mass migration of blue land crabs out of the canal mud flats that was totally eerie. Maybe it was that movie "The Vikings" I saw as a kid where this Viking was captured and tied to a stake on this beach at low tide and when the tide came in, hordes of crabs came with it and ate the guy alive.

* * *

I saw Eddie jump straight up out of the water and for a moment I thought he'd become possessed. Then he reached down into the water and withdrew something dark with legs. Eddie tried throwing it toward us like a discus, but instead of flying to the beach the object sailed off to the seaward side of the sand spit and plopped into deeper water. It was then that

I saw the dark, sail-shaped fin cut through the water a couple of hundred feet from Eddie. It was an unmistakable shape. Eddie was still looking out where the crab had splashed down when I started yelling and waving my arms. Eddie cupped his ear toward me, and I pointed out to the water. At first he didn't see the fin, but a moment later he saw it slicing a path toward the narrow channel.

* * *

Paragraph 3 excerpt from the above letter to Joseph Carr.

My first thought was get back, but then I froze. Then I remembered about noise and splashing in the water and how it was supposed to attract sharks. I kept my eyes on the shark, and the longer I watched it, the closer it came. Then I heard a voice.

* * *

Harry Miles jumped up and ran to the edge of the water. "I would move quickly and quietly out of the water," Harry yelled.

Eddie looked over at him then back out to the water.

Harry said, "Eddie, if you wait much longer...."

Eddie stood frozen...paralyzed. "What if I just stay?" he yelled.

"Eddie," Harry yelled, "don't move Eddie. He's too close. Just stand still."

Eddie stood still in water about thigh deep. Bobdog was screaming hysterically. We watched the fin slice through the water, zig-zagging in quick, sharp turns that still had the shark about fifty yards away from Eddie but getting closer.

* * *

HUNDRED WATERS

Paragraph 4 from letter.

I felt my knees lock and my heart was beating like I had a drum in my chest. I had no voice, just words in my head. I remember the fear. Every time the shark made a quick move in my direction, I braced myself. Then when the fin moved outward momentarily or out toward the tiny island, I felt my insides relax. I saw my friend Harry Miles waving at me to hold still.

* * *

"Eddie," Harry yelled. "Eddie, just disappear."
Eddie looked back at us, and I could see the fear in his body. It was like he was at attention. Harry gestured for him stay still. Bobdog was still screaming and crying at the same time. Then Eddie stunned us.

* * *

Paragraph 5 from letter.

I slowly sat down on the sandy bar. Don't ask me why. But the water was warm under my chin. I remember thinking small and wondering for just a moment if I had the guts to challenge this creature to this piece of the ocean. Something inside me felt defiant or maybe stupid. But I didn't want to give in.

* * *

"What are you doing?" Harry yelled.
Eddie kept his eyes on the shark fin still about fifty yards away, and when it approached the sand bar, the shark turned toward Eddie and moved along the bar.

* * *

DAVID GREGOR

Paragraph 6 from letter.

When it turned in my direction again I thought for sure he was after me. That he'd smelled me or seen me. It was the second most helpless time in my life.

* * *

Eddie started to get up when the shark darted away and headed out to deeper water. But he sat back down when it turned again...now about thirty yards away, moving parallel to Eddie.

* * *

Paragraph 8 from letter.

My heart was racing and for the first time I felt I may have stayed too long. I couldn't move. Inside I think I just gave up. The shark was going to get me. I just stayed sitting in the water...frozen.

* * *

"Don't panic," Harry yelled. "Stay still, don't move."
Eddie didn't move.

* * *

Paragraph 9 from letter.

The shark moved closer, and silently I told it to go away. Go the other way, just get away. It turned, darted and then swung back circling about twenty yards out. Finally it seemed to lock onto the line of the sandy causeway and swam straight for me. I watched until it got too close, then closed my eyes and dug my fingers into the sand, too scared to look.

HUNDRED WATERS

I felt a wave of water wash over my body, and then I heard the cries and calls from behind me. When I finally opened my eyes, the sun seemed even more intense than before, and then off to the left out of the corner of my eye, I saw the dark sail-shaped fin slicing back out in the direction that I had first seen it...out into open water.

* * *

Harry and I went running out to Eddie and lifted him up from behind by the arms and drug him to the beach..

"You're a crazy sonofabitch," I told him.

"You did good," Harry said. "Took a lot of guts."

"Hell," I said. "Pure stupidity."

* * *

Paragraph 10 from letter.

I couldn't speak, Dad. For a moment out there I felt there was a purpose to me staying in the water with that shark. Some personal thing...head to head. Hard to explain, really...like something to prove. I know that sounds stupid, but it's the truth. The good thing is I came out of it okay...or maybe I just came out of it. Who knows what okay is? I know I don't anymore. I did feel relieved but exhausted, and after I got up on my feet, just a little fearless. But don't tell Mom about the shark. She'll just get upset and start worrying about things we have no control over. I know that now.

Your son, Eddie

Part III

The Past Will Set You Free

Carr, MANUSCRIPT. Typewritten on Fort Clayton stationary. There are several drawings of palm trees and banana plants scattered throughout the text. These copied pages are titled, "A History."

The village of Las Cruces sprang up in the early 1530's around Venta Cruz (the Inn of the Cross) which was built as a rest station along the Highway of Gold. The place was thereafter marked on engineer's maps with a cross. The volume of gold crisscrossing the isthmus was so large that more efficient means of transportation were needed. A town, followed by a military garrison, grew up around the new inn, complete with a monastery and several defensive forts facing the Chagres River.

Las Cruces, because it was of higher elevation than the coastal towns and therefore cooler in temperature, quickly became a popular resort for fine Spanish ladies seeking a respite from Panama's sweltering heat.

During the rainy season, wooden boats were loaded with gold and treasures from Peru and floated down to the mouth of the Chagres River. From there the boatmen followed the jagged coastline to the harbor at Nombre de Dios where their cargo was transferred to galleons and shipped back to Spain. For three hundred years Las Cruces was the most important inland city in Panama. The commerce through

DAVID GREGOR

the town's vaults and warehouses was so lucrative that the King of Spain sold the concession to them for ten thousand pesos a year.

From **"Panama: It's History with Spain." NY: 1927. Page 32.**

Carr, *JOURNAL*. December 17, 1968. Written in ink on one side of the page.

Reading up on the history of this place has changed my life. As soon as I read about the gold that moved across this scrawny little country, I got the fever. The day Tompkins showed me pieces of gold coins he had found out on a jungle trail, I wanted some. I want a treasure. I want to find whatever is buried out there. Now I know exactly how gold hunters in California and the Klondike felt. I've got it. It is a fever. Just seeing those coins of Tompkins' has set off a fire inside me. I need to go out there. I need to look. I need to find some of this for myself. I've never wanted anything this bad before. Hard to explain what the gold means. What it will give you. But it's more than its monetary value. I know how the Spaniards must've felt when they first saw the Indians with gold and why they built churches with it. God is gold. They wanted it, and nothing would stop them. It's out there in the jungle waiting to be found, and I want some.

TRANSCRIPT of recorded follow-up interview with James Tepiyac. S-2 offices, Fort Clayton. Dated: May 10th, 1969. Labeled, "Las Cruces."

S-2:	Specialist Tepiyac, today we're going to focus only on your trip to the ruins of Las Cruces. We're not interested in what you came to know after the trip. Do you understand?
TEPIYAC:	Yes, sir.
S-2:	I want you to think back, and tell us exactly what Specialist Carr's interests were in this place.
TEPIYAC:	All Eddie said was he wanted to hike into the jungle and look for this old village.
S-2:	And that was Las Cruces?
TEPIYAC:	Yes, sir.
S-2:	What did you know of this place called Las Cruces?
TEPIYAC:	Nothing sir. I'd never heard of the place. Eddie said he'd found it on some old maps. He said he had read that a lot of old Spanish gold had gone through the place and he wanted to see if we could find something.
S-2:	Something?
TEPIYAC:	Yes, sir. You know...like some old coins or something.

S-2:	Any mention of any Indian groups?
TEPIYAC:	In what way, sir?
S-2:	Had Carr ever spoken of knowing any members of a group called *Cimarrones*?
TEPIYAC:	Not to me.
S-2:	So Carr never mentioned that his reason for wanting to make this trip into the jungle had anything to do with any group called *Cimarrones*?
TEPIYAC:	No, sir. Just looking for old coins and stuff.
S-2:	How about Harry Miles? What was his purpose for going on this trip?
TEPIYAC:	Just for fun. That's my understanding. He was a friend. And he had a van and lots of outdoor equipment. Besides, once he heard Eddie talk about the gold, he wanted to go.
S-2:	Did Miles say why the thought of gold made him want to go?
TEPIYAC:	I can only guess that it was for the same reason as Eddie and myself. Because it would be cool to find Spanish gold in the ruins of an old Spanish village in the middle of the jungle. Just sort of...an adventure, I guess. It was the most exciting thing I'd done after a year in country, sir.
S-2:	No mention of any Indian groups or leftist organizations?
TEPIYAC:	No, sir.
S-2	Subversives who might need money?
TEPIYAC:	No, sir.
S-2:	No group seeking sensitive information?
TEPIYAC:	No, sir.
S-2:	And this prostitute woman named...Bobdog. She was not part of this trip?

TEPIYAC: No, sir. (Laughter) Just us three guys on a day hike. You wouldn't take a whore on something like that.

S-2: So what exactly was your plan?

TEPIYAC: Just to hike to the old site of this town, Las Cruces. Eddie had done all the research. He had some good maps and had figured how far Las Cruces was from the trail head at the highway. He said it was a day trip easily. He asked me and Harry Miles to go, and we said yes. That's all. Did we do anything wrong, sir?

S-2: No other plans?

TEPIYAC: Well...like I said before, there was this mention of gold. Another guy from our unit...Tompkins...had found some old coins a week or so before we went out. So we knew it was possible. Harry was game just for the fun of the experience. That's the way Harry was. He just liked the outdoors. He seemed to know his way around the woods and was real good with survival stuff.

S-2: Survival stuff?

TEPIYAC: Like plants you could eat and where to find water. He did that a couple times that trip. I always felt safe with Harry around...like nothing bad would happen to us.

S-2: Were you expecting trouble?

TEPIYAC: Not especially. But you never know in wild places. Just whatever might be in the jungle.

S-2: Do you recall if Harry Miles or Eddie Carr had mentioned the possibility of danger from someone in the jungle. Perhaps because they knew things you didn't know?

TEPIYAC:	No, sir. Neither of them said anything about dangerous people. I just meant that there are natural things that live in the jungle that can be a danger. Like animals...snakes, bugs, lizards. Or you can get lost. Stuff like that, sir.
S-2:	You mention lizards. Anybody specifically mention lizards to you?
TEPIYAC:	In what way, sir?
S-2:	In any way, soldier.
TEPIYAC:	I just knew there were lizards in the jungle. That's all.
S-2:	Maybe Eddie knew the area.
TEPIYAC:	Just from the maps.
S-2:	Maybe Harry Miles knew some people who lived in the region and could count on their assistance if anything ever happened.
TEPIYAC:	Like what, sir?
S-2:	A rendezvous, perhaps....that maybe got discovered.
TEPIYAC:	I don't know anything about any rendezvous, sir. In fact I don't know who Harry Miles knew or didn't know. He's a pretty likeable guy. Like I said, he knew things about the jungle, like getting water out of this plant shaped like an ice-cream cone. And this root he pulled up tasted like licorice. I was amazed with what he knew.
S-2:	Did he ever say how he knew about those things. Maybe someone had taught him things. Is this possible?
TEPIYAC:	Like who, sir?
S-2:	People he might have known in the jungle.
TEPIYAC:	I don't know where he learned what he knew.

HUNDRED WATERS

	I was just impressed with what he knew. So was Eddie. Eddie told me he thought Harry was the smartest guy he knew. Eddie admired Harry. You could tell Eddie wanted to be like him.
S-2:	Like Harry Miles?
TEPIYAC:	Yes, sir.
S-2:	Did Miles have influence over Carr?
TEPIYAC:	I wouldn't say influence. I never saw Harry make Eddie do anything, if that's what you mean.
S-2:	So what exactly was Carr's relationship with Miles?
TEPIYAC:	Eddie told me he was impressed with what Harry knew and what he could do.
S-2:	So your testimony is that Harry Miles never mentioned any groups or native tribes by name that he knew or had any contact with, in or out of the jungle? Is that your testimony?
TEPIYAC:	Yes, sir.
S-2:	And is it your sworn testimony that Edward Carr had no known contact with any Panamanian groups or Indian tribes in relation to this trip to the ruins of Las Cruces? Is that your testimony?
TEPIYAC:	Yes sir.
S-2:	And Harry Miles?
TEPIYAC:	I have no knowledge of any such contact. Did we do anything wrong, sir?

End of transcription.
Signed, Donald Higgins, Special 4th Class.

Carr, *JOURNAL*. October 27, 1968. Written in what appears to be a red crayon. At the top of the page is the word "~~Mistate~~" followed by "Mistake."

It began as a mistake, like everything in this place. There are those who say there isn't anything here that should be here, and that's why this place is so screwed up. Including the canal that runs from north to south instead of east to west. And nothing that happens should happen, but it does because of a mistake somewhere else, in some other town, some other country, some wood-panelled office high up in a building in some other part of the world.

It made sense to me. This whole place is a mistake, and mistakes have a power of inevitability.

My being here is a mistake. I should have been somewhere else. Some place where men are really tested. Instead I am here where you are only challenged by the amount of rot you can stomach...how far you can stray...how low you can sink before you lose yourself in a case of mistaken identity.

I've heard it said here that life is a mistake that we have to live with. Some live with it better than others. I gave up fighting life here several months ago, when it was easier to forget more about yourself than it was to remember anything you once believed.

All of this came to me standing in the latrine of the Buffalo Cantina staring into the mirror telling myself how

DAVID GREGOR

lucky I would have been if they had given me the War. The enemy here is too willing.

Twice I have asked for the War, but I am not a patriot. Nor a killer. I'm a seeker. At eighteen, I was not prepared to die for anyone or anything. That's how simple life was two years ago.

What I need is to go deeper. I need to go beyond myself. I need to know what is waiting for me. It can't be any worse than the urinal where all this came so clearly. I need a drink.

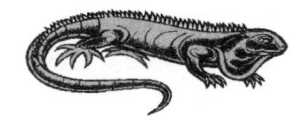

Carr, MANUSCRIPT. Fort Clayton. The words, "The Road to Las Cruces" head the page.

We pulled off the highway into a wide and open parking area adjoining the edge of the jungle. It was a glorious, sunny Sunday and the morning air was heavy with the smell of dank moisture and the hint of promise. Much of the brush around the entrance to the trail had been trampled by visitors so you could see back a ways into the jungle, and it reminded me of some of the trail heads in state parks back home. There was a carved wood sign at the entrance to the trail that read: CAMINO REAL, with a yellow arrow pointing inland.

As Harry and Tepi checked their gear and stretched in the sun, I felt the bowel-knotting sense of anticipation that accompanies any endeavor into the unknown. In the back of my mind, I believed finding some kind of treasure was a very real possibility. There had been a lot of gold here when the Spanish conquered the Americas, and since then some of it had been found. Barry Tompkins, for one, had found five pieces of eight on this same trail just a few weeks earlier. He told me he had found them "just inside the entrance," but nothing more specific. I saw the coins, so I knew he wasn't lying, and I wanted to find some for myself. It is, after all, every kid's dream to go on an expedition into the jungle in search of lost treasure, and I was no different. Even at twenty years old, my insides tingled with the promise of discovery.

DAVID GREGOR

The three of us finally secured the van and checked our modest supplies. When we were certain we had everything, we followed the arrow on the wooden sign until we came to the cobblestone path marking where the Camino Real intersected the highway. I picked up a relatively straight firm limb for a walking stick and quickly found myself poking it into the brush alongside the trail, hoping to glimpse the shine of something gold or even silver.

"So what exactly did Tompkins say about where he found his coins?" Tepi asked.

"He said he wasn't too far onto the trail when he started scraping around on the ground."

"And what exactly are we looking for at this Las Cruces place?"

"I have no idea what's there now," I said. "Map just shows ruins. Means something was there once."

"Used to be a good-sized village," Harry said, snapping on his web belt. "It was a place where gold from Peru was delivered to Panama City, then carried by mule trains cross country to Las Cruces. From there it was ferried down the Chagres and eventually shipped off to Spain."

"Where'd you learn all that?" Tepi asked.

"I'm a student of history," Harry said. "I love this part of the world. The history of the Americas is rooted right here."

"Maybe you'll teach history someday," Tepi said.

Harry chuckled. "You never know. Maybe I'll just live it."

Maybe Harry would, and it made me think about what drew me to him. First of all, he was a man of skill and knowledge. He knew how to find water with none in sight, how to cook without pots or pans and how to trap edible jungle creatures. He was also measured in his approach to doing everything, whether it be choosing his imported pipe tobacco or reading up on the history of a long-deserted jungle village. He was someone upon whom nothing of importance was lost and the one person you would most want as a guide if you were ever in trouble.

Harry checked his compass, and then the three of us stepped off for what was to be a one-day excursion on the Las Cruces Trail.

We each carried a canteen of water, and between us there were two machetes, courtesy of Harry. Harry brought along some fruit, and Tepi carried several portions of what was affectionately called monkey-on-a-stick, essentially cooked meat of some sort always available outside the bars downtown. Inside my camera bag, along with my camera and lenses, I had three beers to celebrate our ultimate arrival at the Las Cruces ruins.

The trail grade began easy, following clearly visible cobblestones, meandering slightly here and climbing a little there, but for the most part the trail was easy to follow. For the first quarter mile the jungle vegetation was not much of a problem, and there was no need to use the machetes. It was apparent that the large number of visitors who had stopped and decided to walk the trail for awhile usually went about a quarter of mile before they had seen enough and walked back, which explained why the jungle growth had been kept off the trail and the stones were so clearly visible. About half an hour in, a huge tree trunk across the trail clearly marked the turnaround place for most hikers. It was at the fallen tree where the trail climbed uphill rather steeply and where the adjacent vegetation was thicker and less trampled. More often than not, the trail stones also were covered with vines and tree debris, and the signs of previous travelers were nearly nonexistent.

The green shroud of the jungle immediately blotted out the sky. I felt invigorated with all the soft shades of green, some of them nearly yellow where the narrow shafts of sun managed to get through the canopy and shine through the broad leaves of plants the size of small umbrellas. The farther back into the jungle we walked, the more the landscape began to change and the layered canopy felt more and more like a huge, leafy cocoon. The first thing you noticed was the light getting darker, though not like night, but a more diffused daylight that took much of the hard edge off of tree trunks and leaves. There were more and more places on the trail where the stones were less uniform in their size or placement, and in several spots you couldn't tell if the stones were there naturally or part of the man-made trail. At these places we would stop, and each of us would move out in different directions, probing the ground with our boots and sticks, looking for strong evidence of the trail direction. Then one of us would locate the trail, and off we'd go again without any idea exactly in what direction we were heading. But that really didn't seem to matter. We knew where we were heading: Las Cruces—the gold terminus. And we knew that the Camino Real went to it. So as long as we kept on the trail, logic told me we would eventually reach Las Cruces. It was just a matter of time.

Sounds engulfed us as though we were traveling under an invisible cloud of chatter. Ticking, whistling, howling and distant knocking swirled around us high and low. The clamor was not especially loud, more a strange and noticeable presence that in no way instilled fear but in a quiet way astonished us with all its complexities and different textures.

We stopped around 10:00 a.m. in a little clearing for a break and rest. The walking was hard enough, but walking on stones was a factor none of us had considered. Though our army boots were designed for hiking, the stones worked against your feet the way flat concrete doesn't. The good thing was that the ground was dry. We were all lying back, taking advantage of the flat ground and the relative quiet, when a sound that was almost a growl, off to the right of the trail, made us sit up straight.

"What the hell was that?" I snapped. It was a sound I had never heard before. We waited...no one spoke. Then the sound of something large and heavy moved through the brush, followed by deep, guttural grunts that did not sound human. Then it was quiet.

"Anybody see anything?" I said.

"Not me," Tepi said, shaking his head.

"Probably a monkey," Harry said, staring intently out into the underbrush.

"Sounded heavier than a monkey," I said.

"They can get pretty big," Harry said.

We paused and listened. My heart was in my throat and pounding hard.

"It almost sounded...like a voice," Tepi said.

"You realize," Harry said, "there are animals that live out here."

"Yeah, but that sounded...big."

"Whatever it was," Harry said, "it's long gone by now. Probably more frightened of us than we are of it."

"I wouldn't be so sure," Tepi said.

"Me neither."

Harry strapped his web belt back on. "Why don't we just head on."

"I don't know," Tepi said. "Maybe we ought to just head back."

"And miss out on the treasure," Harry said. "I think you're making a lot out of nothing."

"That grunting sound was something, Harry," I said.

"You're right," he said. "It *was* something, but the

unseen always seems bigger than the seen. Let's find Las Cruces."

Tepi and I collected our gear and followed Harry to the stone trail. I tried laughing off whatever had made the noise, but my heart wasn't in it. I wasn't so easily convinced it was a monkey, but if it was, it was a monkey I never wanted to meet.

I brought up the rear of the group and found myself looking behind me more than watching the trail ahead. At one point I stopped just to get a clear, unjostled look at what I thought was the movement of a small tree off to the left behind us. My eyes were primed for movement, any sway or shaking...of anything, but I saw nothing move. I took a huge deep breath and sighed with relief. I was glad to see nothing, but a part of me really wanted to catch a glimpse of what I felt in my bones might be shadowing us, so I would know I was right and that I could trust my instincts the way Harry trusted his.

I turned and headed off to catch up with the others when suddenly I heard that sound again. I looked behind me, and off the trail I saw a huge mangrove bush move as though something large was brushing against it. This time I didn't stop. I ran forward as fast as I could on the rounded rocks until I ran up the back of Tepi's boot heels, sending us both to the ground.

"What the hell's wrong with you?" Tepi yelled.
"Sorry," I said, helping him up.
"Sorry my ass. Where ya running?"
"Nowhere. Sorry...thought I...I just got carried away."

Carr, MANUSCRIPT. Titled: "A Little Noise."

We hiked for another hour or so, climbing small rises and dropping down into shallow valleys while following the stone trail even when it narrowed to just a few stones wide. We encountered several small streams that trickled over larger rocks, which were much different in shape and composition from the ballast stones we were following. Now the quiet in the jungle, apart from the sounds we made, was incredible. There were times I could not even hear the wind or the scratch of one limb against another. On several occasions I just stopped on the trail to listen and look back into the jungle. It was like we had walked into a primeval world where the complexities of human advance had no presence...where only the bare elements of life existed, and the jungle felt young and unspoiled. I was struck by the layer upon layer of pattern created by the foliage. I had never seen so many shades of green. After growing up in the Northwest I thought I had seen green, but there were yellowy greens and deep emerald greens and iridescent greens I had never seen before. In places the jungle floor, when it was visible, was like a fluffy carpet so hypnotic in its apparent comfort that on a few occasions all I wanted to do was step off the trail, walk back into the leafy shell of dense green and lie down. Other times the jungle floor was not visible because the brush grew so thick you could not tell where one plant ended and another began. For as far as you could see in any direction, the terrain was green brush—broad leaves as big as elephant ears and huge tree trunks and tree limbs dripping with vines of green foliage like some primordial shawl draped over the landscape.

The one major break in the landscape was water. About four hours in, we came to what could only be called a creek. It was about eight feet across, and in the places we tested with a stick, it was three to four feet deep. By this time my feet were killing me, and my first thought was to get them into that cool water. We agreed to break for lunch, and I was the first one out of my boots. I had just slipped my right foot gently into the water when Harry calmly said, "Crocodiles love these river banks, you know."

"It won't work, Harry. This feels too good."

"Just a cautionary note."

"You expect me to believe that?"

Harry knocked dead ash out of his pipe and repacked it with fresh tobacco. "The Chagres River used to be called the Crocodile River before the Spanish arrived. And this little creek feeds the Chagres."

I scanned up and down the creek's edge without moving my head, and then jerked my foot out of the water...scooting on my butt back away from the bank. I had no desire to challenge Harry's knowledge or his sense of humor.

I settled back against a large tree trunk, opened my can of chili and shared Tepi's Spanish rice, spreading the cold mixture on hard bread. Just being off the stone path was a relief to my joints.

"It's hard to believe people pulled carts and carried crates out here," I said.

"It's hard to believe anybody does *anything* out here," Tepi said.

HUNDRED WATERS

"And in bare feet, too," I said. "My feet are killing me and they've been wrapped in the best leather boots."

"Seems like the heat would get you first," Tepi said. "We've been going about four hours now, carrying virtually nothing, and I'm ready for a siesta."

"Imagine if you were carrying forty or fifty pounds on your shoulders," Harry said, "with some asshole on a horse cracking a whip across your back."

"Maybe the lucky ones were the ones who died early," Tepi said.

"Or the ones who escaped early," Harry said.

"All I've got to say is I hope these Spaniards lost a lot of coins," I said. "I can't wait to get my hands on some Spanish money. Can you imagine..."

I had no sooner spoken when there was a large crash in the brush off behind us. Without moving I looked over at Tepi then Harry, and together the three of us slowly stood up and turned around.

"What the hell was that?" Tepi said.

"Another monkey, Harry?"

"See anything?" Tepi whispered.

"Nope," I said.

"Me neither," said Harry.

I heard what sounded like a deep huff, and I quickly reached down and grabbed my walking stick. I scanned the thick brush for the source of the sound but saw nothing move, not even a twig.

"What the hell is that?" Tepi said.

"Any ideas, Harry?" I said.

"Could be anything."

"No," I said, "it's *something*. And it seems to be following us. We heard it a couple of hours ago and now again."

"Animals live out here," Harry said calmly. "Could be a cat, like a panther. Wild pig maybe."

"How about something human?" I asked.

"Possible," Harry said. "There are people who live out here too, back in the jungle away from populated areas."

"Any reason they would want to follow us?" Tepi asked.

"We have no idea what it was," Harry said, "so let's not get all worked up. Hell, there's an animal they call a *paca*. Means 'painted rabbit' and he runs about 20 pounds."

"Do these *pacas* grunt like men?" Tepi asked.

"Never heard one. Could be anything though. Let's pack up and continue on. We should be close to your Las Cruces."

"Are we really sure we want to continue?" Tepi said. "I mean...this is the jungle."

"Because of a noise in the bushes?" Harry said.

"That was a grunt."

"I'd just like to know what it is," I said. "It's not knowing that's getting to me."

"I don't think we want to let a little noise send us running back to the van," Harry said, calmly.

"Who said anything about running?" I said.

"Harry didn't mean it that way, did you Harry?"

"You're right, we don't know for certain what it is. But we also know that whatever made the noise has made no move against us."

"So we're suppose to relax?" I snapped.

"Some of this could be us, you know," Harry said.

"How's that?"

"Just that we often impact events around us."

"So now *we're* causing the noise?"

"Not causing," Harry said," but maybe affecting. But whatever it is, it has as much right to be out here as we do. Maybe even more. So lets get a grip on and move along."

HUNDRED WATERS

"But I never said anything about running back to the van," I said.

"You're right, Eddie," Harry said. "Why don't we just move on."

I slipped my boots back on while Harry and Tepi collected their gear, but I couldn't get my mind off that noise in the brush. I didn't like the idea of being followed, whether it was man or animal or it belonged in the jungle or not. It struck me as too much of a coincidence that something or someone was tromping along beside us like an unshakable shadow. I wondered to myself what it might be that would stay with you, wherever you go, following your every twist and turn and keeping just out of sight.

If we had taken a vote to stay or leave, I'm not sure I would have voted to continue. But since the trip had been my idea, and I still wanted to find some kind of treasure, I tried my hardest to put the strange sounds behind us.

Carr, MANUSCRIPT. Written in mixed pen and pencil. The title "The Crossing" is at the top of the first page.

    According to my original calculations based on map mileage, we should have already reached the ruins of Las Cruces, but it was clear we were moving slower over the stone trail than I had figured. We picked up the trail again where it clearly skirted the slow-moving creek and headed further back into the jungle. The stream gently wound along a flat stretch of low foliage where there was not much of a middle canopy above us. The effect was that the jungle seemed to open up around us like a large leafy bubble draped with vines and palm fronds. There were stretches of the creek which moved so slowly that a layer of bright green algae covered the surface giving it the appearance of a putting green or a field of clover. It was so appealing in its brightness and carpet-like plushness that, for a moment as we clomped past, I forgot exactly where I was. It was as though we had walked into a nether world—a dreamy, still place splayed with shafts of fuzzy sunlight...an enchanted place where fairy tales or myths might be born. The lushness, the becalmed feeling of the area, the way the light filtered the air—it was near magical in appearance, and I would not have been at all surprised if a unicorn had suddenly appeared off to my right near the stand of banana trees.

DAVID GREGOR

About two hours later the cobblestone trail finally angled off to the north, opening up to low brush and a thinning of trees so that water—a large body of water—was visible through the foliage. We climbed and hacked with our machetes. Howler monkeys began wailing high up above us. We could hear them but see only anonymous limb movements in the highest parts of the trees. Finally the round stones gave way to what appeared to be a wash of rubble.

Harry, who was cutting trail, suddenly stopped and gestured straight ahead of us. "We're there," he said, calmly.

"This is it?" I said. "Where? What do you see?"

"Bricks," Harry said.

"I see a wall," Tepi yelled. "There's another. We *have* found it."

"Let me see," I said running to where Tepi stood. There, in fact, were bricks and what appeared to be a partial wall. When I touched the top of the wall, several bricks fell to the ground.

There were no other towns or villages noted on any of my maps, so it had to be Las Cruces. We were most likely on the outskirts of what had been the town, the place where the gold trail headed out for Old Panama. Glistening through the trees I could see what had to be the Chagres River—reddish brown, about two hundred feet away. None of us said anything at first. We just walked around the site, hacking brush and lifting vines, looking for whatever might be hidden in the overgrowth. Tepi finally sat down on a vine-covered wall but immediately fell to the ground when it collapsed under his weight.

"They just don't make ancient walls like they used to," he said.

Harry walked in the direction of the swift-moving river, then stopped and cocked his head around as though he were listening to some far-off sound. He lit his pipe and filled the still air with the smell of his special English cherry blend.

I continued poking around the underbrush to get a feel for the layout of the place. I tried to determine where the village limits might have extended, where the boundaries might naturally lie, based on the presence of vegetation or lack of tree growth. But it was impossible for me to see anything beyond ten feet. Finally I struck something hard with my walking stick that made a dull-sounding clang.

"Here's something metal," I said.

I turned over a large piece of brick with my boot and poked around with my stick, but it was impossible to even see the dirt for the vines and brush. The tangle of vines was a thick, woody mesh.

Harry walked back toward Tepi and sat down next to him on the remains of the wall. Tepi withdrew his canteen and shook it. "I'm empty," Tepi said. "Who has some water?"

"I still have a bit," Harry said, handing his canteen to Tepi, "but go easy. That's all of it."

"Hell, what's to worry?" I said. "We've got a whole damn river here."

"You want to drink from swamp water?" Harry said.

I looked over at the muddy ground near the edge of the river and took a deep breath.

"Exactly which part of the river are you going to drink from?" Harry said.

"Funny guy," I said. "Funny guy."

Harry walked back down toward the river, and I kicked around the site. To say I was disappointed at what we had found would have been a gross understatement. I wanted to find something like the Mayan ruins found on the Yucatan, buried for centuries in the jungle, but intact. I wanted to find artifacts, doubloons, gold, jewelry...anything of value, but all we had found were several dilapidated clay walls.

DAVID GREGOR

I walked back toward the jungle. Twenty feet out I tripped over a root and fell face first into a tangle of vines. When I looked up, I found myself staring into the eyes of a three-foot long iguana. His sharp tongue darted at me. The first thing I thought of was the Panamanian official I had seen dead outside the La Mar Cantina with an iguana stuffed in his mouth. I rolled over and away from it and crawled around behind a skinny tree. I reached down to push myself up and felt a round metallic object under my hand. The jungle floor was matted with vines and grass interwoven so tightly that they worked much like a rug and made it impossible for me to see what the object was, let alone get at it. I pulled out my knife and slashed at the iguana until it ran off into the brush. Then I clawed at the vines, sawing and slicing, until I was able to reach under them and pull out the hard round object. It turned out to be two rings interlocked like two links in a large chain. They were badly rusted but still intact.

"Hey...look what I found," I said, holding up the links.

"Looks like a chain," Tepi said.

Harry walked over and took the links from me. "Could be any kind of chain." He rubbed some of the rust off, then picked at the ring with the tip of his fingernail. "Feels like there might be some kind of stamping on it." He spit on one of the rings and rubbed it until he could better see the indentation he had felt.

"Well...what is it?" I asked.

"A marking...like a founder's mark. Probably the signet of the foundry."

"How do you know that?" Tepi said.

"I read books," Harry said.

"How old?" I asked.

"No telling. But it's definitely Spanish. You can read the word *marca*."

HUNDRED WATERS

"Any idea what it's from?"

"Could be any number of things," Harry said. "Old strapping chain, harness chain. Could've been a barge chain, maybe even off a set of shackles."

"Like slave chains?"

"Could be something to do with slaves."

"Well, it's not exactly gold," Tepi said.

"So far," Harry said, "it's the only thing we've got to show for this trip."

"Not me," Tepi said. "I've got blisters and stone bruises on both my feet."

"I think I've sweat out everything I've ever drunk in my whole life."

The sun dropped just below the treetops across the river, and while it was still light out, it was clear that night was approaching.

Then out of the blue Tepi spoke out. "Say, you guys, how are we getting out of here?"

I looked at Harry and then around at our surroundings.

"Now that's a stupid question," I said.

"No it's not," Tepi said. He looked down at his watch. "It's 4:30 already, and the sun's going down. Anybody got any ideas?"

"According to my watch," Harry said, "it's taken us about seven hours to get here."

"So what are you saying?" I said.

"Well, we don't have seven hours of light left to go out the way we came in," Tepi said.

"Once the sun goes down," Harry said, "it'll get pretty dark under this triple canopy."

The situation was clear. We needed to find a way out before dark, or else we were in for a night in the jungle with no food, very little water and very little to protect ourselves with if the need arose. There were also those thrashing sounds that seemed to be following us on the trail.

"I'm not spending the night out here," I said.

"I really don't want to spend the night out here either," Tepi said in a calm but forceful tone. "So we need to find a way out, a way that is faster than the way we came in. And we need to find it now!"

"I'm with you," I said. I turned to Harry. "What do you think?"

"I agree," he said. "So let's spread out. If there's another way out, let's find it."

We focused on going across the Chagres River some way, or south for four or five miles along the river bank toward the main highway across the isthmus. Tepi and I walked south, paralleling the river, about ten yards apart, while Harry went toward the river.

Heading inland the brush was thick everywhere and getting thicker the farther away we got from the remains of Las Cruces. The ground was also turning wetter. It was clear we were getting into a bog area. I called to Tepi, and we backtracked with each of us trying to circle the swampy area. Whichever direction I moved, there was mud, and it was getting soggier and deeper with each step. I just couldn't find dry ground going south. Finally I went back in Tepi's direction and met him coming back from down river. His pant legs were wet and muddy from the knees down, just like mine.

"I didn't see any trail this way," Tepi said.

"All I found was mud."

"There might be something back up the trail that bypasses this bog area." Tepi headed off to take a look.

I walked over toward the riverbank where I could see Harry with his hands on his hips and narrow ribbons of pipe smoke rising up from him.

HUNDRED WATERS

"What do you see *kemo sabe*?"

"I see a river about a half-mile wide and nobody on the other side. Any idea what's over there?"

Thick bushy trees lined the far bank of the river. Then the land rose up to gently rolling hills covered with what appeared to be deep-green grass that looked tended, but there were no signs of any structures. Most of all, no signs of people. I pulled out my map and traced our path through the jungle to Las Cruces. I found our site and moved directly across the Chagres River from it.

"It's the Canal Zone Golf Course," I said. "Can you believe it. A damn golf course out in the middle of Tarzan country."

"What's worse," Harry said, "is there's no one there. What the hell good does a golf course do us if nobody's out there playing?"

My hands started sweating, and for the first time since we heard that initial noise in the jungle, I felt concerned. It was quite clear what our situation was. We were within sight of civilization but unable to get across the river to it. I quickly scanned the riverbank for those crocodiles Harry had cautioned me about earlier. I started hearing sounds I hadn't noticed before: cricket chirps, monkey chatter, and raspy sounds from back in the jungle. The farther the sun seemed to sink, the more jungle life I heard, and I didn't like what I was hearing.

We couldn't walk back the way we came, and looking down our side of the riverbank, there was no going south without going inland a ways and with no guarantee that we would ever find another trail. We seemed to be in the best of all possible positions at Las Cruces, which still didn't get us out of the jungle.

"What'll we do?" Tepi said.

"I certainly don't want to stay here," I said.

"Unless you guys want to start hiking back the way we came," Harry said, "I think this is it."

"For what?" I said. "We're nowhere."

"So there's no way out south of here," Harry asked, "along the river?"

"Tepi and I already tried. It's nothing but a swampy bog."

"I even walked back up the trail a ways," Tepi said, "but I couldn't find anything going south."

"Real fucking fine," Harry said.

"We're stuck here for the night, aren't we?" Tepi said.

"Unless you've thought of another way out."

"How about a raft? We could raft across the river." Tepi said.

"Get serious," I said.

"The river may be our only way out," Tepi said.

"Forget it," I said. "We'd need a boat, and I don't see anything like one around here."

"A raft would work," Tepi said.

"A raft?" I said. "You think we've got a couple of days to build one. Hell, it's damn near dark, and we've got two machetes and no flashlights."

"Eddie's probably right," Harry said. "It would take us hours in daylight to build any kind of raft."

"Fine!" Tepi snapped. "So what do we do now...homestead?"

"How about just floating across?" Harry said.

"You mean just float...like swimming?"

"How about on anything that'll float," Harry said, "...like a log."

"Forget that too," I said.

"I don't know, Eddie," Tepi said. "That sounds pretty good."

"No way," I said.

HUNDRED WATERS

"Why?" Harry said.

"Just because," I said.

"We're running a little short of realistic options," Harry said.

"And daylight," Tepi said.

"Why not, Eddie?"

I stared down at the ground, and then I looked up at both Tepi and Harry who were staring at me, waiting. "Because...I can't swim."

Harry smiled. "I never thought about drowning."

"Well I'm thinking about it. A lot. I can't swim a stroke, so I'm not even considering floating out there on a log."

"Hell," Harry said, "I thought you might've been worried about the crocodiles or the water snakes."

"Oh...now don't say things like that," Tepi said.

"The way I see it," Harry said, calmly, "we have three options. We can start back the way we came in and chance losing the trail in the dark. We can spend the night right here and head back tomorrow. Or we can try getting across the river. I say we hit the river and before it gets much darker."

"The safe thing would be to just sleep the night," I said. "Hell, somebody might come by in a boat."

"And pigs might fly someday," Harry said. "But I think the river is our best bet."

"I can't swim," I said. "I can't swim!"

Harry Miles drew calmly on his pipe and blew out a stream of smoke. "Well...since Eddie can't swim, let's look for something big that'll float."

I couldn't move. I was frozen stiff just thinking about going out into that animal-infested river to my certain death. All I could do was stare at Harry and Tepi as they rooted around in the brush and along the riverbank for anything large that might float. I was focused on the river...deep water...water snakes... crocodiles...missing the far bank and floating out into the Panama Canal to be chopped up by a ship's propeller. My mind was swirling on all the ugly possibilities until Harry grabbed my shoulder from behind.

"Eddie," he said calmly, "we found a log. You want to give us a hand getting it into the water?"

"I can't swim," I repeated, following Harry. "I really can't."

"That's okay," he said. "We're really not going to swim. We're going to float and kick. You can do that, Eddie. Just hang onto the log and move your feet. That's all Eddie. No Swimming...I promise."

"You promise?"

We made our way down river a short distance, hacking a path through the low brush to where Tepi was standing next to a partially beached log. It was about ten...twelve feet long and as big around as two telephone poles, with half a dozen smaller limbs stripped bare of any foliage.

"I really can't do this," I said.

"Sure you can," Harry said. "I would strap your gear on tight...get it over your neck so the current doesn't pull it off."

"This baby is really stuck in the mud," Tepi said. "It's going to take the three of us to move it into the water."

"Then let's do it. It's getting dark."

I reluctantly grabbed a limb, and when Harry counted to three, we all pulled with everything we had. The tree trunk inched out of the mud. We pulled again and again and again until after about ten pulls the log finally broke loose from the mud and tangled vines. Harry slowly guided the tree out into the river and bounced up and own on it several times. When we felt sure it wasn't going to sink, Tepi and I waded out and each grabbed hold of a limb. We stood on the up-river side of the tree with Harry farthest out and me in the middle. The sun fell behind the rolling hills of the golf course, and immediately the river was in twilight. The air got still, and the jungle grew uncomfortably quiet.

"I really don't want to do this," I said to Harry.

"I know," Harry said. "Grasp what you're afraid of and make it yours. Trust me, Eddie. I won't let you drown."

"Got you covered on this side," Tepi said.

"Just hold on tight and if the tree starts to roll, just stay with it."

We inched out farther into the river until we were chest deep.

"Okay," Harry said, "here we go." And together we pushed off the muddy bottom and began floating out into the slow-moving river.

The water was cold, and with the chill of the evening air and my fear of the water, I was shaking like a leaf in a strong wind. It was all I could do to hold onto the tree and keep my head above water. We used our legs like a propeller and a rudder. We were able to keep our kicking speed a little faster than the river flow, which allowed us to actually control our direction. The far shoreline was just a flat black wall once the sun went down, and all I could really determine was a ridge line above the river where the dark hills cut sharply against the dark indigo sky. I could also tell we were cutting across the river by the angle the river water was hitting us and the log. But it was hard to have faith in your success when you couldn't tell how far you'd come and how far there was to go. My thoughts started focusing on animals again...crocodiles coming up under us...water snakes swimming after us...lizards and all the unknown creatures under the water I didn't know about. I thought about dying so far away from home and my family, and what a stupid thing it was to go looking for a nothing village that amounted to a pile of overgrown rubble...and who cared about gold coins...what did they matter when you're cold and floating out of control down the middle of a dark, Panamanian river on a tree trunk. None of it mattered. Nothing really mattered except life...staying alive mattered...one more breath...another minute...another day...that's what mattered...and being alive with as much life as you could hold.

I kicked my feet and kicked and kicked...slower and slower, until my leg muscles burned and my arms got tired from clenching the slippery tree. It seemed like we had already been in the water for an eternity.

"How ya doing...Eddie?" Harry called out.

"Tired...cold."

"We're doing good...getting close."

That made me feel good. I looked over at Tepi, and I could only see his dark head bobbing up and down as he kicked.

"Tep?" I blurted.

"Yeah?"

"Good," I said, and faced forward again.

We kicked and kicked, and whenever I started to feel the river cutting across my back Harry would yell for Tepi to kick harder, and then he'd tell me to stop kicking until the water was washing against the side of my face. Then we'd all kick again.

A short time later my leg muscles just gave out and they wouldn't move. I was totally exhausted, and I felt my arms tightening up.

Suddenly I heard a muffled roar. Then we hit something hard, something that made a hollow sound when we hit it. The tree trunk rolled toward me...there were voices...and then I lost my hold. I remember brushing past Tepi and trying to yell, but all I heard was my garbled voice caught under water.

HUNDRED WATERS

Everything was dark and cold, and I felt myself sliding down a deep, black, bottomless hole.

* * *

Carr, *JOURNAL*. December 30, 1968. This entry is in ink, written in Carr's erratic hand. The lines drift all across the page without any symmetry. The word "Drowning" is written boldly across the top of the first page.

>I was still in the water...floating aimlessly, when I suddenly broke the surface. I woke up in the Locos Bar with Bobdog sitting next to me. She looked beautiful and casual...strangely relaxed...looking at me like we had just met. I closed my eyes and thought for sure I was dead. I could've been. There were other people at a table across the bar, but I didn't hear any voices. It was a gauzy scene. For a moment I felt okay...like life was fine. Then I asked myself: what the hell am I really doing? Killing time...or is time killing me? My head is so clouded with bright thoughts...I feel like a lighthouse.
>
>I slip back into the water...floating along until I start to slowly sink beneath the surface. There is an explosion. The air over the river echoes like the voice of a bird. The night is full of echoes. The fear of death is real. A death war. Real bullets. I want to be a part of it. I want everything to be this real. It is all so clear, it is the most crystalline vision I've ever had without drug inducement. The "truth" is the drug. I am in the jungle and shadows are trying to kill me.
>
>I drift farther beneath the surface...until Bobdog's voice is singing my name. I have kept so much of her beauty within me that her voice is like a beam of light. Here I am...I am back. I would like to learn her secret.

* * *

DAVID GREGOR

When I opened my eyes I was out of the water, lying face up on a hard surface, the dark sky above me. I heard familiar voices.

"Everything's okay, Eddie," I heard Tepi say.

"You did good," Harry said.

"Where are we?"

"In a canoe. We hit this guy paddling down river. He's going to put us ashore down near the highway."

A short time later, the man put his canoe into shore just short of a highway overpass. He gave us directions up the hill to the highway and told us where we could catch the bus. We thanked him and gave him what turned out to be twelve dollars we had between us. It just didn't seem like enough, but it was all we had.

As we started up the hill from the river, I turned to Harry who held me up under the arm. "I don't believe it," I said to him. "I really don't. All that water and I didn't even drown."

"Life is good," Harry said.

Part IV

The Call

Carr, MANUSCRIPT. Dated: December 31, 1968. Handwritten with holographic changes made to the text in red pencil. The words "A Radical Proposition" are written along the left margin in blue ink.

It was the first time I had ever gone to a casita in the daylight. I could see it was also uncomfortable for Harry by the tentative way he stepped inside, like he was afraid to touch anything. This bar was off-limits. All whorehouses were, but we had no intention of being with any women. Harry had asked me along for company, or maybe for moral support, on the long drive out to the Las Minas district. That's a funny word: "moral," especially considering who we saw there.

I knew almost immediately that we should not have been where we were, and when I saw the three of them sitting at the far table in the corner of the empty room, I knew that nothing good was coming our way. It just felt uncomfortable. I whispered to Harry that we should leave. He told me he knew what they wanted, and we were safe. But he needed me to be there.

"I have to say 'no' to these people," he told me, "and I need somebody here to hold me up."

It was early enough in the casita for the sweep man to be cleaning up the sawdust off the floor. An older, hunched-over woman was clearing bottles and glasses off the small tables. All the lights were on, and the room was a bright phony blue...harsh to look at. It also gave the second-rate furniture a fourth-rate look. I liked that quality about these places.

Harry and I walked toward the bar, and the man behind it saw us in the mirror and without a word, pointed to the far corner of the large barroom. I knew we were expected but not that expected.

There were three of them sitting at the cloth-covered table, watching us... expressionless. Harry introduced me as a friend. The tall kid was named Pablito, an engineering student at the university. He wore jeans and a red t-shirt with the name "Che" emblazoned on it. We shook hands. The other two, named Moro and Kit, were quiet and wore white t-shirts. They didn't smile or move in their chairs. The small talk didn't last long.

"I can't do that," Harry said.

"You said you wanted to help us," Pablito said. "This is the help we need."

"It's called treason," Harry said. "I can't do that."

"You told me you were sympathetic to us."

"Sympathetic, yes. But I spoke of me personally, not me as a U.S. soldier. There's a difference. I can't do what you ask."

"I see. So those were just empty words you spoke. Nothing but air."

"I meant what I said. But classified material is out of the question. I will give myself, my time, my thoughts, my efforts, but not classified information."

"We don't want no secrets," Pablito said, turning to his two friends. "Do we? We just need information. Like when the Guardia Civil plans to be certain places."

"And how many they are," the one named Kit said.

Moro sat forward. "Little things that are big for us."

HUNDRED WATERS

A telephone rang in the distance.

"Even if I knew, I couldn't do that," Harry said.

"Just another gringo filled with air," Pablito said. "We don't need your air, Harry. If you are with us we need your help, not your excuses."

"I'm not offering excuses. I can give myself, but nothing classified. Hell, it's risky enough just being here now and discussing these things. They could bust my ass right now and put me in Leavenworth just for talking to you guys."

"Panamanian jails are filled with our people."

"One American means nothing," Moro said.

"It means something to me," Harry said. "I believe in what you're trying to do. I want you to get your country back, but I can't give what you want."

The bar sweep interrupted the discussion. He stepped behind Pablito and whispered to him.

"Seems we have visitors coming," Pablito said, and he stood. "I suggest you and your friend leave by the back door. This man will show you out."

"Who's coming?" I said.

"It's just best you leave. I believe we're through talking for now. Adios, Harry."

The sweep grabbed Harry by the arm and pulled him toward the rear of the casita, and I followed. Once out back, the sweep pointed over the rear fence beyond some banana trees. We thanked him and scaled the fence. Harry and I walked down a dirt alley through an area of shacks and shanties overrun with scroungy dogs and little brown children, most without clothes.

"What was that all about?" I asked.

"Revolution."

"No, I mean the visitors."

"Pablito's people have friends in important places.

Clearly somebody knew that somebody else knew about the meeting and was sending some people over to visit us. Pablito is a very powerful player here. We should be thankful that not everybody says 'no' to him."

"But will he take 'no' for an answer?" I said.

Carr, *JOURNAL*. April 1, 1969. Written in blue ink. There is a drawing in the right-hand margin of a man wearing a fool's cap with a harlequin design.

All of this is true. It is the first time I have ever spoken of this to anyone. I can't remember all the truths, and not all the truths are mine, but I make nothing up. Just as every life is a series of fictions, strung together and called truth, every journey is imaginary, and therein lies its power and trueness. There is in this place and these people the fertile ground for truth. I started writing this out of sheer fear: the fear that it hadn't happened. Then out of boredom, that dullness which embraces an unkindled spirit...and now it's desperation. This needs to be remembered, and I don't trust my memory. It is hard to separate what truly happened from what I believe happened. The truth is I can't put it all together in my head...bring order out of the memory. Facts alone are meaningless, so the "real" becomes what is not forgotten. This is what I remember.

* * *

Carr, MANUSCRIPT. Typewritten, with holographic corrections made in red pencil. The title "With Love and Emptiness" written in red across the top of the first page.

DAVID GREGOR

I suppose the first time I realized Bobdog had a love for me was the night she threw the plate of chicken heads at me and chased me naked around her room with a fork.

I had come down with a fever about a week after our near disastrous trek to Las Cruces, and I had clearly lost my bearings. I had also lost a certain confidence in myself. It was also the night Harry Miles failed to show up for work. He was written up as AWOL, and I went into town right after shift change to look for him before the legalities of his absence got out of hand. If there was a pivotal period during my tour in Panama, it clearly had to be that week after our trip to Las Cruces.

I got into town shortly before midnight and hit all the usual places starting with the Red Coat Inn because I knew Harry and Bobdog were friends. But she hadn't seen him, and she was reluctant to speculate where he might be which struck me as odd, especially after I had explained to her how serious the AWOL charge could be for Harry. I sensed in the cool remove of Bobdog's response that there was something deeper going on, but I had nothing more than just a gut feeling.

Since that night on the Chagres River, I had come to feel very close to Harry. He had in large part saved my life on the river when I panicked and later when I got separated from the log and started drifting downriver. He also had a wealth of knowledge, know-how and a certain inner strength that I was drawn to. After our little jungle expedition, something happened with me. There was a strength of character in Harry Miles that I had never known in myself. Since Las Cruces, I felt there were important things I needed to learn from him.

The night Harry missed work without leave and risked losing his clearance or being reassigned stateside, I was desperate to find him before any serious action was taken. It was unlike Harry Miles to miss work and be absent without

HUNDRED WATERS

leave, because it was unlike Harry to do anything that was not according to regulations. He was not the kind of man who took his oath and responsibility lightly. I found that out the first night I met him, the night I ran across the Hitler transmission and he honored his oath of secrecy. To say I took his absence personally would've been an understatement, and that night in the Red Coat Inn Bobdog seemed to take his situation in stride, like she knew something I didn't. Her apparent coolness about his whereabouts made me angry and even more determined to find him.

    I checked a dozen other places—restaurants, bars, dance halls, even BJ Alley where he had once found me. That night I was looking for Harry was a confused time for me. I had looked everywhere I knew for him, and none of the bartenders, the whores or the regular customers had seen him. I had an empty feeling in the pit of my stomach, like I had lost my brother, and everything about the situation felt out of my reach.

    About 2:00 a.m. I ended up back at the Red Coat, tired, angry and not wanting to be alone. Like so many nights before, I agreed to pay Bobdog fifteen dollars to take her out of the bar, and I resented it. I hated the whole night, and I hated even more paying for female companionship. I resented the idea so much I refused to touch Bobdog before I had finished what was left of my bottle of rum. I hated it that Harry was missing, and I hated to pay for a woman but there were no women not to pay for. A guy could go blind holding out for a woman you didn't pay for, the way Jason Marks temporarily lost his sight drinking a bottle of locally brewed rum.

    Every time I went with Bobdog, she told me she was different. She seemed the same each time to me, though. "First give me money," she would say, "then we play." Play was a funny word for it. It sounded like fun. It was never fun with a whore. It was fast, it was convenient, it was cold. It was many things, but after the first few times it was not fun. It was a necessity. And if you were lucky, a whore bought you a moment. A moment's remove from where you were and the emptiness in your life. I found I needed Bobdog and the others like her, like I needed food, to make me feel full for awhile.

    Late into the morning after Bobdog had gone out for the chicken and rice and after we ate it on the bed and washed it down with wine, we drunkenly threw the cleaned chicken carcass around like a football, and then we "played" one more time. It didn't help fill what was missing, but her kisses and her raspy groans sent me off, way off beyond the dull gray walls of her room. Bobdog, in that way, *was* different. Her dark brown skin had the texture of nylon stockings, taut without the softness I remembered from the few white girls I'd been with. Bobdog's arms and legs were muscular but without definition. The tingling she brought to my body had the effect of soft music, and my thoughts went back far away from the shabby room above Delgado Street.

    I could see the corner of that brick building back home again. It always happened that way. I would see the corner of the Stanford House Apartments back on Washington Avenue, and I knew Sara was in there. She had lived there when we were in love, and whenever I felt lonely or empty inside, my memory always focused on her second-floor corner window. Even though the shades were always down in my remembering, I knew Sara was there just beyond the shades, waiting. And while the memory was still good, I would replay mistakes I had made with her...my remoteness...my inability to tell her how much I cared for her...until the good memory began turning sour. But whenever Bobdog's kisses and gentle fingers first brought me back to that second-floor window of the Stanford

HUNDRED WATERS

House, I felt warm inside and wishful of extreme pleasure with a woman.

When that wishful moment inevitably passed and I found myself staring at the bare wood-slat walls of Bobdog's room, the chicken carcass next to the bed and Bobdog's bony butt, my mind snapped back to the smell of rotting fruit and urine and all that was missing from my life. Panama was a rude return. I tried hard to retain the goodness of the memory: the feel of Sara's fluffy white comforter, the searching light off Point Herron in Puget Sound, the distant rumble of an approaching ferry. But the moment passed all too quickly, and an anger shrouded with self-hatred slowly crept over me. I had a desire for more than the emptiness I felt in that desolate room with the skinny whore named Bobdog whom I needed desperately. Rum and wine did that to you. Especially sweet rum. It made you mad...mad like crazy...crazy for everything missing in your life. And now Harry Miles was gone, and with him something of myself.

I suddenly bolted up off the bed. "I need a reason!" I yelled at Bobdog.

She stared at me like I'd just cursed the Pope.

"I need life in my life," I tried to explain, and Bobdog listened. I told her I really didn't give a shit about life, and she told me I was too free.

"What the hell is life anyway...just time, time you spend and things that happen, usually things you don't want to happen which hurt you or cost you money or grief, so what the hell is this thing called *life* anyway? Just a sweaty hangover with a bony whore? And who really cares anyway?"

"What you mean...bony?" she said.

I had been drinking, I admit it, but I really didn't care anymore. I didn't care about the army, about listening to the coded messages of the enemy. I didn't care about Panama or

Panamanians or whether I lived or died. I truly didn't care, and I told her I hated life. When Bobdog heard that her dark eyes hardened like marbles and her lip twitched. And then she exploded. She threw chicken heads at me and cursed in Spanish and English. She straddled my chest and told me she loved me because I was free. When I laughed at being free, she grabbed the fork off the table and chased me naked around her room. I didn't want to be found in that room—stabbed dead and naked. Dead would be bad enough. If she hadn't stuck that fork so deep into the wall, she would have driven it into my chest. That's how much she loved me...that's how free I was. Bobdog's face flashed red from the neon outside her window. I remember laughing and laughing harder with her pressing me against the wall, feeling her breasts heaving up and down against me and seeing her dark eyes wide with anger while she spit curses at me, and it was just too damn funny for me not to laugh. Then she started laughing, and we both tumbled to the floor...sweaty and spent.

There was something about Bobdog's eyes, an innocent softness, that in a remote way reminded me of the girl I had loved and lost back home, the girl on the second floor of the Stanford House Apartments. But that was home, and home was six thousand miles away. I did love sweet rum. But hell, I didn't know I loved Bobdog then. I was in no shape to know anything so important. I did know Bobdog was all I had for a woman, and much more than I deserved. Perhaps Bobdog was my penance for Sara. Maybe Panama was my personal answer to the war I was never given. Maybe Harry Miles was a mirror I needed to see my shortcomings. Maybe...maybe...maybe. Maybe here is where this story began or at least where a part of the whole nasty mess started. With love and emptiness.

* * *

HUNDRED WATERS

Bobdog woke me up the following morning around nine and told me she knew where Harry was and that she would take me to him.

"Where is he?" I asked.

"Not far," she said. "Get dressed and I will take you."

"When did you find him?" I asked

She lowered her head. "I always knew. I was not to tell."

I grabbed her by the shirt and pulled her to me. "You knew last night when I asked you, and you let me walk all over this stinking town looking in every dive and cesspool bar for him?"

"I was swear to be silent. I spoke my word."

"Your word! What the hell's your word when you lie?"

"I didn't want to be quiet, but I had to."

"You had to!"

"Don't be mad. You don't understand this."

"You're damn right I don't." I got up and slipped on my pants and shirt. "Harry's my friend, and he's about to be in deep trouble. And you had to lie to me. Right to my face...stand there and lie and not tell me where he was! Jesus...what a screwed up fucking place and everybody in it. So where the hell is he?"

"In the hills behind Diablo Heights."

"There's nothing back there but jungle."

"A few people live back there. There are friends with a cabin."

"What kind of friends?"

"Harry's friends."

"Friends you knew about," I said. "How is it that you know where he's at and who he's with?"

"Don't be mad," she said. "I just know."

"Don't be mad," I mumbled. "That's an understatement. Come on," I said, throwing her a sweater. "Let's go before it's too late."

DAVID GREGOR

* * *

Bobdog and I took a Chiva bus across town to the last stop, and there we got a taxi. Bobdog directed the driver into the Canal Zone along the Trans-Isthmus Highway. About five or six miles out she had the driver turn off onto a packed-dirt road that wound up the hillside for almost a mile before we reached a wide turnaround where a government access road was barricaded with a heavy chain-link fence secured with a padlock. Off in the opposite direction a narrow dirt path twisted up the hillside and disappeared into the jungle behind a "No Trespassing" sign. Next to the path entrance I saw Harry's Volkswagen van parked in what was clearly a well-used parking area.

"We get out here," Bobdog said. "Pay the taxi."

I paid the man, and Bobdog waited for him to drive away before she started up the narrow path.

"How far is it?" I asked.

"Just a little...not so far...but up."

We followed the path that was just wide enough for two people to walk side by side, and the first thing I noticed was how still and quiet everything was and how removed we seemed from Panama City just a short ways away. It was hot, and the steep incline made me stop a couple of times just to catch my breath. About a quarter of a mile from the turnaround, the path leveled off and spilled out into small clearing atop a hill surrounded by higher hills behind it. But in front was a territorial view of a dense jungle ravine and an adjacent hill that went back into the interior. Right on the edge of the hill and facing the jungle valley was a small clapboard cabin that looked like it could've come out of the rural South.

"This is where Harry is?" I asked.

"This is where he came," Bobdog said.

Bobdog and I started across the open yard when a

HUNDRED WATERS

young man stepped out of the cabin door, and I immediately saw a pistol in his right hand, held down against his thigh. Bobdog and I stopped.

"Jesus," I said to Bobdog, "what is this?"

"It's okay," she said, and stretched her arm in front of me. "*Oye...Ramon. Esta Bobadillia.*" We slowly approached the cabin until it was clear that the man named Ramon recognized Bobdog and stuffed the pistol into his pants. Ramon and Bobdog embraced, and then Bobdog introduced me as an American friend of Harry's.

"*Bueno*," Ramon said. He stretched out his hand. "*Mucho gusto.* I am Ramon Tocal."

"Is Harry Miles here?" I asked him.

Ramon glanced over at Bobdog, then back to me. Bobdog spoke to him in Spanish as he pulled her away from me. I could tell by their facial expressions and their hand gestures that there was more to Ramon's answer than a simple yes or no.

"Just wait here," Bobdog said to me.

"What is it? What's wrong?" I yelled as they walked away. "Is it Harry?"

"I will be right back," she said. "Wait!" Bobdog and Ramon went inside the cabin and closed the door behind them. I went over to the small front window and cupped my hands over the dirty glass, but there was some kind of cloth covering it on the inside, and I couldn't see in. I tried the front door, but it was locked. I lit a smoke and walked around the side of the cabin looking for another window or maybe a back door. There was no other window on the side of the cabin, but when I got around to the backside, the side that faced the jungle ravine, there was a covered porch area with a small handmade table and three wooden chairs. The rear door was open, and I could see Bobdog, Ramon and another young woman bent over the legs of someone on the couch. I didn't recognize the young woman. I went inside the cabin, and the first thing I saw was the large iguana lizard hanging by its tail from the wood rafter above the couch. When I stepped between Ramon and Bobdog, I saw Harry stripped naked and covered in blood. I could see that his eyes were closed, and the young woman was repeatedly pricking his tongue with what appeared to be a needle, every so often dipping the needle into a small vile of brown liquid.

"Is he...dead?" I asked.

"Get him out of here," Ramon said to Bobdog. She stood up and grabbed me by the arm.

"What's happening?" I said.

"Come outside, Eddie."

"What have you done to Harry?"

"Just come with me."

"Not on your life," I said, shaking loose of her grip. "Is Harry dead?" No one spoke. "Will somebody fucking tell me! Is he dead?"

"No," Ramon said. "He is not dead."

"Well, thank you. So what is this?" I said to Bobdog. "Why is Harry covered with blood. And what the hell is this fucking lizard doing hanging here? What has happened?"

There was a foul smell that was pungent like burnt hair, and I gagged twice.

"This is *una otra cosa*," Bobdog said.

"It certainly is something else alright. But what?"

"*Los Indios*. It is from those who live in the jungle...those who want to change things here in Panama."

"This is politics?"

Bobdog shrugged.

"An American GI covered in blood with a lizard hanging over him is supposed to change the country? Do I look that stupid?" I stared into Bobdog's brown eyes and then went back over to Harry's side. I took an old rag off the coffee table and wiped some of the blood off his face. Ramon continued busily chopping a brownish-red root into small pieces. When he had about ten or twelve chunks, he wrapped them inside a blue bandanna he had removed from around his neck.

"What are you doing?" I asked.

Ramon rolled his eyes up to Bobdog and then very coolly continued his task.

"The root is a medicine," Bobdog said.

"He looks dead," I said, "not sick."

"Harry has a poison," she said. "We really should not be talking about this. Come with me, outside. Let Ramon and Tia do this."

"Not on your life. I'm staying with Harry." I turned to Ramon. "What can I do?"

He shook his head. He twisted the bandanna so the pieces of root formed a ball at one end, and then with the handle of his large knife he pounded the root bulb and squished it with the flat side of the blade until the bandanna was wet.

"Eddie, it is truly better that you don't know some things. Some things that can only bring you trouble."

"I'm not moving," I said and continued to wipe blood off Harry's face and neck.

When Ramon finished pulverizing the root bulb, he tightened the knot until liquid oozed out of the bandanna, and then he stuck the bulb end inside Harry's mouth and held his jaw shut around it.

"Now what?" I asked.

"This should change the poison," Ramon said. "Maybe."

"Maybe?"

"Yes...Maybe."

"Come Eddie. There is nothing more to do now but wait. Ramon and Tia will watch Harry. Come. Outside."
"Are you sure he's alive?"
"He breathes," Tia said.
"I mean...you didn't just do something else to hurt him?"
"I would not hurt my friend Harry," Ramon said.

Bobdog pulled at me, and reluctantly I followed her outside onto the covered front porch. The rich dense jungle spread out in front of us like a field of giant broccoli. Bobdog sat down in one of the wooden chairs, and I lit a cigarette.

"What the hell is going on in there with lizards...the blood and that poison?"
"There are people who want to change things."
"People who did this?"
"Those people I said to you with no names...who live in the jungle. Those who took names of the strong so they would be strong."
"You said you did that, or somebody in your family did, with your name."
"A woman far back in my family took the name Bobadilla from a powerful Spanish woman."
"What's a name got to do with Harry in there poisoned and covered with blood?"
"Those who had no names in the time of the Spanish...are those who...still want to change things today."
"With lizards and poison?"
"The iguana is their sign."
"But why Harry? What could Indians in the jungle want with Harry?"
"What I know is Harry and Ramon are friends. Ramon and Tia are like soldiers."
"Are we talking about the *Cimarrones*?"
"Eddie! Do not speak that word."

HUNDRED WATERS

"It's what they're called, aren't they? Why not say it?"

"Because it carries power, and it is not a name to be spoken."

"I saw this once before," I said. "Outside a bar in old town. Some government minister was dead in the street with a lizard stuck in his mouth. It's the same people, isn't it?"

"It is their sign of strength."

"You still haven't said why they would do this to Harry."

"Perhaps to encourage him."

"Encourage him! To do what?"

Bobdog shrugged her shoulders. "Ramon says it is like a show. Of control. Who carries life and death."

"But why? Why do this to Harry?"

"Perhaps because Harry could help them, and these people want his help."

"But how do these people even know Harry?"

"Through Ramon and Tia."

"So these nameless ones, who want to change things, poison Harry to encourage him to do some unknown thing? It doesn't add up."

"I don't know everything, Eddie. But I know these people are very serious. They have survived all these years because they are strong, and people fear them." She stopped and walked to the edge of the porch. I moved some Spanish books off a chair and sat down. "I am of these people, Eddie."

"The people who did this?"

"Those we should not name. They are my people."

"Don't tell me you had something to do with this."

"Of course not. I left them several years ago and came here to the city because I wanted something more. Now I want even more for my son."

"You have a son?"

"Yes. He lives in Colon with an aunt."

"That's who you really went to see the day I ended up in your room...when you left me with your rent money?"

"Yes. But you must not speak of this. I am worried for his safety. That is why he is in Colon and I am here."

"What's his name?"

Bobdog looked at me hard.

"Your boy...he does have a name doesn't he?"

"Raul. His name is Raul. But please do not speak of this. Believe me, Eddie, I have made it dangerous by talking of these things...so it is best we don't speak of this more."

"How would talking about your son or these people be dangerous?"

"Because they can only be stopped if they exist. It is difficult to conquer the nameless. I also wear their mark...here on my neck...and have sworn with my blood to the secrecy of my people. Just by talking of this to you risks the lives of my family."

"And you?" I said.

"I might be found with a lizard in my mouth."

"Just for talking to me?"

Ramon walked out onto the patio and motioned for Bobdog. I lit another cigarette and tried to imagine what could have gone on to get Harry in such a state. I also tried to figure out how to explain to our superiors Harry's absence and his physical state—which was comatose—when I last looked.

"Ramon says Harry is awake now." I started for the cabin door when Bobdog grabbed my arm. "Nothing must be said about what you have seen here."

"No one would ever believe any of this."

"It is very important that what you have seen remains here. For everyone."

HUNDRED WATERS

I went inside the cabin and straight over to Harry who was now sitting up on the couch. He did not look well...like he had been vomiting for two hours straight. His face was a pasty white, his hair drooped in wet stringy clumps across his damp forehead and his pupils were the size of dimes.

"So...you ready to party?" I said.

Harry rolled his eyes up at me, and the hint of a smile crept across his lips. I took the wash rag from Tia and continued wiping the blood off his chest and back. "Say...could I speak to Harry...alone?" I said to the others. Ramon looked at me, then over at Bobdog who nodded and motioned for Ramon and Tia to leave with her.

"Harry...can you move? I mean from here down to your van?"

"I don't know," he said. "I don't know what I can or can't do."

I grabbed Harry under one arm, lifted him upright and held him until he could stand up on his own. He complained of a headache and a cramp in his left calf, but other than that he said he felt able to walk. I very slowly walked him around the cabin until he found his balance and got his mobility. He was eventually able to get into the makeshift shower under his own steam, and with my minimal help, got himself washed up and into some of Ramon's clean clothes. Ramon agreed to help me get Harry down the hill to his van. An hour after I'd gotten Harry on his feet, I had him buckled into the front seat of the van and drove straight back to Fort Clayton. We were almost there when Harry threw up all over the front of his shirt.

The guard at the main gate drove me crazy asking who Harry was and what was wrong with him. I finally just gave up and drove through the gate. I went straight to the base hospital emergency room, and just as I was helping Harry out of the van, two M.P.s pulled up and drew their pistols on us.

Excerpt from a LETTER from Eddie Carr to his father Joseph Carr. Written in blue ink in Eddie's hand on green, lined steno paper. Dated January 13, 1969.

...I can't really go into any detail about what happened because I don't really know everything that happened. But it was weird, Dad. When I found him he was covered in blood and there was this huge lizard about the size of the Bjornson's terrier hanging over him from a rope. It was dead! Some Panamanian friends of his saved his life by giving him some kind of root antidote. I'm not kidding. You want to know how screwed up this place is? His friends said this group of radical Indians who live back in the jungle poisoned him to get him to help their cause. Usually people poison someone because they hate them and want to kill them. Sounds like these people poison you to win you over. That's how messed up things are here.

My friend Harry spent three days in the post hospital, and I guess everything checked out okay because they let him out and sent him back to the company. Harry is a good man and I know he didn't do anything to compromise things. He got off real lucky with the security boys, though. They didn't take away his clearance or anything, and no AWOL charges. But it was real close. They called it something like an unexcused absence...(like in school when you'd skip classes *for a day) and they fined him $200. I thought he'd lose his clearance for sure and maybe get busted back to PFC.*

But get this. Instead of getting in trouble, we've both been assigned to a courier run that goes from Panama to Homestead in Florida and back again. It's only an overnighter, but it's about the only way they can get me back to stateside duty. There won't be much to do except eat, sleep and fly back, but it will be good to at least smell stateside air and maybe catch a glimpse of an American girl. Other than that, I'm in no hurry to hit the States. I wouldn't ask for stateside duty with all the parades and stupid inspections and jerk-headed brass breathing down your neck for anything. All the protests I read about don't make me want to come back anytime soon either. If I want revolution, there's plenty of it down here. We've been on yellow alert about six times in the last month. Seems some of the locals down here don't like us either. There have been some rocks thrown, and a couple of airmen from Albrook AFB got beat-up in town last week, so things are a little edgy right now. They hate us here, and they hate us back home. That's why I volunteered for combat duty. At least the hate there is not bullshit hate, and you can fight back. In my case it would probably be with Morse code, but that would be better than vegetating down here.

So when you ask why I don't put in for stateside duty, that's why. Hell...I'd rather be soaked in blood with a lizard hanging over me. Just joking. Don't tell Mom about that stuff, she'll just worry and think we're surrounded by cannibals. (Well, maybe we are...except they're wearing short skirts and they cost money.) Don't tell Mom about that either. She'll really worry. Well, that's about it for now. Nothing much is new. Tell Cliff I miss him.

Eddie

Carr, MANUSCRIPT. Handwritten in black ink. Printed across the top of the first page is: "Buzzards in the mist: A Courier Run, January 1969."

We were about an hour out of Homestead, heading back to Panama, when a loud voice pierced the obnoxious roar of the DC-10.

"Miles!...Carr!" I bolted upright, as did Harry Miles next to me. "Be advised, gentlemen, we'll be landing into an alert status!"

I viciously rubbed at my eyes, and when they finally started to focus, I was staring up at Lieutenant Farrel's twisted face. I instinctively felt for the .45 strapped around my waist, and then reached for my copy of *The Diary of Che Guevara* as it started sliding off my lap. I rubbed my eyes again. The loud roar of the plane's engines made it hard to make out what Lieutenant Farrel was yelling at the top of his voice.

"I repeat," he yelled, "we have heat on the ground. Do you understand?"

We both nodded, and then I glanced over at Harry and smiled coyly.

"I've been further notified," the lieutenant continued, "an escort will be waiting for us when we touchdown. So pucker up and don't wander off!" He turned and walked up the aisle.

DAVID GREGOR

I turned to Harry. "Did he say not to wander off?"
"I believe he did," Harry said.
"I've wanted something to happen here for a year. Finally something happens, and I'm advised to stay put?"
"Opportunity finally knocks," Harry said.
Lieutenant Farrel returned and looked right at me. "And Carr. Stow that commie rag before we land." I closed *The Diary of Che Guevara* and stuffed it in my travel bag. "Doesn't look good for somebody in our line of work reading that crap." He shook his head and walked back up the passageway.

* * *

The Homestead courier run was a weekly delivery of classified material from Panama up to Homestead, Florida en route to Washington, D.C. and the National Security Agency. The run consisted of two enlisted men and an officer escorting tape recordings, military dossiers, hard copies of intercepted messages about troop movements, shipping news, diplomatic traffic and anything else the military felt too sensitive for unsecured transport. The two-day run had probably been my reward for finding Harry, though the army would never admit to that; instead they told me it was just my rotation. In Harry's case, I'm sure the S-2 boys wanted to put some distance, if only temporarily, between Harry and the elements responsible for his poisoning. When the doctors cleared him after several days of observation, they released him back to duty, and two days later we were assigned to the courier run. For Harry, the run was intended as something of a buffer before he returned to work full time. For me, the diversion of going stateside, if for only a quick turnaround, could have been seen as therapeutic also. If that was the case, the therapy came too late.

HUNDRED WATERS

The army knew I had requested the war as my first choice of duty stations out of school, and now they had to know I had requested it again as my final tour of duty. Perhaps someone thought the flight to Homestead might loosen what they saw in me as a dangerous spring wound just a little too tight for a combat zone. But the courier run was too little time in the wrong direction. I didn't need to get away; I needed salvation.

* * *

Our plane made several banking turns and finally sliced through the white sea of clouds. The blue Caribbean lay beneath us, dotted with small boats and tiny brush strokes of wave caps. The shoreline of western Panama curved like a sandy crescent moon. We swung farther out over the water just east of Panama City, and it was when we banked back over the jungle on our first approach that I caught a glimpse of them far off. They were thin and dark, insect-like just above the city, circling in their all too familiar pattern. I knew then that things had taken a turn.

I pointed out the black marks to Harry. "Maybe this is finally it," I said to him.

"Intelligence has been crying wolf now for weeks," he said. "This is probably just a precautionary move on our part."

"I hope it *is* something," I said.

"I'm sure it is something," Harry said. "Whether it's something we'll understand is another matter. But this *is* something, Eddie. Mark my words."

"I hope so. I hope the whole damn place comes unravelled. I hate this rock-throwing shit and bar fights. If it's going to come apart, then let's do it. I'm ready for the whole damn thing to go. I mean everything!"

"I don't think you do, Eddie. But it's out of our control either way."

"You think so?"

"When it's time for another change down here, change will come. And there will be nothing we can do about it."

* * *

There had always been a certain uneasy edge to the Panamanians for as long as I had been in country, a hangover from the deadly riots a few years earlier. The people only tolerated us because they couldn't afford *not* to, at least not yet. If some Panamanians got the government they wanted, attitudes would change. And we would know it.

I turned back to my window and stared out blindly into the heavy bank of clouds we were passing through, thinking back on just how much I wanted to be where the action was real. Where the risk was severe and the reward significant. Reading the diary of Che Guevara had done that to me. There was something alluring about a ragtag group of revolutionaries roaming the back hills of Bolivia, playing cat and mouse with the authorities, living outdoors, and believing in something so important they'd risk their lives for it. It was a life I could see myself living, trudging along mountain trails or through dense brush with Che, Chino, Pacho and Inti Perez. No matter how bad it got in the diary accounts, it never seemed to be too bad. *I could do it. I could take the heat, the hiking, eating off the land. I could fight if I had to. I could do what had to be done. All I needed was the call.*

* * *

The black marks off in the distant sky above Panama City looked like small aircraft...Cessnas maybe...eight or ten of them silhouetted against the blue tropical sky. We banked gently, and I lost sight of them circling. All I saw was a field of lush green stretching out from my window straight to the far horizon. The jungle was thick and spongy-looking like a green nappy rug. Far off to the north, gentle rolling hills merged with a farther range that blurred in the hazy mist of the distant Caribbean, fifty miles across the isthmus. Several distinct mountains rose up sharply from the sea of lush foliage. One peak, way off to the north, was shrouded in mist and banded with clouds much like a white, wispy hat. The jungle down below us looked clean and bright, shiny fresh, like everything had just been rinsed by a heavy rain.

Our plane banked again, and we began our slow descent. The horizon shrunk and the ground drew closer. Brown patches pocked the vegetation. I glimpsed small lone structures, then clusters of wooden shacks with people moving around them. Suddenly something metallic caught the sun, reflecting a flash of light up into my eyes, and there was smoke below...layers of smoke and tongues of fire, curling up from the jungle...

God, how I wanted it, how I wanted the War. I wanted it so badly my palms got sweaty just seeing the smoke. The thrill was deep and intoxicating; it grabbed my bowels and wrung them tight. I want the test. I don't fear it now...I need to know things about myself...

Off ahead of us, closer now, the dark thin figures were circling Panama City and Panama Bay. We passed over several tankers of different sizes approaching the mouth of the canal. Farther off, the Pan American Bridge arched high over the canal entrance just beyond the city. We banked hard and passed over a string of waterfront warehouses, one with the name United Fruit Company in large, banana-yellow letters on the roof. We dropped lower, and as we swung back over Panama Bay for our final approach to Tocumen Airport, I could see more clearly what I thought I had seen earlier. The buzzards over the city were as thick as sea gulls over a garbage scow. *What kind of city can this truly be where its major air traffic is buzzards?*

But then I saw beyond the buzzards and there were three...no four...helicopter gunships circling downtown Panama City. The pall of smoke that I could see off in the distance was clearly coming from several fires in the streets below. There were large crowds of people running through the narrow city streets, and then quickly we were beyond the smoke and fire. We dropped down to building level where the view vanished, and we were at eye level with six-story apartment buildings. Suddenly our tires bounced twice off the tarmac, and we were back.

We taxied out to the far end of the runway, away from the commercial gates and the cargo terminals, and finally came to rest near a concrete revetment with a large sign marked: NO TRESPASSING. U.S. GOVERNMENT VEHICLES ONLY!

Harry gently tapped my arm. "The quickest way to assess the proximity of danger," he whispered, "is in the actions of those around you. Stay alert."

Just then Lieutenant Farrel approached us. "All right gentlemen, let's saddle up." He hurried us to the exit door and led us down the portable stairs onto the tarmac.

The smell of change was unmistakable. It hung heavy in the air. The putrid smell of burnt wood and rotten food mixed harshly with the biting, pungent odor of tear gas. My eyes immediately began to water. Lieutenant Farrel, looking nervous with a large leather briefcase handcuffed to his wrist, wiped tears from around his eyes. Harry and I followed suit. The lieutenant frantically searched the airfield for anyone who looked like they were looking for us. Finally a green army sedan raced out onto the runway and pulled up next to us.

HUNDRED WATERS

The driver called out the lieutenant's name. Farrel got into the front with the driver; Harry and I slid into the back seat, and off we went.

"You call this is an escort?" Lieutenant Farrel asked the driver.

"That I don't know, sir. I was just told to pick up the couriers at the airport."

"Hell, they made it sound like things were really cooking down here. I don't see anything but a little smoke."

"Just precautions I guess, sir."

"So driver, are you saying there's no uprising? No riots!"

"There's been trouble, but nothing too serious yet. Some cars overturned and set on fire and a few rocks thrown, but that's it so far. They haven't marched on the Zone or anything. All the action's been in town. That's why I'm taking the back way in."

"Damn it!" I whispered under my breath.

"What's that, Carr?"

"Nothing, sir. Just wishful thinking."

Lieutenant Farrel argued with the driver about which road would take us out of the airport and get us back to Fort Clayton most directly.

Harry Miles nudged me and pointed out the side window at a small group of Panamanian soldiers working over two young men with the butts of their rifles. "No need to wish," he whispered. "It's happening."

The civilians were still down on the ground, flailing under a dusty cloud, as the group of soldiers kicked and plunged their rifles down on the bloodied young men.

"It just won't be what anyone expects, that's all."

"How do you know this?"

Harry smiled. "It's our job to know...remember?"

Carr, MANUSCRIPT. Dated: January 1969. Titled, "The Perez Communique."

It was early Sunday morning, about 1:00 a.m., and I had just completed my assigned missions for the night. I had no further scheduled transmissions to monitor, so I began rolling through the frequencies as we were always directed, listening for unknown or unscheduled radio transmissions. I rolled and rolled, stopping occasionally to listen to weather or shipping traffic, just to hear something besides static or gray noise. After about twenty minutes of rolling, I suddenly I caught a blip and stopped. I rolled forward and then back, got the signal clearly tuned, and when I heard the code I listened for just a moment to make sure it was "good" code—not "canned" or automatic. When I was sure it was good, I started typing. The code was coming out in plain-text Spanish, and I could tell by the subject matter that I had missed the important message address which gave the *to*, *from*, and what *priority* the message carried. I kept on copying and called out for a linguist. Billy Donner, our shift DF operator, came up beside me, checked the frequency and walked back to his direction-finding station.

"Let's hope he's got a lot on his mind," Billy yelled from across the room.

I knew immediately Billy was going to try to get a

directional shot on the signal to see where it was coming from. A moment later Harry Miles leaned over my shoulder.

"What do we have here, partner?" he said, lifting up my sheet of copy as it came out of my typewriter.

"A UFO," I said.

"No I.D. at all?"

"I've locked him in back here," Billy Donner called out.

"Call in for a shot, Billy," Harry yelled.

"Beat you to it," Billy replied.

I continued to copy the slow, often ragged and periodically faint transmission. I saw the words "guerrillas...rifles...Cuba...help."

"This looks good," Harry said.

"At least interesting," I said during a pause. The sender keyed up again and sent a quick burst of words including *"peligroso"* and "Panama."

"All we need is "Castro" or "invasion" and we're in for medals," Harry said.

From the modest Spanish I knew, I got the rough idea that somebody needed help and quickly, and from the sound of things, also medical supplies and weapons. But without the message I.D. information at the beginning of all standard Morse transmissions, we had no idea who the message was from, where they were at, or to whom it was being sent. Without at least a city of origin, some military or diplomatic organization name, or an official's name, nothing would make any sense. We received a lot of messages without identification, and though the people in "traffic assessment" never discarded them, these messages were rarely of any significance.

The message wound down by asking for a reply to the sender's request via *"la Churo frequencia."* The word *"Churo"* made me pause for a moment. I was about to write off the whole event when the sender signed off with his name...Inti Perez. I looked up at Harry and smiled.

HUNDRED WATERS

"What?" he said.
"You don't recognize that name...Inti Perez?"
"Should I?"
"It's on the shelves of bookstores. As a matter of fact I was just reading about an Inti Perez on our courier run."
"So who's this Perez I should've known about?"
"He was one of Che Guevara's men in Bolivia. I can't tell you any of the others' names, but for some reason I remember Inti's."

I explained to Harry how Inti and several others survived and escaped the ambush that led to Guevara's capture. That group had not been seen or heard from since. Until now, that is, if this was the same Inti Perez.

"Perez is a pretty common name down here."
"And Inti?"
"If there's one, there could be five. And we don't even know where this message is coming from. He could be right down the street for all we know. Besides the Bolivians killed most of those guerrillas earlier this year."

Just then Billy Donner walked up and handed Harry the coordinates from the three-way direction shot. "Guantanamo says north central Bolivia, most likely the mountains near the Chilean border."

"Bingo," I said. "How's that for a rendezvous?"

Government DOCUMENT 27. U.S. Army Security Agency, SOUTHCOM. Labeled: "Locos Bar. Panama City. January 1, 1969." Written in ink in Edward Carr's hand on both sides of three large bar napkins.

This is a confusing time and a confusing place. Another winter of the War, and I'm still here. The weirdness continues.

Lyle Boggs blew his intestines out his navel from convulsions when he found out he'd eaten dog meat sold as beef outside a bar last week.

Panama is the only true home of vampire bats.

A family of six Panamanians died from a grenade thrown by a Panamanian Ranger on alert who mistook them for Cuban guerrillas landing west of Rio Hato.

You can buy a twelve-year-old girl here for an hour for five dollars.

Marijuana is potent, plentiful and cheap, like the whores and the fevers.

Dickey Brewer watched a scratch on his leg abscess until it ate away a lemon-sized chunk out of his calf.

The streets of this town smell like piss and the daily news reads like bad history:

"Governor Villarte Ocente, who recently conducted a three month campaign to eradicate voodoo priests, was officially pronounced dead yesterday after a two week bout with an unknown fever."

DAVID GREGOR

Reading that newspaper account was my third encounter with "Los Cimarrones". Harry Miles knows them...I'm certain of that...as does Bobdog, I'm sure, bless her heart ...and I'm feeling stupid from the rum. I've been in country for fifteen months and all I have to show for my stay are sore kidneys and a bad attitude. Jesus...if the army doesn't send me to the War after doing time in this stink hole, there's no mercy in the world.

Happy Fucking New Year!

Carr, MANUSCRIPT. Dated: January 15, 1969. Titled: "Riots, Panama City, Panama." Typewritten on Fort Clayton stationary.

We sat in white wicker chairs on the second-floor veranda of the Tivoli Guest House drinking Bloody Marys, waiting for the start of the revolution.

Down the veranda from us and beyond a waist-high wood partition was a group of six men with a battery of cameras (still and moving) and binoculars all around. The men wore suits and ties and had long sideburns. They were clearly not military, and we had a good idea who they were. We had known something was coming for weeks. Rumors picked up throughout our Operations Building as soon as the Panamanian Guardia Civil was put on alert. Then when the advisories were posted putting town off-limits indefinitely, we knew something was imminent. Exactly what was going to happen no one knew for sure, but it was clear something could happen and given that, certain people wanted to know everything they could. So we weren't surprised to see the CIA represented. That's why the three of us had checked into the Tivoli early the first morning of our two-day break; something important could happen and the best place to be, outside the event, was at the Tivoli Guest House. It sat right on the Avenida 4th of

July across from downtown Panama City. In fact the street marked the border between the country of Panama and the U.S.-governed Canal Zone. The Tivoli had been built in 1906 during the American construction of the canal and was where visiting dignitaries stayed. Situated on beautifully manicured grounds, it was a grand old structure, complete with employees dressed in white colonial uniforms. It was an ideal place from which to watch a revolution.

Harry, Tepi and I took a large room on the south side of the building that looked out across Avenida 4th of July. We ordered a portable bar and waited for our lives to get interesting.

* * *

About ten in the morning Bobdog arrived with two of her girl friends from the Red Coat Inn. I recognized the blonde one known as Bicycle, but the young girl with East Indian features Bobdog introduced as Naja, I had never seen before.

"Help yourselves to something to drink," Harry said and gestured toward the portable bar.

"This is very nice place," Bobdog said. "Everything is so...clean...so white."

"Not exactly the rooms above Delgado Street," I said.

"Not exactly Panama," Harry said. "That is, Panama as they know it."

"Or as we know it," Tepi added. "It took three of us to afford this room."

"And well worth the expense," I said, "if anything develops across the street."

"Well," Tepi said, "if the guys down at the end of the porch are any indication of what might be coming, then we may be a little too close."

"The closer the better," I said.

HUNDRED WATERS

Bobdog walked over and stood next to me. "Why do you want to see such ugly things?" she said.

"I don't want to see *ugly* things. But if *ugly* things are going to happen, I'm not going to look away."

"My dear Bobdog," Harry said, "if Eddie wanted to see ugly things, none of you young ladies would be here."

"I love you very much, Harry Miles," Bobdog said. "If I did not have some love for Eddie, I would spoil you for some women. But wanting to see fighting and to see people hurt, I do not understand, Eddie. None of my friends want to see these things."

"Then why did you come here?" Tepi said.

"I'm afraid to be with my own people."

* * *

Carr, *JOURNAL*. Noted as "Entry 9." Fort Clayton, Canal Zone. Dated: January 14, 1969.

Bobdog is a chameleon. She's so many things and yet she's nothing in particular. When I think of her, I think of so much else. I guess that's why I keep coming back to her. She reminds me of me. Maybe that's all anyone is—a reminder of ourself. Harry is someone I want to be. Harry is the hole I feel in my existence. He is what I am missing in myself. I need what Harry has. And Tepi. I guess I need him too. And why not? What's not to like about him? He has history. I like that about him. History gives him something I lack. And he is so damned careful. I guess he can afford to be careful; he has so much behind him that is solid. His girl back home. If he only knew the thoughts I have about her. They are so together, and that makes me feel so apart. But Bobdog brings me back. What would I do without her?

* * *

DAVID GREGOR

Carr, MANUSCRIPT.

Bicycle leaned over the railing like she was modeling her tight shorts. "I never been here," she said. "I like to see what is new to me."

"I can't believe there is much that is new to you...Bicycle," Harry said.

"You make a good joke, Harry."

"No," he said. "Your reputation far outreaches your beauty."

"My name is known in many places?" Bicycle asked hopefully. "I love you too much, Harry. You speak nice things to me."

Harry smiled. "You are known far and wide, for your...how should I say this...your pedaling skills."

"Are you speaking of her ability to transmit motion...." I started to say.

"...Or peddling...as in moving from place to place and offering things for sale?" Tepi said.

Bicycle feigned a look of hurt and then peered at Tepi with squinted eyes. "I don't recognize this one," she said. "I remember many GI's but this one is not known to me. And all GI men who want the best come see Bicycle. No? I have GIs waiting in line for Bicycle, but I never see you before." Tepi smiled. "Are you cherry boy?"

Harry and I laughed. Tepi had made it a point to avoid going with the whores out of his strong allegiance to his fiancée back home. While I supported his personal belief, I couldn't help but laugh at Bicycle's crafty way of turning the tables on him.

"Touché," Harry said.

"I don't need to stand in line for a woman," Tepi said. "Or pay money for that matter."

HUNDRED WATERS

"You must be married," Bicycle said, "or perhaps there are other pleasures you like much better."
"What the hell's she mean by that?" Tepi snapped.
"She's pulling your chain, Tep."
"She's not pulling anything of mine...that's for damn sure."
Harry stepped in between Tepi and Bicycle. "Tep, I think we could use some more ice. Why don't you call down for some. "
"Take Naja with you," Bicycle said. "She is lonely for company."

***

Shortly before noon, the tenor of the day changed. Far off back in the heart of the city, a low undulating roar echoed off the narrow ancient streets. The sea of voices grew louder and more intense. People chanted repeatedly in a low rhythmic roll that blurred the individual words into a frightening wave of sound that continued to grow in intensity.

I stared nonchalantly out across the manicured lawn, listening calmly to the thunder of distant voices. No crowds were visible, just the uniform chants of thousands of voices. Suddenly streams of people began pouring out of the narrow streets that spoked into Independence Plaza, waving banners and Panamanian flags. Huge photographs of stern-faced men danced above the throngs of people spreading into the plaza like a human tide. Trumpets blared, drum beats ricocheted off the concrete walls and competing chants met above the plaza in a cacophonous roar.

From our vantage point we could see most of Independence Plaza and the main streets that led into it. We also had an unobstructed view of Avenida 4th of July, which was now closed to traffic. Hundreds and hundreds of people continued pouring into the central plaza until every piece of open ground was covered, including the benches, the small built-in tables and the concrete dividing walls. People cheered whenever one of the huge photographs passed by or when they were instructed to cheer by one of the many people with a bullhorn.

Harry and Tepi and I quietly watched the event unfold without violence or interdiction from the Panamanian military. Just thousands of people cheering and making noise in a loud display of exuberance and anger. One man with a bullhorn climbed up onto a makeshift platform, and with people behind him holding a long banner and others with picture placards bobbing riotously, he called out to those gathered to elect their man to the presidency and get the U.S. out of Panama. It was impossible to hear the speaker's every word, but key words of anger and passion were quite clear. I scanned Independence Plaza, down the surrounding streets, and across the tops of buildings encircling the plaza.

The dark silhouettes of soldiers with rifles quickly started materializing on the rooftops. Everywhere I looked I saw small groups of helmeted soldiers with weapons, standing dark against the blue sky. I pointed them out to Tepi first, then Harry. The civilians at the end of the veranda had their cameras aimed toward the rooftops and were clicking off pictures. Down below the demonstrators were chanting a slogan followed by the name of a popular opposition leader. The huge crowd seemed to swell and contract like some giant breathing organism, then sway from side to side the way a changing tide moves.

Suddenly a company of mounted Guardia Civil came into view on Avenida 4th of July. The soldiers were in a formation of six horsemen abreast and about twenty deep. From our vantage point we could see both the civilian rally and demonstration in Independence Plaza off to our left and the approaching mounted Guardia Civil on our right. A block of tall old buildings, including the main cathedral on the edge of the central plaza, blocked the demonstrator's view of the quickly approaching mounted guardsmen. In the plaza there were several thousand Panamanian civilians gathered in front of a statue with a few men in white shirts standing on its base, some of whom waved large red banners. From the side streets that angled off from Independence Plaza, like so many veins running off from the heart of the city, several platoons of black-bereted soldiers, rifles held across their chests, jogged at quickstep toward the plaza.

"Looks like we've got ourselves a show," Tepi said.

"This could get ugly," Harry added.

Bobdog ran to the porch railing and stared across the highway toward the plaza. "*Mio Dio*," she said in a hushed voice. "This is not good."

"I'll call room service for more ice," I said. I walked back inside the room and phoned the front desk and ordered ice and mixers.

I returned to the veranda and moved my camera tripod to the railing next to Harry. I looked up from the viewfinder of my Pentax and aimed the telephoto lens in the direction of the mounted Guardia Civil, still moving down Avenida 4th of July. Through my camera I could see the faces of the soldiers—young, gaunt and scared. They bounced in their saddles and glanced from side to side, concerned with their positioning and probably wondering what possible dangers awaited them in the plaza.

The civilians down the veranda from us leaned into the viewfinders of their bank of cameras, sporadically clicking off frames of military movement and faces in the crowd. The armed soldiers, silhouetted against the sky, moved across the building rooftops, grouping in threes and fours along the corners of the buildings surrounding the plaza and the main streets. Off to our right, the mounted soldiers rounded the corner of Avenida 4th of July and then came to a halt outside the Biblioteca Nacional. The mounted Guardia stood there in ranks of six, and they waited.

* * *

Harry continued to scan the crowd of demonstrators for the faces of Panamanian nationals that he knew. He repeatedly expressed concern for the whereabouts and well-being of his two closest Panamanian friends. Tia and Ramon were like his adopted siblings, which explained why they had been at his side after he was poisoned. Harry knew them from the University of Panama where he had taken several advanced Spanish classes which Ramon taught. Tia taught classes on the political history of Latin America. Tia and Ramon were young idealists with a strong desire to change the political direction of their country. On several occasions Harry had met with members of the their revolutionary party just as an observer, an uninvolved witness with an interest in history and grassroots activism. He once told me that it helped him put a perspective on his army work. It struck me as an excuse, but one with some intellectual integrity. Harry confessed to me he had some concern for his newfound friends because their political activities were very dangerous. People like them were abducted, beaten, even publicly assassinated for their beliefs and their activities. To be politically engaged in Panama was like being an unpaid combatant in a war zone. The duty was hazardous to your health, and you knew it going in. I could hear in Harry's voice, whenever he talked of Tia and Ramon, that he admired their political commitment. Harry understood why they rallied, why they protested, why they risked having their pictures taken or being seen at public demonstrations. Without their belief, they had nothing, Harry said many times. So belief became very important to Harry. Something, he said, he had not honestly known before coming to Panama.

When rumors of civil unrest began spreading through our operations building, I noticed right away the impact they had on Harry. He was visibly concerned for the welfare of his friends with their strong beliefs. Harry knew if there was any civilian uprising, Tia and Ramon would more than likely be an integral part of the action. For that reason he was more upset than anyone else at the Tivoli at the sight of the soldiers on the rooftops and the approaching mounted guardsmen.

* * *

Bobdog brought two cold beers and set them down on the railing between Harry and me. "Some trouble yet?" she asked.

"Nothing yet," Harry said, lowering his binoculars. "But I don't like what I'm seeing. These soldiers up on the roofs are not there for defensive measures. Something is cooking, and it doesn't smell good." Harry put the binoculars back up to his eyes and continued to scan the ever-growing crowd.

"Are you sure they're out there?" I asked Harry. "I mean...they could be anywhere."

"Of course I'm sure. This is their show. This is what they want. Tia and Ramon would not be somewhere else. This is where the action is. Believe me, they're out there somewhere."

"Why you look for them?" Bobdog asked.

"Because those guardsmen there on horseback were probably shown photographs of them and other leaders and given special orders."

"What kind of orders?"

"It's no coincidence the number of stray bullets that find their way into the backs of organizers and party leaders down here."

"Come on now, Harry. Do you think these guys are going to just start shooting unarmed civilians, for no reason with...with those guys at the end of the porch watching and photographing everything that's going on?"

"I know of the Guardia Civil's special orders. Trust me. They're not brought in to negotiate. Besides, the CIA has no jurisdiction over these dictators. To them this is all just information. Not about right or wrong...or living or dying. It's just cold data."

"How do you know of their special orders?"

"We're not here just to listen to weather traffic."

The Black Berets spread out at the north end of the plaza, encircled the area and stood at parade rest. The voice of one of the demonstrators echoed out from a speaker across the plaza, drawing cheers from the crowd. The cheers were quickly followed by rhythmic chants which overlapped at first, then became synchronized into a powerful, threatening roar.

I looked up from my camera and surveyed the scene from the Black Berets on my left, across the thousands of people in the plaza, to the mounted soldiers to the south on my right. The demonstrators began chanting in Spanish, punctuated by arms thrust in unison into the air and banners waving.

Then suddenly, off in the distance, there was a POP! There were several screams, followed by loud, painful wails. Then another loud POP! A cloud of smoke rose up from the crowd on the far side of the plaza, and a rippling wave of bodies surged away from the billowing smoke.

"Oh, do we have ourselves a show," Tepi said.

"I was afraid of this," Harry said. "What did I tell you?"

The civilians at the end of the veranda scurried around

and sprung into action. "Who fired?" one of them yelled. "Anybody see who fired?"

"Doesn't matter now," I said under my breath to Tepi. "Did anybody see it?"

"I heard the pop, that's all...then saw the smoke."

The mounted guard quickly moved into the plaza from the south and at the north end the Black Berets pinched their way forward, pushing demonstrators inward with their rifles and lashing out with their rifle butts at anyone who refused to move. From the side streets, covered half-ton army trucks pulled up, and riot police with night sticks poured out and rushed toward the crowd. Small explosions echoed off the walls of the buildings surrounding the large plaza, followed immediately by clouds of tear gas. Demonstrators covered their faces with bandannas and shirt-sleeves, running aimlessly for safety, but everywhere were armed soldiers, riot police and the mounted guard pushing, beating and flailing their sticks. Sporadic rifle shots popped and pinged off the walls surrounding the plaza. Within moments of the initial tear gas explosion, dozens of people lay on the cobbled square, red stains clearly visible on the white shirts of many of the men and women, arms reaching to no one, bodies writhing with pain, some being assisted, others lying alone, still others being stepped on by those trying to escape the batons of the riot police.

"This is ugly," Harry said, lowering his binoculars. "Insanely ugly." He continued looking through his glasses, scanning the sea of bodies swirling in every direction, looking, I knew, for his friends. They were out there. Harry knew that, and he was clearly concerned for them.

"Any sign of them?" I asked.

"I thought I saw Tia earlier, near the base of the statue. But nothing now."

DAVID GREGOR

I aimed my telephoto lens into the crowd, and though I had only met his friends on the one occasion, I hoped I might recognize them if I saw them again. Cameras were clicking all along the veranda, and people were yelling. There was a man on a radio relaying information either to another intelligence site or to Army Headquarters at Fort Amador.

My eyes were watering from the drifting tear gas, and there were a lot of people on the veranda coughing. Naja and Bicycle pulled towels off the service cart and held them across their faces. Tepi held his head down and rubbed at his eyes.

"There...there they are!" Harry yelled. I squinted through the tears flooding my eyes in the direction of a clump of trees just off the main plaza. Harry kept pointing toward a small group of people dodging the baton attacks of several mounted guards. I looked through my viewfinder and saw the demonstrators trying to keep a tree between themselves and the mounted soldiers. Then three more horsemen arrived and sent the group scattering in all directions.

"That's them!" Harry yelled. "Tia's wearing a red scarf around her head."

"I see them," I said, "they're coming across the highway."

"Jesus," Harry yelled, "run you guys...run!"

Harry's friends, along with several other protestors, were running as fast as they could, chased by two mounted guardsmen. They got to Avenida 4th of July and ran across the street into the Canal Zone, but the mounted guardsmen followed them.

"Hey...hey...," Harry yelled and lowered his binoculars. "No jurisdiction. Canal Zone. This is the Canal Zone."

But the mounted guardsmen didn't slow a step and continued to follow Tia and Ramon and two others up the street and onto Canal Zone property.

"That's it!" Harry said. He dropped his binoculars,

HUNDRED WATERS

ran to the outside stairway and flew down the stairs to the lawn.

"Harry!" I yelled. "Harry, stay here. Stay out of it." I watched Harry run out onto the lawn and wave his friends toward him. The horsemen galloped after the pair, following them onto the Tivoli grounds. One of the guardsmen galloped hard and cocked his right arm to strike with his club. I ran down the stairs after Harry and yelled at him to get off the lawn and out of the way of the horsemen.

"Harry. Come back! Get out of the way."

"Come on!" Harry yelled to his friends. "Come on...you're safe here."

The horsemen kept coming, mere steps behind Harry's friends. As the horsemen drew closer and were clearly poised to use their batons, Harry ran down the grassy slope waving his arms and screaming, "Don't...don't do it!" One guardsman swung and hit Tia hard from behind with his stick, knocking her to the ground. Ramon stopped and, joined by Harry, ran back to get Tia while Harry waved his arms, apparently trying to get between Tia and the horseman. I ran down and helped Ramon drag Tia up the hill toward the hotel, while Harry danced around the horseman, delaying him just long enough for us to get Tia into an outside hallway of the hotel. I ran back outside just in time to see Harry running toward the horseman, yelling and waving his arms, sending the rider's horse rearing back on its hind legs and throwing the rider head first onto the ground. The horse ran off, but the thrown rider did not move. The second horseman dismounted, knelt down and gently rolled his partner over onto his side. The thrown rider still did not move.

"Get your friends out of here," I yelled to Harry. "Go on, get them out!"

"My things?" Harry said. "My stuff upstairs?"

"Don't worry, I'll get your stuff. Go on. Just get them out of here."

Harry and Ramon carried Tia to the rear parking area where Harry's van was parked. When I heard the van start up, I ran back inside the Tivoli, up to our second-floor porch area.

"Did Harry make it?" Tepi asked.

"I heard the van pull out. That girl Tia didn't look too good. She took a nasty hit to the head."

"I think we better get out of sight. That guardsman down there doesn't look good either."

"Soldiers will come soon," Bobdog said.

"I don't need trouble," Bicycle said. "Come, Naja, let's get a taxi."

"Bobdog's probably right," Tepi said. "If that soldier is as hurt as he looks, the Tivoli is going to be swarming with soldiers pronto. I think we want to be somewhere else."

I quickly broke down my tripod and collected my camera gear, while Tepi packed his overnight bag.

"You know," I said to him, "my dad once told me to stay away from things like this. Stay away from mobs and demonstrators, he told me. Now I know why."

Newspaper clipping from *The Miami Herald*, January 16, 1969. Dateline: Panama City. Headline reads: "Thirteen Panamanian Demonstrators Killed in Riots. Hundreds injured."

Panama City's Independence Plaza exploded into violence yesterday when anti-government demonstrators clashed with armed Panamanian military troops, leaving thirteen civilians and one civil guardsman dead in the aftermath. The demonstration by members of the leftist PTN party in opposition to the ruling military junta included speeches and a call for social reforms. The estimated 5000 demonstrators also called for the end of U.S. military and civilian control over Panamanian sovereignty. The march through the narrow streets of downtown Panama City began at approximately 10:00 a.m. in the morning and ended a short time later in Independence Plaza in the center of the city. Panamanian Guardia Civil General Armando Trupillio blamed the riot on radical provocateurs who he claims opened fire on his troops. The Guardia Civil and elements of a special military group returned fire in self-defense and used tear gas grenades to break up the unruly mob. Six of the demonstrators died from gunshot wounds, four from head injuries suffered during mob control, two were trampled by mounted guardsmen and one woman was crushed by stampeding demonstrators. One mounted civil guardsman died from head injuries when he was thrown from his horse. No American citizens were reported injured according to U.S. government sources monitoring the situation in the Canal Zone. This is the first civilian uprising since the deadly march on the Canal Zone by radical PTN demonstrators in 1965, which ended with twenty-four deaths including three Canal Zone residents.

Carr, MANUSCRIPT. Handwritten in blue ink, with holographic changes in the text in red ink. A small pencil drawing of a cabin is in the top right-hand corner of the first page. The words: "A Bit of Inside Luck" are written next to the drawing.

Two hours after the riots broke out, Tepi and I made our way to Ramon's remote cabin back in the Diablo Heights area. We took a cab a few miles out of town and then walked the half-mile from the highway up to the cabin perched atop the jungle plateau. It was quiet, except for an occasional monkey scream and the squawk of a cockatiel. We passed a fresh anthill teeming with fire ants, and we both gave it a wide berth. When we reached the top of the hill and entered the clearing around the cabin, Tepi saw someone sitting on the porch, and he tapped my arm. As we approached, I slowed down and cautioned Tepi about going too fast. I called out Ramon's name and waved my arms so he would see we were not a threat. Ramon looked startled, stepped up to the cabin door and called to someone inside.

"It's me...Eddie," I said. I waved again and called out for Harry.

Bobdog came out onto the porch, and I could clearly see the pistol she held at her side. "Don't shoot," I yelled only half jokingly.

"Ramon didn't recognize you at first," Bobdog said. "Come on."

"Expecting bad guys?" I said.

"Harry taught me how to use it," she said, stepping down off the porch. She walked over and embraced me.

Tepi kept looking down at the pistol hanging loosely in Bobdog's hand. "Is that *really* necessary?" he asked.

"Harry kept it for the pumas and wild hogs."

"I'd really feel better without it," Tepi said.

"Okay," she said, clumsily stuffing the pistol inside her back pocket. The three of us walked up to the cabin and went inside. Bobdog removed the pistol from her pocket and laid it down on the wood table.

"How's Tia?" I asked.

"She is asleeping. Her head...right here...above the ear...has deep cut. Her ribs, too. They are black and very large."

"Broken?"

"I don't know. She is very, very sore right there and much swelling."

We talked about the riots and how lucky Ramon and Tia were that Harry pulled them out from under the horses of those guardsmen.

"So...where's Harry?" I asked.

"He's not here."

"When is he coming back?"

Bobdog turned and slowly walked to the back door. I followed her out into the sun and lit a cigarette. "Harry's not coming back," she said.

"You mean he's not coming back here...to this cabin?"

"Harry's gone away. He's not coming back."

"What do you mean he's not coming back? He has to be back. He's scheduled to work tonight."

"He told to me he had new plans, that's all."

HUNDRED WATERS

"What new plans?"

"Work," Bobdog said. "He say to me he want to do something good...something strong."

"He's gone AWOL?"

"I don't know this AWOL. I just tell you what he say to me."

"Which was what exactly?"

"Harry wants to help some people here. To be free. That's all he say to me."

"Oh Jesus, Eddie," Tepi said.

"He's gone and done it," I said. "He can't help anyone by going AWOL. All he's done is screwed himself. Desertion is serious business."

"So what did Harry actually say he was going to do?" Tepi asked.

"He did not say...exactly...but I believe it is with those I spoke to you about from before."

"Who's that, Eddie?" Tepi asked.

"Some locals who have this thing with lizards."

"What locals...and what lizards?" Tepi asked.

"Harry said to me he wanted to help them."

"I hope this isn't what I think it is," Tepi said. "If so, he's crazy, Eddie. Fucking crazy."

"We don't know anything for sure yet," I said.

"He's gone over the hill," Tepi said. "He's going to desert the U.S. Army...to join a bunch of wild natives...so he can help them. I can't believe this is the same Harry Miles I know."

"Harry would never betray his oath or his country," I said. "That's not in Harry Miles."

"They'll go after him," Tepi said. "You know they will. With his clearance and what he knows, they can't let him just drop out of the system."

171

"Harry wanted you to know he is not doing wrong thing for his country."

"So why didn't he tell us?" Tepi said.

"He said you are his friends and you would try to stop him. He said for me to tell you, so you would know the truth about him. Harry also wanted you, Eddie, to have his van."

"His van?"

"I have the papers for the *autobus*."

When Bobdog went inside the cabin, Tepi rolled his eyes at me. "I don't believe this. How can a guy that smart do something this stupid?"

"I don't know. I'm as confused about this as you. S-2 is going to come unglued."

"Hell...I'd just like to grab him and drag his butt back to the post before he does something really stupid."

"For some reason, I don't think we would find him anywhere nearby."

"Where do you think he is?"

"I have no idea, but I think Bobdog knows something."

"What could she know?"

"She knows...believe me. I think what we need to do is request some emergency leave."

"And...?"

"And try to find Harry. Get him back before this thing goes too far."

"You think we can find him?"

"There's a chance. The army won't do anything for at least thirty days. After that, it's desertion and things will get serious."

"So how do we begin?"

"We need time. Like a week's leave and a bit of inside luck."

"What kind of inside luck?"

HUNDRED WATERS

"The kind of luck a Panamanian whore with a lizard tattoo on her neck can give you."

"And you think Bobdog knows and will just tell you?"

"She loves me," I said.

"What whore doesn't love her GI?" Tepi said.

"Bobdog wants me to be a father to her boy. And she wants something better for herself. She'll help us. That kind of love can make you do things you normally wouldn't."

"And if we can't find him?" Tepi said.

"Either way, Harry's in deep. If he deserts and they have to go after him, Harry's looking at Leavenworth if he's lucky and MIA if he's not. These people won't fuck around."

"So what's the plan?" Tepi said.

"Time," I said. "We need an emergency leave, and we need it now."

Part V

The Search

Beyond the Chagres River
'Tis said—the story's old—
Are paths that lead to mountains
Of purest virgin gold;
But 'tis my firm conviction,
Whatever tales they tell,
That beyond the Chagres River
All paths lead straight to hell!

"Panama Patchwork"
by
James Stanley Gilbert

U.S. Army DOCUMENT 10. Transcript of tape recording, Sony 60-minute cassette. Recorded on one side only. Written in ink on cassette label: Spec. 4, Edward Carr. Recorded at Fort Clayton Hospital, March 23, 1969. Interviewed by Lt. Daniel Hofster, U.S. ARMY SECURITY AGENCY. CONFIDENTIAL.

(Excerpt beginning at foot meter 021)

CARR:	*I know it was crazy but she was the only answer I could think of. I told her she had to help me find Harry. I knew she could help. She knew Harry and she knew the country and the language and the people and she....*
HOFSTER:	*And she what?*
CARR:	*She...ah....*
HOFSTER:	*She what, Carr?*
CARR:	*I knew she liked me.*
HOFSTER:	*She liked you? What does that have to do with this issue with Harry Miles?*
CARR:	*Well...not just like...but more....*
HOFSTER:	*Are you telling us that this prostitute named Bobdog had strong affections for you?*
CARR:	*Yes, sir. I believe she did. She had a son in Colon. She told me she wanted me to be his father.*

HOFSTER: So based on this feeling, you felt you could ask her to help you find Harry Miles?
CARR: I felt I had a good chance of getting her help, sir.
HOFSTER: You said earlier you sought her aid because she knew Harry Miles, the country and the language.
CARR: Yes, sir.
HOFSTER: I am told that Harry Miles had many friends who knew the language and the country, yet you chose to seek the help of this prostitute. Why?
CARR: Because I thought she was the best person I knew who could help.
HOFSTER: Is it possible that she could have had specific information about Miles' whereabouts?
CARR: Specific information, sir?
HOFSTER: Let me be more direct. Did she have personal knowledge of an indigenous group referred to locally as Los Cimarrones?

[LONG PAUSE]

HOFSTER: Did you hear the question, Carr?
CARR: I'm not feeling well, sir.

[Note: SUBJECT'S EYES APPEARED AT THIS TIME TO NARROW AND GLAZE OVER AND HIS ATTENTION SEEMED SCATTERED]

HOFSTER: Did she ever speak of the group called Los Cimarrones?
CARR: They are mystery.
HOFSTER: Los Cimarrones?
CARR: They are the dark...like the shadow to the man.
HOFSTER: Are you speaking of Los Cimarrones?

HUNDRED WATERS

[LONG PAUSE]

HOFSTER: *Carr! Carr! Did this prostitute tell you this about them?*
[LONG PAUSE]

HOFSTER: *Answer me, Carr! Damn it, answer me!*
[LONG PAUSE]

[END OF RECORDING]

Carr, MANUSCRIPT. Typewritten with changes to the text made in red ink. The word "Portobello" is written across the top of the first page in blue ink.

Tepi and I both had thirty days leave coming to us, and first thing Monday morning we went down to operations and each requested an emergency leave. But since we were both only three months away from our change of duty station, we knew they would never allow a thirty-day leave in that brief period of time. When the clerk asked for the nature of our emergency, Tepi turned to me and I stared blankly at the clerk, thinking quietly to myself...*redemption*.

"It's personal," Tepi said, "you know...personal stuff."

"There's somebody sick," I said. "Really."

The clerk glared at Tepi, glanced over at me, and then typed "family illness" in the appropriate spaces, on our respective forms. Impromptu requests for emergency leave without an obvious medical, emotional or family crisis were rarely ever considered and usually choked off with mounds of paperwork.

"How much leave are you requesting?" the clerk asked.

Tepi and I looked at each other. I knew thirty days was out of the picture, so I thought of the next best number.

"Ten days," I said.

DAVID GREGOR

"You've got seven," he countered.

"We'll take it," Tepi said.

The clerk hand carried the forms into the officer in charge, and thirty minutes later we had our seven days of emergency leave. The clerk calmly handed us our request papers and showed us where to sign.

"Good luck," he said. "I hope you find him."

* * *

By noon we had packed our gear into Harry's VW van, gassed up in Balboa and were waiting for Bobdog downtown in front of the Buffalo Cantina. When she finally came downstairs and slid in between us, we headed northwest on the Trans-Isthmian Highway for the fifty-mile drive across the narrow neck of Panama to the Caribbean side. Bobdog asked that we stop briefly in Colon at her aunt's house so she might see her boy who was about to turn three years old.

We got to Colon about an hour later, and Tepi and I agreed to wait outside in the van while she visited her son. When Bobdog came out onto the covered wood porch about twenty minutes later with a rather large dark woman, she was carrying a light-skinned boy, hugging him tightly. Then she abruptly put the boy down and ran out to the van. I could see that her face was wet with tears. Tepi got out so she could sit between us, and when she got in she cried loudly and refused to speak. All she did was point her finger in the direction we should go to get out of Colon and travel northeast up the coast in the direction of the once notorious village of Portobello.

* * *

THE PROVINCE OF COLON: AN HISTORICAL ABSTRACT AND THE SPANISH SEARCH FOR A WESTWARD PASSAGE. [An Excerpt, pages 6, 7] Headquarters,

HUNDRED WATERS

Department of the Army. DA Pamphlet 7321—51. Historical Research Division. Fourth Edition 1965.

*On the Caribbean coast of Panama just east of the mouth of the **Chagres River**, and beyond a wooded peninsula lies **Limon Bay**. This body of water was previously named the **Bay of Ships** by its first visitor, Christopher Columbus, in 1502 because the inlet appeared large enough to hold the entire navies of the known world. Columbus believed this enormous bay was the entrance to the Westward Passage to the Indies, but his belief was proven wrong, and he headed further east. The location on Spanish charts was later misread by English sailors and wrongly translated to **Navy Bay**. The present day port city of **Colon** (named after its founder Christopher Columbus) was built on the shores of **Navy Bay** around the **Island of Manzanillo**, first charted and named by Columbus.*

*Approximately five miles northeast of Colon lies another large recession also explored by Columbus, where once again he believed he had located the entrance to the Westward Passage to the Orient. While Columbus did not find a water route there, he did discover from the locals that there were gold deposits mined by the natives. Columbus charted the body of water, **The Bay of Mines**. Approximately 15 nautical miles northeast of **The Bay of Mines** lies another large natural harbor flanked by open, rising country populated by natives who maintained a multitude of orchards and vegetable gardens. Columbus and his small fleet of four ships took refuge in this large protected harbor for a week until a raging storm subsided. Columbus charted and named this harbor **Porto Bello**, the beautiful port.*

*Columbus and his squadron of ships left **Porto Bello** with the weather change and sailed toward the westernmost* *charted coastline some seven leagues northeast, still in search of the Westward Straits to the Orient. When Columbus finally crossed the longitude charted two years earlier by his predecessor Rodrigo de Bastidas, he found no evidence of a strait or a water passage to breach terra firma. Frustrated and disappointed that there would be no Strait of Columbus, he charted his geographical location at that moment and named it based on his feelings at the time:* **Nombre de Dios**, *Name of God!*

In the year 1509 Diego de Nicuesa, a successor to Columbus, established the first successful European city on the mainland of the Americas at Nombre de Dios.

* * *

Carr, MANUSCRIPT. Handwritten in pencil. A continuation of the section named, "Portobello."

Tepi, Bobdog and I approached the village of Portobello from the west, along the unpaved road that for now was dry and passable. This was the same route that Morgan the pirate had traveled when he surprised the Spanish in his sack of the great gold port in 1669. About twelve kilometers from the village, we came to a river and quickly found out why no outside visitors had been to Portobello by car or bus in over ten years. The river was in a flood stage, rushing fast and wide. And there was no bridge. There was evidence that at one time a bridge had existed on our side. The heads of several posts, once driven deep into the ground, stuck up from the mud, and chunks of large beams were strewn along the shoreline.

"So what do we do?" Tepi said.

I turned to Bobdog. "Is there another way across?"

She shook her head and told me to turn off the van.

HUNDRED WATERS

She calmly got out and walked down to the river's edge and stared out over the water. Then she casually took off her shoes, rolled up her jeans and stepped into the river. She called for Tepi to join her. After complaining for a moment, Tepi got out and slowly followed her into the river. Bobdog took his hand and they stretched out their arms and inched their way forward, side by side, until they reached midstream. Though the river was swift, it did not prove to be very deep, knee-high at most. Then suddenly Tepi stepped into a hole and dropped to his chest, but he quickly regained his balance and stepped back onto higher ground. I could see Bobdog testing the riverbed with her feet and adjusting her direction based on the depth underfoot. She and Tepi snaked their way across the rushing river with only two other deep dips up to their waists, but each time they quickly found higher riverbed. After they reached the other side and spent a few minutes in conversation, Bobdog stepped to the river's edge, cupped her hands and yelled to me.

"Okay, Eddie, now you drive across."

"Have you lost your mind?" I yelled back. I stood at the water's edge and watched the river rush by. "You've got to be kidding."

"Everything will be fine," she said. "You watch me. I will walk you across."

I stepped into the water and looked downstream where the river got wider with no sign of shallow white water or evidence of a more accessible shoreline, just thick jungle brush down to the water's edge. If anything went wrong out in the river and the bus got washed downstream, it would be hard for the others to reach me by land. I also thought about the crocodiles Harry had spoken of, living along riverbanks, and for the first time since Harry had disappeared, I felt my desire to go farther diminish—if for only a moment.

"No," I shook my head, "I don't think so."

"This *is* the way," she yelled.

"No," I yelled back, "this is *not* the way."

Tepi stepped out into the water and cupped his hands to his mouth. "She's right, Eddie. This is it and I think you can make it."

"You *think* I can make it."

"Okay," he replied, "I'm *sure* you can do it."

"This bus will float you know," I informed them. "Volkswagens do that. If I drive off into a hole out there, my next stop will be Bermuda."

"You can do it!" Bobdog yelled. "Come on before we lose the light. *Venga!*"

I looked out at the swift moving river, then downstream again. This is *really* stupid, I told myself.

"There's no other way, Eddie," Bobdog yelled out.

I got back in the van, took a deep breath, and against my gut feeling, I turned the engine over. Tepi and Bobdog walked back out into the water, holding their clasped hands outstretched. I gently eased the van down the bank and out into the river. I could feel the rock bottom and that somewhat eased my fears. A mushy river bottom of sand or mud would have been bad. Bobdog and Tepi guided me out into the strong flow of the river with arm and hand directions. Slowly I kept inching the van out into the water, turning ever so slightly according to directions, following the shallow bed they had followed. For the first few feet into the river, I watched out my window at the water level around the front tire. As long as it did not cover the tire, I felt everything would be okay. A water level above that, the engine in the rear might flood, and then I'd be stuck. I didn't dare stop for fear of stalling, so I just inched the van along. About midstream I felt the right front tire start to roll down steeply, and

HUNDRED WATERS

I quickly turned left until I felt the tire roll back up onto bedrock. I didn't realize how hard I had been clenching my jaw until the muscles in my face began to ache. My hands were so tightly gripped around the wheel that even my forearms started to cramp. I continued inching the van forward, watching Bobdog's directions and rolling with the uneven riverbed, until the nose of the van dipped way down. I saw the water level rise up the front of the van, quickly approaching door level, and my first thought was that I'd slipped into the hole that Tepi had stepped in. I was too scared to stop, so I gave the van more gas. I dropped down immediately but quickly bounced out of the hole back up onto level river bottom. I floored the accelerator, felt the back end dip way down into the hole and then quickly rise out of it. I wound my way across the last stretch of water and pulled up onto the bank far enough from the river that I was on flat ground before I stopped and just laid my head onto my arms and sighed deeply.

Tepi and Bobdog cheered and embraced one another then ran around the van and climbed in.

"Very good, Eddie," Bobdog said, kissing my cheek.

"Don't get any ideas, Tepi," I said extending my hand.

"Straight ahead," Bobdog said. "To Portobello."

* * *

The road, which was little more than a wide path with faint wheel ruts that were mostly overgrown, wound along following the curve of the coastline. The jungle grew right up close to the edge of the road, and I found it hard to believe we were anywhere near what might be called civilization. There were no signs of people or the trappings of progress like light poles, antennas or houses. Not even another car or a cart. Bobdog told us that with the bridges washed out for over ten years now, anything not grown or built locally came to Portobello from Colon by boat, including outsiders—whether they be Americans stationed in the Canal Zone or the occasional tourist off the big cruise boats that docked in Colon.

We continued on the narrow road surrounded by thick jungle growth until we came around a sharp corner where I slammed on the brakes. Suddenly there was a large group of people in front of us.

"Jesus Christ! What are all these people doing in the road?" There were forty or fifty people of all ages moving slowly up ahead of us, much like a procession but without singing or music. Our presence startled several older women in the rear of the group, and when they turned and saw us driving up behind them, they were momentarily stunned... motionless, like deer caught in oncoming headlights. When I pulled off what was now just a wide path to a spot where the jungle thinned out, the group of old women turned and continued on their way. Far up ahead I could see more people streaming forward. I shut down the van, and we got out, watching the procession snake through the tall grass in the direction of smoke and music. I could just see to where the jungle suddenly appeared to stop and the landscape totally opened up. We walked across the dirt trail out into the tall grass, and suddenly before us was a view of a beautiful, green coastline with what seemed to be the mouth of an inlet and the ocean stretching out from it. The dark blue water, the light blue sky, and the lush green jungle. It was breathtaking.

"We are here," Bobdog said. "This is Portobello."

"Jesus," Tepi said. "No wonder they named it *bello*."

"What are all these people doing out here?" I asked Bobdog.

"Wait here," she said. "I will ask." She walked up ahead where she stopped an older woman with two children.

HUNDRED WATERS

A moment later she came back with an orange from the old woman.

"I should have known," she said. "This is the Festival of *El Christo Negro.*"

"Black Christ?" I said. "What the hell's that?"

* * *

COLON PROVINCE: AN HISTORICAL ABSTRACT ON THE FOLKLORE OF THE REGION. [An Excerpt, page 20]. Headquarters, Department of the Army. DA Pamphlet 27-1092. Historical Division, Wash. D.C. Fourth Edition. 1965.

According to local history, a Spanish galleon en route back to Spain with riches from the Americas visited the harbor of Portobello in the year 1660. A sudden, unexpected storm arose and the galleon tried on five occasions to enter the protection of the fine harbor at Portobello, but on each attempt the ship was beaten back by the strong winds and a raging sea. On board the galleon, in addition to gold and silver, there was a life-size statue of Jesus Christ carrying the cross. The statue was carved out of a local tropical wood called cocobolo, a hard, heavy, and durable wood used in making furniture. The wood, which is naturally dark, has a tendency to blacken with age and does not float. Historians have recorded that superstitious sailors on board believed the statue was the cause of the foul weather and keeping them outside the safe harbor, so several of the crew threw it overboard. On its next attempt, the Spanish galleon cleared the heavy seas and was able to enter the harbor of Portobello.

The statue, according to historians, was found washed up on the shore by local natives of the village, and they quickly set it up in the church of Jesus of the Nazarene in the center of town. The statue quickly acquired a reputation as a healing shrine, which gained world renown in the year 1821 when a cholera epidemic swept over the isthmus of Panama, killing thousands in its path but leaving Portobello untouched. The festival of the Black Christ is an annual pilgrimage for thousands of Panamanians, many of whom report the occurrence of miracles.

* * *

Carr, MANUSCRIPT. Typewritten, with holographic changes made to the text in red ink.

We left the van, and the three of us joined the flow of pilgrims moving along the road to the town of Portobello, and before long we came to the ruins of Santiago Castle. I pulled Bobdog over to the ruins. It was an Old Spanish fort that had been built to protect the harbor in the days when Portobello was one of the three richest cities in the New World. Much of the grounds were now overgrown with tall grass. Several old cannons lay along the ramparts, their rusted steel barrels pitted, their wooden casements long ago rotted away. Down below, several boys were playing and chasing each other among the ruins. We walked along the central rampart, and I couldn't help consider the historical significance of where I was standing, and how three hundred years earlier to the day some Spanish soldier, perhaps twenty years old like myself, must have stood in this exact place and looked out on the same view. He too was far away from his home, his family and a more hospitable landscape; he was here in this backwater village on the edge of the jungle, looking out onto the blue Caribbean waters, dreaming perhaps of gold or a woman, or hating some sergeant who was making his life miserable. Someone had stood *here* in this exact spot and remembered, dreamed, and gazed out to sea. He too was involved in a search, and for a brief moment, in the quiet of those ruins, I felt the undeniable reach of history.

Across the bay I could see the remnants of San Felipe Castle, a turret and pieces of plaster walls sticking out of the overgrowth of jungle. It was clearly abandoned with no sign of life.

I turned to Bobdog. "How do we get over there?"

She shook her head. "Only by boat," she said.

"Do you know if there is a road on that side? My map doesn't show any."

"I bet there are a lot of things over there," Tepi said.

"I don't know," she said. "I don't remember any, but that was years ago. There are big holes in the ground, and I think a road would be too difficult."

"Holes from what?" Tepi asked.

"The Americans came here and took rocks to build the canal, but nobody lived over there."

"If you can't walk or drive to it," Tepi said, "I doubt that many people have been there since. If there were any...artifacts...they could still be around."

"We're here to find Harry," I said.

"I was just supposing," Tepi said.

"Let's go into town and make some inquiries," I said.

We followed the procession of people across a modest stone bridge that must have dated back three hundred years. We wandered past stone houses that faced the narrow streets of the town; their doors were open with old men sitting on the single steps looking at us without expression. The farther into the town we got, the more it felt like the carnivals I had gone to back home as a kid. Shirtless children wearing dirty shorts ran up and down the streets barefooted, dodging in and out of the hordes of pilgrims. The air was hot and thick with the rich, pungent smells of wood smoke, stale beer, dirt and sweet fruits—all mixed with human sweat. The humidity was so high that your clothes hung heavy and damp. The air quickly made you thirsty. We looked up and down the narrow street for a cafe or a *Cerveza* sign before we turned and followed people down toward the water. Tepi saw the sign first, so we sent him in for three cold beers.

While we were waiting, Bobdog pointed out places she remembered from when she was young and had come here with her father.

"Down the street there," she said, "is the Church of the Nazarene where the *Christo Negro* is kept. You will see it if we stay. There will be a procession with the statue through the streets. It is very beautiful."

Tepi came out with three beers, and we crossed the street to a place with some shade, sat down and watched the flow of people. We could see a crowd of squatting men playing dice in a dirt side street. Opposite the men was a woman selling painted pots, but her attention was focused on the men and their dice game.

"How do we find out anything about Harry in the middle of a carnival?" Tepi asked.

"That's a good question." I turned to Bobdog. "How do we find Harry?"

"I said to you before, it would be hard. This makes it more hard."

"So what's that mean?"

"Nothing, Eddie. Just more hard." Bobdog said that it would be impossible for her to find out anything with Tepi and me around. She would need to make inquiries discreetly and alone.

"How long?" Tepi said. "We don't have a lot of time."

"I told you this was not for certain," Bobdog said.

HUNDRED WATERS

"No guarantee. I said that to you. I don't know what I can find out, but I will try. This is very dangerous, Eddie, to find out these things."

"It's going to be dangerous for Harry if we don't find him and get him back."

"Harry knew what he was doing," Bobdog said.

"Let's not argue about that again," I said.

"So what do you want us to do?" Tepi said.

"I will meet you at the Volkswagen tonight," she said. "Enjoy the festival. I will see you later."

Bobdog kissed my cheek, and I watched her walk up the narrow, crowded street until she disappeared into the crowd.

"Well Tepi," I said, "I guess it's you and me."

* * *

It was a little after five o'clock when we separated from Bobdog, and we resigned ourselves to the fact that we were in Portobello at least for the night and maybe longer, depending on what Bobdog found out. Tepi and I sat in the shade and finished our beers. Radio rhumba echoed out into the cool, evening air and mixed with music coming from all directions: heavy drum rhythms...horns...singing...guitars... howling...shouting... and laughter. There was no moment that night without a sound.

Both of us were hungry, and the air was filled with the smells of cooking meat, so we walked the narrow, crowded streets looking for a place to eat. We found a small cafe not far from the church, near the wharves. It was outside under a makeshift tent, and the woman inside was serving chicken halves and rice. We both ordered plates.

A group of three small boys came up to us offering trinkets for sale. There were wood carved figures and small woven blankets. The tallest boy thrust out his hand offering a large silver coin in his palm.

"Five dollars," the boy said. "Five dollars."

I looked at Tepi and smiled. For over a year, ever since the day we had arrived in country, we had been accosted by children and older beggars to "give" or "buy" everything from gum to treasures. Usually at grossly inflated prices.

I shook my head. "No, *gracias*."

"Five dollars, *por favor*. Very beautiful, " he said in Spanish.

"No," I said.

"Four dollars, Gringo. Just four dollars."

"I'm eating," I said. "No! Go away!"

"*Viego. Muy viego. Mira!*" The boy thrust the coin at me again, forcing me to look at the face of it. I took it, and he was correct. It was old. I rubbed at the date and read 1763.

"Kid's right," Tepi said.

"Too much," I said.

"Three dollars. Okay. Three dollars."

"No *gracias*," I said to the kid. Then I turned to Tepi. "All they want to do is rob us. I refuse to pay them a dime more than it's worth."

"Two dollars, señor. Only two dollars."

"Hell," Tepi said. "It's got to be worth the two dollars."

"You're missing the point, Tep. It's not the amount. It's the idea that we're full of money, and we buy everything. Gringos equal money. Well we don't, and I'm not buying it."

"Well, hell, I will then. They're only kids."

"No you won't," I said. "If it's worth so much, let the locals buy it."

"One dollar, señor. Only one dollar."

"I said no!" I grabbed the coin out of his hand and threw it up the street. "Now get lost. *Vamonos!*"

HUNDRED WATERS

* * *

After we finished our dinner of chicken and rice, Tepi and I walked the streets of the fair. They were still crowded into the night, and the air was muggy, so we decided to get out a ways where things were less congested. I looked up and around for anything that might be a relief from the crowds of people, and when I saw the hill that seemed to be right in the center of town, I grabbed Tepi, and we headed off in its direction. We wound our way through the narrow streets with the vendors, the kids, the singing and pushing and the pungent smell of smoke and meat cooking. There were card tables with jewelry and crafts, open doorways and little makeshift tents in between buildings. Just as we were working our way clear of a clog of people singing and dancing in the street, a voice called out like a raspy cough.

"*Oye Gringo.* You *Americano!*"

I turned, and next to a building wall a woman sat at a rickety wooden bench and table under a cloth tent cover. She motioned us over. Tepi and I looked at each other.

"Yes, you my friends," the woman said in Spanish. "Come here and sit with me. Let me speak to you of your fortune and your future."

"Oh, I don't think so," Tepi replied in Spanish.

"What is the danger of the words of an old woman," she insisted. "*Venga agui*! Come!"

I looked at Tepi and rolled my eyes.

"Maybe she could tell us something," Tepi said, "about where we might find these people."

"Hell I doubt it," I said. "Bobdog stands a better chance. Besides, what could an old woman under a blanket know? This is like carnival stuff back home."

The woman said something in Spanish that I didn't recognize.

"She says she's been expecting us," Tepi said.

"Expecting us," I said. "Hell, she doesn't even know us. How could she be expecting us?"

"I'm just telling you what she said," Tepi said.

"Come inside and for *poco dinero* you can know what an old woman knows. I could know things of your woman and others in your life."

"What do you mean 'know things of my woman?' What does that mean?"

"Come! Sit here and join me. It would be good for you to know things...perhaps."

Tepi and I stepped in under the blanket tent and slowly sat down on the wooden bench across the table from the woman.

"What things do you know about my woman?" I asked straight out.

"I am named Sata," she said. "For two dollars I will speak of your future."

"Does this woman have something to do with my future?"

"Two dollars please, señor."

"Give her the two dollars," Tepi said.

I slowly reached into my pocket and pulled out two dollars.

"You have come on a journey," she said, sliding the two bills from my fingers, "but have found nothing."

"I paid two dollars to hear that?"

"Your woman asks some questions."

"So?"

"But your journey ends here."

"How do you know she asks questions? Did she speak with you?"

"This is a small village. If you speak with one, you speak with many."

HUNDRED WATERS

"We are looking for a friend," Tepi said.

"An American," I added. "You would know if an American was here...wouldn't you?"

"Perhaps."

"No," I said, "you would know."

"Where can we find him?" Tepi asked. "It's important we find him."

"There are those who don't wish to be found."

"Our friend is confused," Tepi said.

"We just need to find him, fast."

"There is a danger in looking some places. Perhaps your woman inquires, and perhaps there are those who do not like those questions."

"Perhaps this, perhaps that. Get to the point!"

"Questions are dangerous. I suggest you leave your friend to his own life."

"Well I can't do that," I said. "Do you know anything about him?"

"He has a large mustache, bigger than his," Tepi said pointing to me. "He smokes a pipe."

"Beware of lizards," the old woman said.

"Lizards?"

"Sata offers *buenos noches. Gracias, señors*."

"But wait. What do you mean, beware of lizards?"

"What about the future you spoke of?" Tepi asked.

"I know things about lizards," I said to her.

"Good night."

"But you haven't told us anything."

Sata turned quickly and disappeared through the back of the tent. Immediately Tepi and I stepped around the table and followed her out. There were five bare-chested black men sitting around a small fire right behind the tent. Their skin glistened in the firelight like varnished ebony. We stared down at their shiny dark faces looking up at us, and then watched the woman called Sata disappear around behind a building.

"Excuse us," I said to the men. Tepi and I slowly stepped back into the tent.

"So much for fortune telling," Tepi said.

"So much for my two bucks."

"She knows something, Eddie. She knew about Bobdog and Harry."

"Anybody could've seen us come into town. As far as knowing about Harry, she didn't say a damn thing."

"Yeah," Tepi said, "that's what's bothering me."

I looked around the narrow, crowded street for any sign of the woman Sata, but it was impossible to see through all the people. The crowds were getting to me, and I was mad about losing two dollars to a fortuneteller. I bought two more beers from an old woman with a worn Coleman ice chest, and we continued on to the hill where the old customhouse once stood.

It took us about twenty minutes to scale the mass of brown, tangled vines and tall grass. Once we got to the top and perched ourselves on the only visible section of one of its crumbling stonewalls, we opened our beers and looked out over the gaily lit village. Portobello was a sea of rusted tin roofs, accented by a dozen ribbons of blue smoke rising straight up from the festivities below.

"What do you make of that old woman?" Tepi said.

"Hell, I don't know. She didn't tell us a thing new."

"She did know about Bobdog and her asking around though."

"That's not fortune telling. That's gossip."

"What do you think she meant by 'some people not wanting to be found'?" "Think she meant Harry?"

"If she did, why not just say it. She's just a hustler, and she hustled me for two bucks."

HUNDRED WATERS

"I'm not sure I like that lizard shit, either. I hate lizards and frogs and snakes."

"It's part of the image. Fortunetellers, mysterious mumbo jumbo, throw in a lizard here and wild talk about spells and lost souls. It's bullshit for two bucks."

We sat quietly atop the remains of the ancient customhouse and took in the view of lights, the smoky smells of open-air cooking and the raucous sounds of festivity. I found myself seeing this same scene occurring several hundred years earlier with hoards of Spanish sailors crawling these same streets, pawing and groping the great, great, great, great grandmothers of some of the women down there. Spanish adventurers drinking and eating and playing their games of chance while, right where we were sitting, tons of gold bars stood in six-foot stacks waiting to be loaded onto galleons for shipment to Spain. There were old men and old women down there on the sides of those narrow streets whose ancestors had seen those bars of silver and gold stacked like cordwood and the bay before us, jammed with a hundred Spanish galleons, their wood masts like a denuded forest growing out of the water. The thought of being in such close proximity to that historical event sent shivers through my body.

Tepi who had been uncommonly quiet, suddenly nudged my side. "I think I just saw Bobdog."

"Where?"

"Out there," he said pointing toward the jungle on the edge of the village.

"Out there? Alone?"

"No, there was someone else. Two of them out there, by the tree line."

We both agreed that it was probably not the safest place for Bobdog, so we made our way down the vine-covered hill and headed out in the direction of what appeared to be a small park on the edge of the village. By the time we climbed down the hill, wound our way through the village streets and reached the jungle edge, Bobdog was nowhere to be seen or heard.

It was nearing twilight, the night sky just turning dark blue, when we reached the outskirts of town where the main dirt street narrowed down to a wide path. The path crossed an open field and then passed what we had thought was a park, but turned out to be a cemetery with several big trees in it. As we approached the cemetery, we could see through the vines and tall grass the rusty remnants of a wrought-iron fence around the grounds. A tall, iron archway stood over the main gate and while there was a date over it, too much of it had rusted away to make out what it was. We walked inside and examined the irregularly placed headstones. The masonry was pitted and darkened with age, but on several we found dates in the late 1600's and the 1700's.

We passed the cemetery and followed the well-worn dirt path out a little farther, up toward the Cascabal River, which flowed into Portobello Bay. In the dimming light Tepi tripped, stumbled and fell onto something solid. When I reached down to help him up, I saw what had tripped Tepi: several rounded stones protruding up in the trail. The same kind of rounded stones we had walked over on our trek along the Camino Real to the ruins of Las Cruces. We walked along following the rocks as best we could in the dying light with the help of our pocket lighters, and then we lost the stones where the trail seemed to split off and the jungle overgrew everything. We continued on, each of us taking a different path, once again feeling for the stones with our feet, until suddenly I heard something out a ways that sounded like a cough.

"Tepi. That you?" I called out ahead of me.

HUNDRED WATERS

"What?" he replied, from off to my right.

"That you coughing?"

"I didn't say a thing. I thought it was you."

"I'm not finding the trail over here. How about you?"

"Just jungle and mud. Let's head back."

There was a deep protracted growl, this time off to my left, and I quickly turned and headed back out to the clearing where Tepi and I had separated. Tepi came walking out, brushing at his head and neck.

"Ran into something back there," he said.

I tried to see what he was slapping at, but the light was gone, so I struck my lighter in front of his face. Little red ants were scurrying around the large red welts on his neck. He pulled off his shirt, and I brushed at the ants with my hand, then I used my bandanna. When I got Tepi cleaned of the ants, we both stood at the edge of the jungle where the path that Tepi thought he had seen Bobdog on disappeared into the thick brush; we called out her name. We called and called until we stilled the howler monkeys and wild parrots, then we stopped.

"I don't like it," I said. "We should've kept a closer eye on her."

"Hell, she wanted to go out alone."

"But we should've kept an eye on her."

"You like her," Tepi said. "Don't you?"

"Now that's a stupid question. Of course I like her."

"You know what I mean. You're worried about her the way I would worry about Angela."

"She's a good person, and I don't want to see anything happen to her. That's all."

"Yeah, sure," Tepi said. "So what do we do now?"

"I don't know what we can do."

"Well, she's from around here. Maybe she found

somebody with some information...maybe an old friend. Who knows?"

I called her name again and again, then listened for her response, but none came.

"She said she'd meet us at the van," Tepi said. "She's pretty savvy. Maybe we should just go and wait. I really don't want to wait around here, especially around that old cemetery."

As much as I hated to think of Bobdog out in the jungle, with who knows who, I agreed with Tepi. We headed back past the cemetery through the narrow streets and back out to where we had parked the van, just outside the village, and we waited.

* * *

Tepi and I were sitting inside the van shortly after midnight playing cards when Bobdog finally returned. She looked exhausted and her clothes were filthy.

"Where have you been?"

"It is not so easy to know things here."

"We saw you out near the cemetery," I said.

"Me?" she said. "*Impossible!*"

"I'd swear it was you," Tepi said.

"It doesn't really matter," I said. "Did you get any word on Harry, where he might be?"

"I learned he is not near Portobello. Can I have some water?"

Tepi slid over so Bobdog could sit down at the table, and I got her a cup of water from the cooler.

"It is how I thought," Bobdog said. "Nobody likes to talk about these things. But I did find a man near the dock, and he spoke to me of some things."

"Well, if Harry isn't around here, what did he know?"

HUNDRED WATERS

"He knows a man up the coast, he said, who maybe could help us."

"Where up the coast?"

"The place is Nombre de Dios."

"And who is this person up there?" said Tepi.

"He is the local civil guardsman. A sergeant named Huertas."

"Sounds like a vegetable."

"What's the road like?" Tepi asked.

"I hope there are bridges this time," I said.

"There is no road," Bobdog said.

"A place farther down the coast with no road to it."

"That must mean...no bridges. How do we get there?"

"One gets there by water."

"Oh fine," I said. "We've got a van, and we really need a boat."

"Where exactly is this place?" Tepi said.

While Bobdog explained that Nombre de Dios was some twenty to twenty-five miles northeast of us by water and that we needed to hire a boat, I felt we were being drawn deeper and deeper into more than we understood. With the festival going on, boats and a boatman were not so easy to hire, but Bobdog said she had secured the services of a local fisherman named Señor Lemos. We were to meet him with the morning sun down on the wharf.

We turned in, listening to the hypnotic sounds of music and drums late into the night. Like so much else—the heat, humidity, the flow of beer, the music and the chanting—Portobello had crept into our blood and like sweet rum, it had its own intoxication.

Carr, MANUSCRIPT. Holographic corrections to text made in red ink. The title "Over Drake's Bones" is written across the top of the first page. There is a crude drawing of an old Spanish galleon just below the title.

The boatman named Lemos was waiting for us on the Portobello dock when we arrived, just as the sun was coming up. He was a short, wiry man in his early thirties. He wore a straw cowboy hat with the brim rolled up on the sides, and his face had the color and texture of tanned leather. The grip of his handshake was firm, which gave me confidence we were in good hands. The air was already warm, and Lemos wore shorts and a white sleeveless t-shirt that stood out brightly against his dark skin. I looked around the wharf for a boat large enough to take the four of us up the coast.

"So where's his boat?" I asked Bobdog.

She shrugged her shoulders and then went over and spoke with Lemos.

"Well?" I asked when she returned.

"It's not a boat. It's a *cayuco*. That's it tied up at the end of the dock."

I walked down to the end of the wharf, and my heart sunk. It was a fifteen-foot canoe, hollowed out of a log, with an old Johnson outboard motor on the back.

"We're going in the ocean in that?"

"He is very sure it is safe. This is how everybody here gets up and down the coast."

"But it's so...small," Tepi said.

"Did he say how far it is we have to go?"

"Just a little over twenty miles. He said he wants us to leave now so we can go with the tide."

We threw our bags into the *cayuco* and sat where Lemos directed us according to weight. Me at the bow with Bobdog behind me and then Tepi behind her. Lemos sat in the rear at the motor. Bobdog tapped me on the shoulder, and when I turned around she handed me a six-inch crucifix. It was made of dark wood and was heavy like a stone.

"I got this last night for good luck," she said. "Put it at the front of the canoe."

As we pulled away from the dock and glided over the smooth bay waters, my initial apprehension over the canoe and its modest size eased. I was quickly overtaken by the primitive beauty of the rough shoreline...the rich green jungle reaching down to the bay shore and behind us the rusty-brown square buildings hugging close to the ground with a thin, gauzy layer of blue smoke suspended over the village.

The water in the bay was calm and blue and the village quiet and quaint-looking, very pastoral like a harmless color postcard from the exotic tropics. The green softness of the jungle as it met the water was soothing, uncomplicated, undisturbed, and friendly in a primordial way. Even the tiny, square buildings of the village lost much of their hard-line shape against the color and foliage. The farther away we moved, the more serene and pleasant Portobello looked, with several slender ribbons of smoke trailing upward and suspended like a wispy blue lariat against the darkness of the jungle backdrop.

Out in the middle of the bay, I recalled what I had read about the number of galleons that once filled the harbor

HUNDRED WATERS

during the festival, three hundred years earlier. Right where we were passing, over a hundred ships of all shapes and sizes had anchored. Ships waiting to fill their holds with the bars of silver and gold from Peru—bars stacked like firewood in the streets of Portobello, gold filling the custom house, the structure where Tepi and I had sat the night before overlooking the village. Trying to imagine this entire bay full of ships created in me an overwhelming picture of wealth and congestion that must have been frightening to the local inhabitants of the day.

As we approached the mouth of the bay, the water picked up a chop, which quickly turned a smooth ride into a bouncy romp. We crossed out of the protected bay into open water and angled as close to the shoreline as the rock-dotted coast would allow. We got out past the point rocks in the general area where the bones of Sir Francis Drake were laid to rest, and I immediately wondered if we had made a big mistake. I turned to see how Bobdog was doing and caught a glimpse of Tepi gasping deeply, perhaps from the splash of the cold water or as an expression of the same concern I was feeling. Either way, his eyes were wide, and he did not look relaxed. Bobdog, on the other hand, appeared to be taking everything in stride. She seemed loose, and I even caught a glimpse of what could have been a smile, while huge frothy breakers splashed violently against the rock islands just offshore.

Going out beyond the rocks removed any protection we had near the coastline and put us directly into the ocean. The bow spray was heavy and constant, and I was soaking wet only moments after we left the smooth waters of Portobello Bay. All I could do was clutch the gunwales as tightly as possible and hope that Señor Lemos truly knew what he was doing in deep water. And that the black crucifix carried only the strongest luck.

Lemos kept the canoe out away from the rocky outcroppings that dotted the shoreline, keeping us farther out in the deep water than I was comfortable with. I could not swim, and the farther out we went, the more concerned I got. The waves were running five and six feet around us, and I watched with awe as they crashed violently against the rocks between us and the shoreline. Huge pillars of spray shot high into the air, spreading so much froth against the rocks that they looked momentarily like they were covered with snow. From out of nowhere, a tremendous wall of water hit us broadside and sent us skidding into a deep trough. I turned around to Bobdog.

"If we sink" I yelled, "I can't swim."

"*Que?*"

"I said if we sink, don't bother with me. I love you."

"*Que?* I don't hear you."

"Forget it," I yelled. "Just forget it."

The fifty-horse Johnson whined loudly against the roar of the rushing sea around us. We rocked, rolled and tumbled, and we pitched and tossed, plunging deep into watery troughs, heaving skyward to skim the crests and then drift sideways, only to tumble as we were buffeted by the dark rolling water. We were at sea, out of our element, and I was scared shitless.

I had never been in such malicious water in such a small craft. The way we were being shaken and pitched, tossed and dropped with water coming at us from every direction, I did not believe we were going to make it to shore alive. There was just so much violent water, and we were so small and so far offshore, that I knew if we got swamped or capsized, it would be the end.

This is not what I had in mind. I hated deep water and this was as bad as deep water got. I kept looking back to see how Lemos was holding up. Tepi's face looked like it was being stretched out away from his nose, his mouth frozen in a permanent grimace. On several occasions, when we took some heavy swells broadside, I checked to see if he and Lemos were still with us. Tepi held his ground, and Lemos continued to impress me. He looked intense and in control, and I liked that. It didn't ease my fears of where we were and the danger around us, but it didn't cause me additional concern.

We continued up the coast, moving slowly but steadily past huge rock formations that were being pounded hard by the heavy seas. I stared off ahead, hoping to see something of a village—buildings, smoke, even other boats, but all I saw was the churning blue-green sea rolling out beyond us for miles. There was so much mist around the rocky outcroppings that it was no longer possible to make out anything of the shoreline. I turned around looking for some assurance or consolation in Bobdog's face, and in her own way she gave it, or at least I took her unemotional response to the threat of danger as a consolation. Bobdog was invaluable for that quality alone.

The sky was still slate gray and the wind cold and stiff. About forty-five minutes out, we turned sharply landward, and I looked back to make sure Lemos was in control. I followed his intense stare, trying to see where he was aiming us. Finally, as we rounded a rock the shape of a tall smokestack, I could see where the land dropped down to what appeared to be the entrance to another bay. While I felt a moment's relief, the waves were still very high and violent, heaving us fore and aft and side to side.

The closer we got to the mouth of the bay, the more I felt a different pull on our canoe. There was an undertow pulling at us from below while the surface waves bounced us sideways. Lemos never lost his concentration. Each time I looked back at him, his eyes were fixed on the water, never once showing any fear of the thundering sea. He worked us in close to the mouth, coming at it from an angle, flowing in the troughs and then riding those troughs—much like a surfer waiting for the right wave. Then suddenly he whipped us around, facing shoreward, and we skimmed along on the crest of a large wave, like a surfboard, rolling and dipping, but all the while being pushed by the power of the surf into the quiet bay.

* * *

When we suddenly whooshed out of the heavy waves, like a hot knife through butter, and glided effortlessly into the smooth bay waters of Nombre de Dios, Tepi and I cheered with great relief, and Bobdog laughed loudly and then let out a series of shrieks. Lemos, unemotional except for a tiny smile, guided us straight toward the crescent-shaped sandy beach. It was high tide, with the water level right up next to the jungle, allowing only a ten-foot stretch of sand high up on the beach. Lemos gunned the engine and took a straight ahead run at the beach and then cut the engine, and we glided up onto the shore.

For a moment I just sat still. I was never happier to be touching solid ground. My body still rocked and rolled inside, even though we were beached. I finally climbed out and held the bow rope while Bobdog stepped out, followed by Tepi. We unloaded our canteen belts, knapsacks and sleeping bags, and then stacked them on the sand. It felt good to be off the water and on solid ground. The air was moist with humidity, but fresh-smelling, still and warm. Coconut palms lined the beach, and not far beyond them, thick, dense jungle covered the hillsides. With no wind coming off the water, my face began to burn and I noticed the red faces of the others. Lemos told Bobdog that because the tide was high and he wasn't sure when we would be leaving, he was going to anchor the heavy *cayuco* out a ways so that it would not be left high and dry when the tide went out. He stripped off his shirt and sandals and then pushed off. About twenty yards out, he threw the cement-can anchor overboard and then swam back into shore.

I flopped down on the beach and lay back, staring up at the pale blue sky. It was quiet and still, except for the faint wave lapping of high tide and the buzz of sand fleas. I had never been so scared in my whole life. I thought for sure Tepi or Bobdog would see the violent way my muscles were trembling on the inside. I clenched my fists trying to quell the shaking I felt sure was clearly visible.

"Eddie," I heard Bobdog ask, "you alright?"

"Fine," I said opening my eyes. "Just a chill." It felt awfully good to still be alive, even with the huge sand fleas nipping at me.

"That was close out there," Tepi said. He sat down next to me.

"I still can't believe we were out there in that tiny canoe."

Bobdog sat down between us. "Señor Lemos told me the big sea was unexpected."

"Unexpected is right. There were several points when I didn't expect to make it at all."

"What were you trying to say to me out there?" Bobdog asked.

"It was nothing," I said.

"I just could not hear you," she said.

"Forget it," I said. "It was nothing at all."

"At least twice I thought we were goners," Tepi said. "I don't know about you, but I was scared shitless."

"Well I know about me," I said. "I was too."

"I'm glad to know it wasn't just me," Tepi said. "It really feels good to not be bobbing."

DAVID GREGOR

Lemos stepped out of the water, put on his shirt and sandals, and then addressed Bobdog in Spanish. She listened intently then told us that while he did know the local police official, Señor Lemos would be nothing more than our guest. That left Bobdog as the ranking member, since she had been born in these parts, and even though it had been some time since she had been back, she was the best ambassador we had. We grabbed our gear and started up the beach.

Carr, MANUSCRIPT. In the top left corner of the first page there is a small drawing of a man wearing a large straw hat down over his eyes. There is a dialogue balloon coming from the man's mouth that reads: "*Yo No Se Nada.*"

"What exactly are we looking for here?" Tepi asked, as we walked up the beach.
"Harry."
"Yeah, but you don't expect to find him just stretched out on a hammock drinking a margarita."
"Somebody around here knows something. If not about Harry, then something about these *Cimarrones* that he might have joined." As soon as I said the name *Cimarrones*, Lemos' head snapped around sharply, and I saw a fear in his eyes that I had not even seen all time we were coming up the coast.
I tapped Bobdog on the shoulder. "Ask Lemos what he knows about the *Cimarrones*?"
"I don't think he knows anything," she said.
"That's not what I asked you to do. I saw the way he looked when I said their name. He knows something. Just ask him."
She spoke to Lemos quietly, and the way he shook his head and waved his arms, as though he were trying to push her words away so as not to even hear the question, told me

more than anything he could ever say. "*Yo no se nada,*" Lemos said. "*Nada!*"

"He says he doesn't know anything."

"That's interesting. He knows the name when he hears it, but knows nothing about them. How can that be?"

"I told you Eddie. This is not a small thing. It is very serious, and there are those who are very superstitious about things. He is clearly one of them."

We walked up the sandy beach for about a quarter of a mile before we heard the distant sound of drums and people chanting. I immediately looked over at Lemos and then Bobdog.

"*Cimarrones*?" I asked.

Lemos' face fell...expressionless.

"I don't think so," Bobdog said. "Most likely the villagers here." She turned to Lemos, spoke with him and then turned back to us. "These people also celebrate something like the festival in Portobello. But here is with the Virgin Mary. Lemos thinks it might be the celebration we hear. But he is not certain."

We picked up a well-worn trail leading inland from the beach and followed it through low brush and sparse jungle forest. The sound of drums and rhythmic clapping along with chanting grew louder and louder, filling the air with an intoxicating pulse. The smell of wood smoke greeted us long before we reached the edge of the village which was marked by an old stone bridge much like the one we crossed outside Portobello. Bobdog pointed out that the bridge dated back to the first Spaniards. It spanned a modest river running low on the banks, with much of its rocky bottom exposed. A little boy about two or three stood naked, peeing, down below near the river bank, staring up at us without a moment's shyness. When he finished, he ran up the riverbed and joined a woman walking up river.

HUNDRED WATERS

Small children were the first to greet us after we crossed the bridge. With wide-eyed amazement, little boys and girls peeked at us from behind large-trunked palm trees. I smiled at the kids and waved. The bolder ones laughed, while the more timid stayed well behind the trees.

"The children are very shy," Bobdog said. "They don't get many outsiders up here. No tourists or travelers. Every once in awhile some government people or scientists. But no white visitors. Especially Americans. I remember what it was like when I saw my first white person. I thought he was sick."

We stopped to watch a procession of young girls wearing white cotton dresses cross in front of us on a hard-packed dirt trail that clearly headed into the village proper.

"This is an old village," Bobdog said. "Very poor, very simple and very old. The ancestors of these people lived with the Spanish conquerors. This was a very important place for many years. Much gold came through here on its journey to Spain."

"Is that what this celebration is for?" I asked.

"No, this festival is for the people here."

I looked back and saw Tepi squatting down offering a stick of gum to a little boy peeking out from behind a tree.

I turned to Bobdog. "Do you know anyone here?"

"No, no one. But Lemos will introduce us to the guardsman who has lived here many years. His house is supposed to have a large porch. He should still live here. We'll see."

The procession of young girls in their white dresses continued on through the village. They were immediately followed by four men carrying a wood platform upon which rested a brightly adorned statue which Bobdog said was the Virgin Mary. The statue wore a crown of sparkling stones and was covered with red and white fabric. Four men pounding on drums followed the statue, and they in turn were followed by two men playing horns that looked like bugles. It was all very lively and up-tempo, and as we watched, I found my mind magically carried away from our original reason for being in the village. When the horn players at the end of the procession passed us at the bridge, Bobdog gestured that we should follow.

The village consisted primarily of small, mud huts with thatched roofs and high peaks that Bobdog said were called *bohios*. Large coconut palms dotted the well-worn grounds, their drooping, bushy fronds gently rustling high above us in the warm breeze. The heat made the earthy smells of the village even stronger. Dogs barked from open doorways; women and men stared at us from porches and windows. We walked down through the village grounds looking for a house with a big porch. A short ways into the village, a group of local men approached us. One of them was dressed in something of a military uniform; he straightened his jacket and adjusted his hat as we got closer. He was larger than the other men of the village, and he had not shaved for several days. His face was shiny with perspiration, and his clothes smelled of old sweat. Lemos stepped forward.

"I have brought you some visitors." he said.

"*Bueno*," the uniformed man said. He turned to us. "*Buenos Dias*," he said, and tipped his hat. "I am Sergeant Huertas. Welcome to our humble village. We don't receive so many visitors here."

"They are soldiers of the *Estados Unidos*," Lemos said. "The woman is with them."

The policeman Huertas spoke very rapidly first to Lemos then to Bobdog, and then she translated for us.

"He says he is pleased that you are here," Bobdog said. "He is curious about what brings soldiers of the United States to the small village of Nombre de Dios?"

HUNDRED WATERS

"Just tell him we're here on vacation," I said. "Nothing official."

Bobdog spoke to the policeman, and he laughed when she said vacation. He turned to the other residents around him and repeated what Bobdog had said, emphasizing the word "vacation." There was spotted laughter.

"Señor Huertas says he cannot understand why anyone from the *Estados Unidos* would come to this poor village for vacation. Maybe Panama City or Colon, but not Nombre de Dios. He finds that very humorous."

"Tell him we're just a bunch of funny guys who don't know any better."

The sergeant spoke to Lemos and gestured for us to follow him. He led us through the village announcing to everyone we passed that we were American soldiers from the United States and we had come to vacation in their village. The blank, disbelieving expressions on the faces of everyone said it all. It was a statement that made no sense to the villagers. I couldn't believe that any of them had ever taken a vacation, as we understood vacation, and to do something like that in a place like this would register as pure nonsense. There was absolutely nothing of special interest here, and they all knew it. But that did not stop the policeman from telling everybody that we were *touristas* as we walked by. Besides, Tepi did have a camera around his neck, and that was certainly some evidence of being a vacationer.

We eventually came to the biggest house in the village and the only one with a raised, wooden porch. The policeman led us up the porch stairs, gesturing for us to sit while he called to someone inside to bring refreshments. He spoke to those standing around the house to go about their business and waved them off.

I asked Bobdog if it would be appropriate for us to inquire about Harry, but before she could answer, a large woman stepped out onto the porch with what looked like lemonade. She was quickly followed by a girl, perhaps sixteen or seventeen. The girl handed out the drinks. She was shy, but clearly intrigued by us North Americans. She kept her eyes down and smiled almost painfully. Tepi took his glass, smiled broadly and thanked her.

The sergeant spoke, and Bobdog said that this was his wife and his daughter, Malique. We greeted them both courteously. Tepi raised his glass to the pretty Malique, and she looked down and smiled briefly, then went back inside the house.

The sergeant spoke. "To our visitors," he said. "*Salud!*"

"*Salud!*" we replied. The lemon drink was cool and tart.

"I trust you will honor my house with your presence tonight," Bobdog translated for us. "We do not have so much, but you are welcome to share it."

"That's not necessary," I said to Bobdog. "Tell him we're just looking for information about our friend."

Bobdog did so and provided us with his reply. "He says he insists. It would be an insult to refuse, Eddie."

I turned to Tepi, and he looked around at the house and the porch. "We could do a lot worse."

"He *is* the police," Bobdog said. "If anyone knows anything about Harry, it is Señor Huertas."

"We've got to stay some place," Tepi said.

We agreed to accept his hospitality, though my imagination started working overtime. Here we had just arrived by boat to this out-of-the-way coastal village where outsiders never come, and we'd just agreed to stay with the village cop stationed, for God knows how long, in this remote outpost as the lone symbol of law and order. For the briefest moment I

HUNDRED WATERS

feared the possible complications of being so far removed from the world we knew.

We finished our refreshments, and the sergeant's wife showed us to the covered back porch area where we would be staying. We stored our bags, and once we had made up our beds and were settled, Malique came to speak with Bobdog. Bobdog told us Malique was to act as our guide in the village since her father had some official business to attend to before dinner. Lemos and Tepi joined Malique; Bobdog and I followed. As we stood and watched a group of fishermen repairing their nets, I pulled Bobdog aside and asked her about Señor Huertas and how he might help us find Harry Miles.

"If he knows something about Harry and if Harry is anywhere nearby," she said in a hushed voice, "then this man knows why we are here."

"Did you say anything to him?" I asked.

"No. I would not have to. These people are not stupid. Some of them may be *Cimarrones*."

"You think so?"

"Their world is like the web of the spider. That is how they survive."

"How would we know them?" I asked.

"You wouldn't. We have probably passed many in the last two days without knowing."

"Then why has no one tried to stop us? If they know who we are and what we're doing, why not just do something?"

"The lizard does not strike until it is hungry or trapped."

Tepi turned around and came over to us. "What's that about lizards?"

"What the hell's that got to do with anything?" I said to Bobdog.

Bobdog turned her back to Lemos and Malique. "They can do whatever they want at any time," she said in a whisper. "That's all."

"So what about this policeman? Do you think he knows anything about Harry?"

"He is the law here. He knows everything."

"Then he's the man to ask."

"We can ask at dinner."

* * *

At about six o'clock, dinner was announced, and the three of us followed Malique inside and sat down at the oblong, wood table. Bobdog sat across from *El Jefe*, as she affectionately referred to the policeman, and Tepi and I sat on either side of her. Lemos sat next to Señor Huertas. The plates and utensils were wooden, and the plates were decorated with colorful paintings of crudely drawn animals.

Dinner consisted of a bowl of figs, fried plantains, white rice soup with curassow, and slices of meat. When Tepi asked what the meat was, *El Jefe* answered in Spanish with a slang term Bobdog did not know. The policeman reached over, pushed some slices of bread aside and pointed to a monkey painted on the plate. After a brief period of what could only be translated as "cordial bullshit," *El Jefe* changed the subject.

"So tell me," Bobdog translated for the sergeant, "why is it that you vacation in my modest village?"

"To be honest," I said through Bobdog, "we are looking for someone. A friend."

He laughed. "And you think this friend is in Nombre de Dios?"

"We don't know where he is, but we think he might be with some people called *Cimarrones*."

HUNDRED WATERS

Lemos coughed, and the policeman's eyes darted from side to side.

"How is it that you know this name?"

We all looked around at each other, then Bobdog spoke up. "From me. I spoke of them."

"And how is it that you know of these people?"

"I was born near here, in the village of *Casa Maropa*."

"That village is no longer," the policeman said.

"Yes...I know," she said. "I left some years ago, but I know something of the people and this region."

"We are just trying to find our friend," Tepi said.

"Here is his picture." I handed him a black and white photo of Harry, but *El Jefe* said nothing before handing it back. "We are not here to cause trouble or disrupt anything. We're just looking for our friend. Can you help us?"

"This is a small village. We are apart from other places, as you found out today. We have learned to keep to ourselves. There are those in the world who must keep to themselves. For safety reasons. I suggest you do the same. Have some more soup."

"We have come a long way to find this friend, and we have every reason to believe he is in this area, involved with these *Cimarrone* people. We just want to know how we can find them. Where to begin looking."

The policeman dismissed his wife and daughter, then went to the windows and cautiously looked around outside.

"There are those in this country who want to be unknown," he said through Bobdog, "and they exact a high price for that. These people require obedience, and people respect that. Even if I knew where such a group of people were...who might know of your friend...I could not say. I might be in your next bowl of soup. And my wife and my beautiful daughter would not like that."

"Are you trying to scare us?" I asked.

"He's succeeding with me," Tepi whispered.

"Scare?" *El Jefe* said through Bobdog. "No, I don't think so. There is no need to scare you. Fear is such a luxury. Around here...either you are alive or you are dead."

"If you cannot help us, is there anyone else here who can? We must find our friend."

"Do you know anything of these people you are looking for?"

"Some things."

"I have spoken to them of things," Bobdog said.

"You live on the blade of danger."

Bobdog looked over at me, then back to Señor Huertas. "I know what I am doing," she said.

"Then you know of their past," Huertas said to me. "Where they came from."

I looked at Bobdog then Tepi and shrugged.

"Listen to me then! There are some things not to be known. If your friend is with these people, it is for him to decide. Not your concern. If he is still alive, it is their wish. Not his. So you can do nothing to change anything now. Everything is in the hands of the Father Boco."

"What is Father Boco?" I asked Bobdog.

Bobdog leaned close to me and whispered: "Father Boco is like a priest, a holy man, but of voodoo."

"So...it would be best if you forget this friend of yours who is now lost. Just turn around and leave now while you can."

I spoke to Bobdog. "Tell *El Jefe* he doesn't scare me. I'm not leaving without my friend."

"Eddie," Tepi whispered, "maybe this guy knows what he's talking about. We can't help Harry if we're dead."

"If it's so dangerous, how did we get this far? Why did they let us leave Portobello? Ask *El Jefe* about that."

HUNDRED WATERS

Bobdog told the policeman what I had said, and he just stared at me, as though he were sizing up my determination. Or maybe my craziness. Then he slowly sat back in his chair and lit a cigar.

"What those of the jungle do is decided by them," *El Jefe* said through Bobdog. "I have no explanations for their actions. And as I say to you before, I have no knowledge of an American in these places. I could not take you to those you seek if I wanted to. We live in separate worlds. I have made it my business to leave the untamed to their own life."

El Jefe called for his wife to bring him some wine, and when she came out he filled his glass and offered the bottle to Bobdog. *El Jefe* massaged his stubbly face, drawing his deeply creased fingers slowly and methodically across his darkly tanned skin, clearly considering very carefully not only his thoughts, but his impending words.

"There is only one thing I can offer these 'tourists'," Bobdog translated, "in finding their American friend. That is a direction... more an area than a place."

I sat up closer to the table. "Where is this place? Ask him that."

"*Aguas Cientos*," he said crossing himself.

Just then, Señor Lemos stood quickly and nervously crossed himself.

"Hundred Waters," Bobdog said.

"*Pardonome*," Lemos said. "I must go and check my canoe. Excuse me." And he quickly left the table and scampered down the porch stairs.

"That was abrupt," Tepi said.

"So what exactly is this Hundred Waters?" I asked. "A village?"

"A place of strong magic for some people," *El Jefe* said.

"Well...who is there, then?" I asked.

"There is no 'there,' so there can be no one exactly...yet so many."

"How will we know this place that is not really there?" Tepi asked.

"It will know you," Huertas said through Bobdog. "If you are meant to find those people where you think your friend is, then perhaps this place called Hundred Waters will be where you need to be."

Tepi leaned toward me and whispered, "That was clear as mud."

"It is a place of beginnings. For those with no names, it is where their new life began. For others, it is an ending place. I would think hard about looking for such a place."

"How do we find this place? Where do we start?"

El Jefe smiled and slowly took a drink of wine. "So it is," he said and drank again, wiping his chin on the back of his hand. "You go on the old trail of gold. It is some distance from here; I myself have not been on that part of the trail since a child, but I can direct you with a map. Do you have a map?"

"Of course," I said. I quickly pulled our map from my back pocket and opened it on the table between us. *El Jefe* found Portobello then his village up the coast. I pointed out the dotted line that represented the old gold trail. He referred to an old lighthouse from which, he said, by looking inland, we would see a mountain, and it was somewhere along the base of the mountain that the place called Hundred Waters was supposedly located. It was an even older route than the one shown on the map, he said, because it was abandoned after the Spanish slaughter of many slaves, and a new stretch of cobbled road was laid.

"If you go this old way, perhaps you will find what you are seeking."

HUNDRED WATERS

"Maybe we'll find them," Tepi said.

The policeman laughed hard. "No, my young friend. You would not find them in a hundred years. The army does not even look for them anymore. The Americans came here on one occasion but left. The 'untamed' have survived all this time just because no one can find them. They are like the rustling of a distant bush...the whisper in a coward's head. What you are seeking is the heart of belief. The best you can do is to help them find *you*."

"How will we know the place when we see it?" I asked.

"You won't," *El Jefe* said. "It is not a place to see."

"Well, how will we know it is them?" Tepi asked.

"Believe me, you will know. There will be no one else."

"Then what?" Tepi asked.

"Then...well...you are there. But I encourage you to leave this alone. You may think you understand, but trust me, you do not. It would be better to forget this foolishness. Forget your friend. He is a luxury now...like fear. Whoever he is, he has forgotten you. Just go back to your world. Even if your friend is with these people, he may not be as you remember him."

"Why...what do you know?" I asked. Then I said to Bobdog, "Ask him why he says that?"

She asked him and he replied, with a half smile, "Nothing remains the same in the jungle. Even you will not be the same."

"That sounds like a threat, Eddie," Tepi said.

"It's only been two weeks," I said. "How much could've happened to him with his friends?"

The policeman smiled again, then spoke to Bobdog.

"What did he say," I asked.

Tepi turned to me. "He said he thought Bobdog had told us about these people."

"I told him you've been told," Bobdog said, "but you won't listen."

"You thank *El Jefe* for his help, and tell him we'll head out first thing in the morning."

Bobdog translated what I had said, and after we finished our coffee, I collected our map and the four of us retired to the rear porch area of the house where we were to sleep.

Tepi and I laid out our blankets side by side on the floor, at a right angle from the handmade bench that Bobdog would sleep on. Before we called it a night, Bobdog leaned over and whispered my name. I sat up and scooted over to her.

"This policeman knows," she said in a hushed voice.

"Of course he knows...but what?"

"Too much, and he was giving us his warning."

"And you think we should turn back...forget about Harry?"

"I want you to know how serious this is."

"You can wait here if you're afraid. Tepi and I will go on."

"No, Eddie. I am here because of you. I will go with you. But I worry...for my boy...for Raul, if anything happens."

"Why would anything happen to your boy? He's in Colon."

"You are so...simple sometimes, Eddie. That's why I like you. Maybe if things are good..."

"...What?"

"I would like my son to know something of a man like you."

"Like me?

"Promise me, Eddie, if anything happens you will speak with my son. Tell him how we were."

"Exactly how are we?"

"You are free, Eddie. And now...I think part of me is too."

"How's that?"

HUNDRED WATERS

"Coming back here. I don't have a fear so much, like when I was young and was told to fear many things...like those who look dead. It is as Señor Huertas said. For me there is not so much fear now. My heart is very full, Eddie. I fear only for my son."

"You worry too much," I said. "You can tell your son all he needs to know."

Bobdog wrote something on a piece of paper and handed it to me. "This is my aunt's address where we stopped in Colon. Please let my son know. Promise me, Eddie."

"You worry too much."

She clutched the collar of my shirt. "Promise me, Eddie!"

"Okay," I said, "I promise. But it won't be necessary. You'll be able to tell him. Now go to sleep. And stop worrying."

Carr, MANUSCRIPT. The words, "Something That May or May Not Exist" are written across the top of page one.

    I woke up with the roosters and the sound of pigs rooting around in the dirt pen beneath the porch where the four of us had spent the night. Bobdog and Lemos were already up and gone when I reached over and gently tapped Tepi awake. I walked down the porch steps and around the side of the house to where a huge rain barrel stood under a gutter pipe. I splashed a few mosquitoes off the surface, dished out a pan of water and washed up. Dogs barked in the distance, and there was a faraway sound of a baby crying. It was already getting warm, and a strong smell of coffee wafted through the thin morning air. Several older women walked about the village grounds carrying loads of clothing to the large communal washtubs; a one-armed man chopped wood with a hatchet outside his doorway. A dozen other men collected their fishnets and were walking down the path to their boats on the beach.

    I felt a million miles away from the army and the joy-boy world I had fallen into and had come to hate. I hadn't been drunk for four days, and my body was still a little sluggish. I took a deep breath, and the earthy smells of decay that a few days before would have turned my stomach didn't seem as pungent anymore. I wasn't sure if the odors had diminished or if my senses had dulled, but for the first time in awhile, the air smelled rich and invigorating. It smelled like a good day to find Harry Miles.

* * *

Bobdog and Lemos eventually showed up and joined Tepi and me at the large dining table. We ate a light breakfast of fried eggs, fried plantains and bread prepared by *El Jefe's* wife. We drank several cups of black coffee while Bobdog told us that she and Lemos had walked down to the beach to check on the *cayuco* and had found it pulled way up on the sand.

"Señor Lemos said it would take six men to move his canoe," Bobdog said.

"But it's still there, right?" Tepi said.

"Yes, of course, but it makes it difficult for any one or two individuals to get it back into the water."

"Well I'm sure some of Señor Huertas' people will be happy to help us."

"Any idea how the boat got moved up onto the beach?" Tepi asked.

"No...but Señor Lemos was very distressed."

"Maybe our ship's captain had planned on leaving early...without us. That might explain his concern over this," I suggested.

"Well," Bobdog said, "we're still going to need someone's help when we need to get the boat back in the water."

Just then, Señor Huertas returned from some early morning police duties in another part of the village. His daughter Malique was beginning to take an interest in Tepi, and it was quite clear from the way she kept refilling his coffee cup, and not mine or Bobdog's, that she could not stay away from Tepi.

HUNDRED WATERS

Finally *El Jefe* had the dishes cleared, and on the heavy wood table he laid out our map and started marking out our route with a red pencil.

"He says," Bobdog began, "that he is sorry that he cannot show us the way himself. He says the way is a bit steep, and he is too near retirement for such a trip. He offers the services of his daughter instead. Malique knows the way, he says, as far as the old Spanish trail, and she will be quite helpful to us."

I looked over at Tepi. He half smiled and then shrugged his shoulders innocently. "Tell *El Jefe* that will be fine. And thank him."

Señor Huertas described the trail as overgrown but discernable for much of the early stretch, and after that his daughter would not be of help since she had never been beyond the region north of the lighthouse. From that point on, we would be on our own, Huertas told Bobdog. Malique was instructed to return once she reached the lighthouse. We were to travel in a southeasterly direction always looking for signs of the old stone trail.

I turned to Bobdog. "Ask him how long we should travel in that direction?"

She asked and during his reply, he crossed himself when he spoke the words *Aguas Cientos* again.

"He says he does not know," Bobdog translated. "He himself has never been to the place called Hundred Waters. It exists for him in name only. But as he knows of it, that place should be on this part of the trail. He says the trail was changed many years ago because the natives were afraid to travel that route, as are the Panamanian soldiers now. No outsiders go there. And there has never been any reason for anyone to go in that direction. Unless, like us, they are looking for something that may or may not exist out there."

"What does he mean by that?" I asked.

Bobdog asked and the policeman's reply was a smile and the shrug of his shoulders.

* * *

Within an hour we had full canteens, several sacks full of bread, some dried fruit and meat, all provided by *El Jefe*, that we slung across our backs.

We asked Lemos if he wanted to go along, but he shook his head, clearly not wanting anything to do with this part of the excursion. He also crossed himself when he said the name *Aguas Cientos* and began to speak in short, rapid bursts. The crossing gestures surrounding the mention of Hundred Waters made me nervous, and I wasn't sure what to make of it. We paid Lemos half of what we owed him for the ride up the coast and told him we'd pay the rest when he delivered us back to Portobello. Lemos told Bobdog he would wait for us in the village for no more than two days. After that, he said, we would be a "dead account."

"What the hell does he mean by that?" I asked.

She asked and translated his response. "He didn't mean anything," she said. "He says only that after two days, it will be a bill he will not collect."

"I'm not sure I like the sound of that," Tepi said.

"He wishes us a safe journey," she added.

"That I like."

El Jefe walked the four of us through the village and out past the small cemetery. All that remained of a once large fence were a few wrought iron bars, standing like lone sentinels watching over the dead. The place didn't leave me with a very good feeling as we reached the end of the village proper and the beginning of the jungle. *El Jefe* hugged his daughter, whispered something to her and then kissed the top of her head.

HUNDRED WATERS

"*Buenos suarte*," he said.

He continued to speak to us in Spanish, with Bobdog translating. "There are many things out there," she said. "He says he hopes you find what you seek."

"Thank him for me," I said.

His daughter stepped ahead and started off down the path into the jungle.

"*Vaya con Dios*," *El Jefe* called out.

"He said...," Bobdog began, but I interrupted her.

"I know what he said. I just hope he means it."

Carr, MANUSCRIPT. Titled, "Embraced By Angry Arms."

Once we were out in the open, the morning sun quickly became an additional member of our party. Shirts came off, and the gnats, mosquitos and huge horseflies quickly joined us. Within minutes there was a thin layer of moisture covering my entire body. My feet slipped in my boots, and beads of sweat ran down my face.

The path we were on was fairly well established, like a narrow crease cut through the thick brush on either side of us. The grass was not trampled, only pushed aside, and looking back where we had just walked, it was hard to tell that anyone had passed. I figured by the end of the day no one would be able to tell that we had walked this path at all, and I found that notion just a bit unnerving. Not that I was overly worried, but it was comforting to know that at least the people of Nombre de Dios knew who we were and where we were headed.

We followed a line through the single-canopy jungle where the land was pretty much flat and dry. After about an hour the path got steeper and rockier, and the shade of light changed from gauzy pale green to a deeper, darker olive color. I started to feel the heaviness of my pack about the time I experienced my first dizzy spell. We took a short break for water and salt pills, and I wrapped my shirt around my head.

DAVID GREGOR

The trees overhead grew thicker and so did the underbrush, as the ground got wetter. I could smell the dankness of the earth as we walked farther inland and climbed higher, and I found my thoughts focusing more on where my feet were stepping than on how the terrain was different from just twenty minutes before. I kept looking up toward the open sky in hopes of getting a glimpse of the lighthouse we were headed for—as a sign of progress—but all I saw was a layer of green overhead with only infrequent glimpses of blue sky and the constant yellowness of the sun.

I thought about Harry a lot, wondering what he was doing and where he was exactly, as we plodded up steep, rocky grades while razor-edged bamboo leaves sliced the insides of my fingers. For some reason I pictured Harry lying in a native hammock tied between two trees, swinging gently in the jungle breeze. He was drinking something cool from a bamboo cup. Maybe that was just where I wanted to be, maybe that was what I was imagining for myself. Maybe that was what the harsh yellow sun did to you.

After almost two hours of climbing and winding back and around, following a marginal path at best, we broke out of the thick overhead canopy. A hundred yards away rose a badly weathered lighthouse with a glass top. Señor Huertas said we would find it, and there it was.

The jungle grew right up its sides and covered the lower level of what was clearly an outside ladder that wound around the badly weathered structure up to the top observation level. We cut and hacked our way to the base of the lighthouse and then cleared a way around the ladder.

The metal ladder was rusted from the humidity and salt air, but after banging on the rungs, we concluded that they were sturdy enough to hold us. Tepi climbed up first then helped Melique and Bobdog up; I followed. We gingerly wound our way up to the top outside observation level.

HUNDRED WATERS

The view was breathtaking. For as far inland as you could see, the jungle landscape was a soft looking, fluffy green that seemed harmless and primordial, completely devoid of human life. Down below the Caribbean stretched out crystalline blue with only the single gray profile of a merchant ship breaking up the straight line of the horizon. There were no signs that anyone lived within a hundred miles: no buildings, cars, trucks or planes, no smoke, no pulsating industrial hum...no voices but our own. Just the distant chatter of monkeys and an occasional breeze that whooshed through the treetops. We decided to stop for a break, and we all took advantage of the rest to dry out our feet in the sun.

"Hard to believe this still exists," Tepi said.

"This is what Columbus and Balboa saw. Nothing much could've changed. What we see is probably what they saw."

"Tell me, Eddie," Tepi said, "you think Harry's really out there?"

"I do."

"I mean...just look around us. I bet you could throw a rock out there and not come within five miles of another human being."

"He's out there, Tepi, and so are those *Cimarrones*. If we find them, we'll find Harry."

"Well, that's kind of what I'm a little worried about. Malique told me none of her people ever go out much farther than this lighthouse. They're scared of these *Cimarrones*."

"She's right," Bobdog said.

"Well, they can be as scared as they want. I'm not. We're not here to cause anyone trouble."

"But being here could cause trouble," Tepi said.

"I just want to talk to Harry. Give him a chance to rethink what he's done and come back. That's all."

"We're a long way from our world, Eddie. And...well,

hell, it's pretty damn wild out here. I mean...primitive, Eddie. We don't know what the hell's going on out there," Tepi said, lifting his arm and making a wide sweeping motion in the direction of the jungle. "And this is as far as Malique goes. From here on, we're on our own. If we go tramping through that jungle...you know...hell, we'll be out of our element. And into somebody else's."

"What's your point Tep?"

"Point is, maybe we ought to reconsider what we're doing out here."

"You mean forget Harry and go back?"

"Not forget Harry, just rethink hiking out into the Stone Age. We might be biting off more than we know. I just don't want us to make a mistake, that's all."

"It won't be a mistake to find Harry and bring him back. Trust me."

The policeman's daughter was speaking with Bobdog and pointing inland, in the direction of a jungle-covered hill that clearly rose up higher than the lighthouse and appeared to have a cloud-halo around its peak.

"Is that the mountain her father spoke of?" I asked Bobdog.

"She thinks so. It is the highest place."

"And from here to there, there's no trail?"

Bobdog spoke with Malique. "There's a stone trail, she's been told. We just have to find it."

I took a compass bearing on the mountain, and after our half-hour break, Tepi and I put our boots back on, and the four of us started down the lighthouse ladder. On the ground, the jungle was again in our face and right overhead.

I turned to Bobdog. "Tell Malique we appreciate her taking us this far."

While Bobdog spoke to Malique, Tepi stepped up close to me. "I've got a bad feeling about this, Eddie. We have no idea where we are...where we're going or how to even get where it is we don't know we're going. I say we go...."

Before Tepi could finish his sentence, Bobdog interrupted him. "Malique says she will stay with us."

Tepi whirled around, the hint of a smile on his face.

"I thought her father didn't want her to go beyond the lighthouse," Tepi said.

"He didn't," Bobdog said. "But I told her about Harry and that you were trying to save him, and she wants to help us."

"Today's our lucky day," Tepi said, smiling broadly.

* * *

We each took a direction and poked around looking for any sign of a trail inland. Malique found what looked like a path, and with no other options, we started out in the direction of the cloud-capped mountain.

How Malique decided that was the trail was beyond me. I saw no evidence of wear to the brush or the ground, but gave her the benefit of the doubt. She led the way with her own machete, followed by me, then Bobdog and Tepi. The light changed almost immediately, going from a bright, harsh yellow to muted, grayish-green that made everything feel a lot closer to night, even at midday. Periodically I'd pause and check my compass reading to see that we were indeed still traveling in a southeasterly direction toward the fog-draped mountain.

After about an hour's walking, we were all ready for another break. We stopped at a wide spot fronted by several large fallen trees. The ground had gotten wetter the farther inland we traveled, and the air was thicker and heavier with the humidity. I lay back on one of the fallen logs and closed my eyes, listening to whistles and hoots of the birds and the screams of howler monkeys high up above us. Bobdog spoke softly in Spanish with Malique, and Tepi rested silently across the trail from me. Suddenly I realized how quiet the jungle had become. The sound of birds was gone, as was the ever-present chatter of monkeys and whirring of flies and gnats. Everything went still. A bit of a breeze moved through the high upper leaves, but that was the only sound. I sat up, looked at Tepi, then over at Bobdog and Malique, first for confirmation, then for an explanation.

"What is this?" I said.

Bobdog shook her head. "I don't know." She turned to Malique and spoke to her. "She does not know too."

Then off to our right, back in the thick underbrush, was the sound of something—apparently very large—pushing through the brush, followed by a deep guttural growl.

"I've heard that before," Tepi said.

"On the trail to Las Cruces," I said.

"What was it?" Bobdog asked.

"No idea."

"Holy Father and Mother of God," Malique said in Spanish and crossed herself. She babbled on in Spanish and Bobdog tried to comfort her.

"She says it's the spirits of dead slaves. They live out here and haunt the places where they were tortured and killed."

"It's probably a boar or something else rooting around out there."

"Perhaps we should go back," Bobdog said. "This girl is truly frightened."

"It's really nothing. Just some animal moving around. Tell her there aren't any spirits flying around. Besides, Tepi and I are here."

"But she believes they're spirits. She can't just stop believing."

HUNDRED WATERS

"Well, we're not turning back. We're this far and we're going on."

Suddenly the sounds of monkeys and birds returned, and the jungle seemed normal...friendlier.

"See," I said, taking in a deep breath. "Just some critter checking us out." I took another compass reading and pointed off in a southeasterly direction. "You know," I said to Bobdog, "this is the jungle. There are animals that live out here."

We started out again, and after about a mile, we came upon a small stream. We crossed it and found stronger evidence of the trail. Though not laid out in a thick pattern, rounded stones, like those we had seen on the Las Cruces trail, stretched out ahead of us. They were clearly imported to this place because of their uniformity of size and shape. I traded places with Malique and took the lead. We were able to follow the sporadic splay of round stones for the rest of the afternoon, but before we knew it, the daylight had passed into dusk. One entire day of walking and we had not seen anyone else or any evidence of other people or a village. It was impossible to see the mountain through the thick canopy overhead, and we had no idea how close or far away we were. Or whether we might have passed it. We continued on a little farther until the darkness made it impossible to see where we were stepping.

We agreed to stop for the night and make camp. Once again we found a place with some fallen trees. We stretched both of our ponchos between two crossed logs in case of rain and built a fire for the night. After we had eaten some cold rice and dried *paca*, we settled into after-dinner smokes and hot tea. Once we felt comfortable with our surroundings and had sufficiently fed the fire, we paired off for warmth. I was happy for Tepi that Malique had decided to come with us beyond the lighthouse or else it would have been awkward with the three of us trying to keep warm. This way it was only awkward for him, and even that only lasted a few moments.

    I lay awake for what seemed like an eternity, just listening to the night sounds of those creatures whose waking life begins when the sun sets. I was equally concerned about the small things: creatures with lots of legs and antennae that could deliver nasty bites, creatures that I couldn't see or hear that lived and moved on the ground. I hated spiders and anything resembling centipedes. Just thinking about snakes and lizards with their darting tongues sent shivers up and down my back, but I did finally fall asleep.

    Sometime later the sound of pouring rain woke me, and the chill from the damp ground made it hard for me to fall back asleep. I found myself staring out into the blackest darkness I had ever experienced and found that even when it's that dark, there is a certain amount of light that somehow is emitted. I knew I was tired and my legs and feet were sore, but the idea of seeing things, like hallucinations, caught me off guard. Because I did see what I thought was the silhouette of a figure off in the distance, standing, then crouching as if trying to get a better look at something. I blinked repeatedly and then rubbed at my eyes, trying to help them focus on the unclear shapes off in the distance. Immediately my heart began to race, and in my fear of the possibilities, I felt frozen, unable to move or even speak. All I could do was stare out into the deep dark, secretly hoping the longer I stared, the more likely whatever it was out there would just disappear. In the meantime, I tried to focus on a recognizable form so that I would know for sure what I was seeing, but each time I thought I was focused, the form went fuzzy, blurred then dissolved into the shapeless black night. At first I was too frightened to move, then too frightened to try to wake Tepi for fear of seeming paranoid if it turned out to just be my imagination. It was like a dream; I just wasn't sure what was truly real.

I closed my eyes, squeezed the lids tightly hoping the pressure would wash away the fuzziness of sleep and make everything clearer when I opened them again, but the black jungle night was still very much unfocused. Whatever I thought I had seen earlier was not out there now. At least I didn't *see* anything. The longer I kept looking, the more I prayed that the jungle night would stay empty, that it just would have been my imagination or some optical illusion that occurs in the dark. I felt my body relax; then it got cold, and I started to shiver so hard that Bobdog woke up.

"What's the matter, Eddie?"

She wrapped her arms around me and pulled herself tighter against my back. I listened hard for any sound of movement—anything that might sound like a person or an animal—something that might identify what I thought I had seen, but deeply hoped I hadn't. The last thing I wanted was a surprise in the dark in the jungle. Surprises were best encountered, if at all, in daylight.

* * *

I bolted up and awake with the screech of a howler monkey high above us and the sight of yellow light. The darkness of the night had changed to the blue of morning. I looked over in the direction where I thought I had seen the figure, just to see how close it might have been, if in fact something had been out there. The trees and brush looked less threatening in the indigo morning. I climbed out of our sleeping bag and tried stretching the soreness out of my legs and back. My whole body felt tightly strung, and I didn't feel very rested at all. I quietly stepped off in the direction where I thought I had seen the shadows moving. I was pawing around in the dirt looking for human or animal prints or any other evidence, when out of the corner of my eye I saw movement on the ground beneath a bush about twenty feet away. I froze momentarily, then slowly turned my head. I saw a black object, about the size of a softball, that could have been a foot inching out from under the brush. My heart was pounding so hard I couldn't swallow. I stood dead still and waited for someone to jump up, but as I watched the dark object move the leaves, it suddenly began coming toward me, and then I saw the furry legs and thick round body of a tarantula as big as a baseball hat. I backed up, then reached down and grabbed a small stick and threw it at the spider. It stopped and then began walking away from me.

"What's up out there?" Tepi called out.

"Nothing," I lied, not wanting to scare the others. "Just taking a leak."

I grabbed some wood for the morning fire and quick-stepped back to the others.

"What were you looking for?" Bobdog asked.

"Thought I saw something last night, so I was just checking around."

"And?" Tepi asked.

"It was nothing."

We ate a quick breakfast and made orange juice out of Tang and started out again on the scattered trail of rocks.

By midmorning it felt like we had already walked a hundred miles. The bottoms of my feet ached from stone bruises, and what little weight we were carrying felt ten times heavier than it was. It was all I could do to keep plodding along, and for the first time since we had set out searching for Harry Miles, I began to question my desire to go farther.

I began to think of the jungle as a living entity at which I could aim the anger I was beginning to feel. The tiredness

HUNDRED WATERS

in my body made my mind focus on the pain and exhaustion; I began to hate the jungle like you would an enemy. I wasn't even sure where we were anymore. It had been over a day since we had last seen the mountain we were headed for. All we had was the compass bearing, and for all I knew, we could have stumbled on past the base of the mountain, heading farther inland into a true no man's land. From my memory of the map, there were no indications of any villages inland from the coast. All I could remember were hills, mountains and the myriad of streams that cross-hatched the map as they made their way down steeply from the mountains to the coast and out to sea.

At what point would we know we were past our destination and off into the great green unknown? I couldn't answer my own question, which told me we were already lost. I could tell the others were as trail-weary as I was, and when we finally stopped near another small creek to rest and soak our feet, I put the question to Malique by way of Bobdog.

"Ask her if she knows where we are?" I said.

Bobdog asked and replied, "She says she is following the stones as before."

"Well, how do we know these are the stones? That she's not lost, that we're anywhere near where we're supposed to be? Ask her that."

"Why are you yelling at Malique?" Tepi said. "It's not her fault we're out here stomping around in the damn jungle. Hell, she's going against her father to help us this far."

"I just want to know where the hell we are."

"Malique says she does not know if we are lost or not, because she did not know where exactly we were going."

"That's some help! Hell, I give up!" I stomped away from the others and sat down on a large moss-covered rock.

"What do you mean give up?" Tepi said.

"Our guide doesn't even know where we are, and I'm not even sure we should be going anywhere. That's what I mean."

"This is a fine time to not know," Tepi said. "I asked the same question back at the lighthouse. But you said we had to find Harry. That if he was here, we would find him."

"I thought it would be easier to find Harry. At least track him. You know, a village somewhere. See somebody who might know something. But hell, we don't even have that. Just more rocks and heat and brush and things crawling around."

"I didn't expect to hear this from you," Tepi said.

"Seems to me if there were people out here, we would have seen or heard them by now. We haven't seen a soul. Hell, we could be ten miles from the nearest human."

"So what are you saying?"

"All I'm saying is that we don't know where we are or where we're going. And for that matter, if we can even get back out of here."

"Do you want to turn back? Forget about Harry...just write him off?"

"I don't want to write him off, but I don't think we're going to find him by wandering around the jungle hoping we just run into him. Hell...maybe Harry really wants to be out here, playing in the woods with the natives. Maybe we should just let him be...do what he wants. He's old enough to make his own decisions. Shit...I don't know. Besides, we're running out of time."

"Maybe we should take a vote, then."

"Who's to vote? You and I are the ones who wanted to come out here. It should be up to us, and I say let Harry call his own shots."

There was a long pause.

HUNDRED WATERS

"If that's the way you feel, Eddie, I vote with you."

We decided to call off our search for Harry right there in the middle of nowhere. We agreed it would be best to spend the night where we were and start back fresh in the morning. We stretched our ponchos again into something of a lean-to and made a fire for the night. It rained again that night, and for the first time since we started out, I enjoyed the sounds of the jungle night. The rain hitting high up in the trees and dripping down on the layers of leaves below created an echoing effect that was strangely hypnotic.

Bobdog and I snuggled up under our poncho. I lit a cigarette for each of us, and we just stared out into the darkening jungle.

"I am happy we are going back," she said. "Before something happens."

"That's our problem. Nothing has happened...except we got lost."

"You tried Eddie. Harry would like that. A good friend is not so easy to find."

"But I didn't find him. Hell...we didn't even get close. All we did is get lost and tired. Some achievement."

"The truth may be that Harry is where he wants to be."

"That doesn't change how I feel," I said. "He's my friend, and I miss him."

"I'm sure he knows that," she said. "Maybe now you have to go your own way."

We finished our cigarettes without saying anything more, but I couldn't stop thinking about Harry Miles and where he was, while we huddled under our ponchos lost in the jungle.

I finally fell asleep to the gentle sound of the rain. It would be far into the night, after the rain had stopped and all you heard were the steady drips of water from high above,

DAVID GREGOR

when I would again awaken to see what I thought was another dark figure moving in the jungle. I squeezed my eyelids closed, then tried again to focus on distant objects in the blackness. I thought of the tarantula I had seen that morning, and I didn't like the thought of another one crawling around out there. Every time I closed my eyes and reopened them, shapes changed or dissolved into some leaf or tree form. I no longer felt threatened by things I thought were out there and accepted the fact that in the dark your eyes can play tricks on you. I fell back to sleep with the patter of the rain as it began to fall again.

Then came the explosion. Voices...deep growls, and screams from Malique and Bobdog. Someone grabbed me from the back and held my arms behind me, while someone else wrapped cloth around my eyes and mouth. All I heard were screams and wild grunts of people struggling. The cloth around my face smelled of smoke and something pungent that made my head hurt. Even though I tried scrambling to my feet, my back felt unjointed and my legs like rubber. I couldn't stand up, my head throbbed, and then everything went coldly dark like the night had embraced me with angry arms.

Carr, MANUSCRIPT.   Titled, "Distant Voices."

When I opened my eyes, a flickering yellow light danced above me, and I felt like I had been away for a long time. I had no idea where I was or if I was alone. My body felt like cement...heavy and unmovable. I tried lifting my arm to shield my eyes from the light, but it wouldn't move. It was like I was alive, but my arm was dead. The same thing happened when I tried moving my legs. They felt attached to the dirt. I saw myself dead. No...I knew it. It wasn't what I expected of being dead, but it seemed like death. I tried to speak but the words were only in my head. Only my eyes worked...or seemed to work...at least I thought I saw things. That struck me funny, that only my eyes would work and nothing else. I could see the yellow light dancing about me, but that was all. I closed my eyes and my head spun around and around; the spinning made me feel sick to my stomach. I couldn't roll onto my side in case I had to throw up, and I panicked thinking I would choke. I knew you could choke on your own vomit, and I didn't want that. But I was dead. And dead people can't vomit or worry about choking or any of that stuff. I was delirious, and my stomach was turning inside out...but I finally fell asleep, and I was gone again.

* * *

DAVID GREGOR

Suddenly bright blue light, and I heard voices...distant voices...voices like you would expect from angels, not very clear, but comforting, and the light around me was very blue...almost warm. My eyelids would not open, and after a-while that was okay. I could hear things, and the pictures that came with the sounds were very pleasant. There were people dancing...men and women...without clothes, and they were dancing in the dark shadows cast by the bright light of a huge yellow fire. I could not see their faces...they had no faces, just featureless bodies that moved like sea grass in a sway I felt move through my body. I too was dancing. I saw myself in the shadow of the great yellow flames...yellow tongues of fire shooting skyward...away from me lying flat on the ground.

The pounding was loud, like drums...a pulse beating like blood rushing through my veins. It was no sound I had ever heard before. The sound went on and on like an image reflected into a mirror back into itself and back again. I wanted to walk with the sound. The sound was haunting as if coming from a place far away...a sound that grabbed at the base of my neck and pulled at my spine like it was a rope connected to my feet, lifting my body off the ground. It was a very pleasant feeling, and I wanted more of it.

Then there was the face in my face and the voice that was not mine...words stretched out in a chamber of echoes that I heard and loved but did not understand. I bolted straight up into the face, though my body never moved, and I knew I was someone else.

A loud forceful voice spoke to me. "You have come to find out," followed by shrieks of laughter. The voice was strangely mine.

I knew then I was not dead, but something dangerous had touched me and with the weight of extreme finality.

* * *

HUNDRED WATERS

The first thing I consciously remembered upon waking was the grossly tattooed face of a green man. His head was hairless, round, smooth and shiny green, and in the firelight long shadows danced across his eyes and mouth. The shadows around his eyes were so deep that his gaze seemed a mile long. The light green skin over his head was covered with small, crudely drawn images of black spiders, coiled snakes and concentric circles. A large black spider emanated down from the crown of his bald head, and other marks, much like horns, were crudely etched around his eyes, nose and mouth with dark ink, as if done in a child's hand. His yellow eyes were hard and penetrating. They had the glow of death in them. I could feel the intensity of his gaze, as if he were reaching inside me just with those eyes, drawing out what he wanted to know of me. Then he laughed, baring yellow front teeth that had been filed to sharp points. He laughed hard again until his voice sounded like a growl, and then he blew some powder from his open palm into my face. He laughed even harder, spitting out words in a language I had never heard before. Slowly the green man turned away to face a loud voice behind him. Then before everything went dark, I saw the letters...I N T I...tattooed across the back of his neck. I realized, for just a fleeting moment, that I knew those letters...from another crease in history.

Where I was, how I got there and where the others were, I did not know. Everything I remember occurred in darkness and to me alone. I did see people or the figures of people, but except for the green tattooed one, I only saw them at a distance, and they never spoke. They would be in the place where I was...off in the shadows, looking over at me, but I never had contact with them.

I remember being incredibly hungry and thirsty, and without ever asking for food or water, someone would be at my side in the dark, lifting my head; I would feel liquid flowing into my mouth, followed by a kind of paste that tasted much like rotting wood smells. Things moved in my mouth, but I swallowed anyway.

I was never sure about time or place. It seemed like I had been lying in one position on my back for an eternity. I saw figures move in and out of sight and heard indiscernible voices but always in the darkness, never in the light. No matter how hard I tried to move my arms and legs, they were unmovable like huge chunks of steel. Only my head moved, and that made me feel very detached from my neck down, like I was two different people: one a lifeless body, the other a living head. And sleep! There was always sleep, though I did not feel tired. I was truly lost.

Then I finally saw light, but I had to close my eyes immediately because it was so painful. I was carried out of my hut into what appeared to be a large village square where people with painted faces were standing around the edge of the open area. They were looking at me as I was carried across the compound on a bamboo bed. As my eyes grew used to the surroundings, I realized it was either daybreak or twilight because the light outside was muted, with tiny patches of blue in the sky. I was set down and approached by the green, tattooed man. He muttered something again that I did not understand, sprinkled some powder around my stretcher, and then began to chant loudly while thrusting a wooden stick in my direction.

Suddenly the head of my stretcher was hoisted upward and secured from above in a near vertical position. I thought I would fall, but my body was lashed to the bamboo slats; the rope vines dug into my wrists, ankles and bare chest. What I saw next has stayed with me like a bad dream.

Stretched between two tree-sized poles and a cross beam was the naked figure of a man, his body smeared with a white paint, which made him look ghostly. He was about ten feet off the ground. Below him were several dead animals laid out in a row; they had been gutted and their insides exposed. Smoking sticks were stuck in the dirt beneath the hanging man, along with what looked like fruit and flower heads. The man was attached at the wrists and ankles and also from around the ears, causing blood to run down the sides of his head, staining the white paint a deep, dark red. He just hung there pinned in the air, not moving, and I was certain he was dead.

I saw myself up there, and my heart pounded like a drum. That was the only reason I could think of for why I was brought outside to see that man. I did not want to be strung like that to die, and I started to cry. A short while later, my stretcher was lowered to the ground and I was left outside not very far from the suspended man. A black and white dog slowly approached me. My heart pounded hard inside my chest. The dog stood at my feet. He bared his teeth and growled loudly. I was afraid he was going to bite my foot or leg. I wouldn't be able to defend myself while he ripped at my flesh. He began to sniff me, and then licked my toes and wandered off.

Tears streamed down my face, and every joint in my body felt limp. I looked around for Bobdog and Tepi but saw no sign of them. My pants felt damp, then I felt my bladder slowly empty, and I didn't care.

Dark people painted white wandered around just outside the firelight, keeping a distance from me. I waited anxiously for something to happen...for someone, maybe the tattooed one, to reappear and do something with me. But no one came near me. The longer I lay there, the cooler the night air became, and the more relaxed I got until I finally lost consciousness.

When I woke up, I was back inside the structure again, and off in the far corner I saw Bobdog. I was never so happy to see anyone as I was to see her. I looked around for Tepi, but he was not there. I tried getting myself up off the ground and quickly found that only my arms worked. My legs would not work. I called to Bobdog, but she did not move. I rolled onto my stomach and dragged myself over to her side. I whispered her name and shook her, trying to get her to come to. She looked so helpless, and I prayed that she was not dead. Finally her eyes opened, and I kept repeating her name. I held her hand and told her over and over how good she looked to me.

We lay there, side by side, in the dark hut, while all around outside there were the sounds of drums and chanting. Bobdog couldn't move, and she kept blinking her eyes like she was having difficulty focusing. I asked what they had done to her, and when she was finally able to speak, she told me it was probably caused by potions or drugs they had given us. I asked Bobdog what had happened to Tepi.

"I have not seen him since that night in the jungle," she said.

"And Malique?"

"I last saw her asleep next to Tepi."

I brushed her hair away from her eyes. "Do you know where we are?"

"I think the place you were looking for. The place of *Los Cimarrones*."

"So the old policeman was right. They did find us."

"They always knew," she said. "Since I first asked about them in Portobello."

"Why are you here and not Tepi or Malique?"

"They know who I am, Eddie. And this place is taboo. Outsiders are not allowed."

"So why did they bring me here?"

"I don't know, Eddie. I only hope you are not sorry."

"I don't want to die. I don't want anybody hurt."

HUNDRED WATERS

Bobdog told me that from what she had heard and could pick up from the festivities, there was a sort of initiation ceremony in progress, and that's what was happening with the person hanging between the poles. We would not be dealt with until that ceremony was finished. I asked her about the tattooed, green-colored man, and she said he was probably the chief, or the medicine man, or both.

"Have you seen Harry?" I asked Bobdog.

"No," she said. "But you must know. This is very, very serious."

"Of course."

"No Eddie. I mean like death."

Carr, MANUSCRIPT. Typewritten. The words, "A Murmur Followed by a Long Cold Shiver," written across the top of the page in pencil.

Sometime in the middle of the night, three men came and dragged me by the arms out across the village compound to another small hut back up against the jungle. I was taken inside and dropped at the foot of a bed of thatch and palm leaves. A small candle lamp flickered in the far corner near the head of a bamboo bed. When my eyes adjusted to the dim light inside, I saw Harry Miles propped up in the bed staring at me blankly....full-faced. There were streaks of white around the edge of his face and blood around his ears. I felt sick inside when I realized it had been Harry hanging up between those trees. His hair and mustache had been crudely shaved with large chunks chopped out so that he looked like a dog with mange. I just stared at him. Then a painful half smile crept over his face.

"Eddie," he whispered, his voice hoarse and barely audible. "You shouldn't be here."

I tried to talk, but nothing came out. My mind felt jumbled, like the words were all stacked on top of one another. Then slowly I felt the inside of my head begin to clear. Words suddenly fell out of my mouth, like they were so much heavy syrup, with no particular rhyme or reason. I could hear the sound of words I was making, but I knew instinctively they were not making sense. A broad streak of bright light flashed behind my eyes, and some of the hushed roaring I had heard in my head suddenly quieted.

"You...don't...belong...here...Eddie," I heard Harry say. The words came out very slowly. "You...have...not seen me...and know nothing...of my whereabouts."

"We came...," I said, "to help you back...Harry."

"N-o-o-o," he said. The word echoed deep inside my head. "No-o-o-o."

"It's...not...desertion yet. There's...still time...to...get back."

Suddenly I felt dizzy and my stomach began contracting. I retched and spewed a thick white substance down my chest.

"This is...a dangerous...place," I heard Harry say. "If you want...to help me...forget me."

Harry's words were getting clearer and coming out closer together.

"I can't do that," I said.

"You have no choice."

"I'm here, Harry."

My words were coming together now, too.

"This is not...kid's stuff. This is where I want to be...and you're making it hard."

"I don't know what these people promised, Harry, but it can't be enough. Running off into the jungle and joining these people is just bullshit. You need to come back, take the AWOL charge...get on with real life."

"This *is* real life."

"This is the fucking jungle, Harry. These people strung you up like an animal."

"Is real life doing what you believe is wrong? Is real life spying on your friends or supporting leaders who butcher their own people?"

HUNDRED WATERS

"Real life is not getting painted white and hung up by your ears. I know that for damn sure."

"I'm dead Eddie. The Harry Miles you knew before is gone."

"Don't say that, Harry. We can slip out of here and be back in two days."

"You still don't get it, do you Eddie."

"Get what?"

"You may be dead too. Jesus, Eddie...these people are serious."

"Too many people know we're out here looking for you."

"Do you think these people give a shit what anybody knows about you? As far as they're concerned, this is the only world, and you're still in it and still breathing by their choice. No one else's. So when I say you're dead, Eddie, I mean disappeared, departed. Gone without a trace." He paused a moment, clearly in pain. "You see...they own *this* world of theirs and everything in it. If they say something's gone from their world, it's gone. So if you want to see daylight again, you better listen to me and do exactly what I say."

Harry winced and closed his eyes. I dragged myself up next to him where I could feel his shallow breath against the back of my hand. I was still experiencing flashes of light behind my eyes and a crackling sound in my ears, like radio interference. I took a cloth from next to his bed and wiped at the blood trickling down the sides of his face. The holes in his ears were nasty. They must have burned through the cartilage because the flesh was blackened and seared. There was even a sour...dead...smell around him.

He opened his eyes again. "No outsiders can know this place," he whispered.

"People know of this place," I said. "The guy who brought us up the coast knew of these people, and a village policeman knows something. Hell, he sent his daughter."

"They may know of it, but you don't see them here."

"So why are we here?"

"Because you asked about me. Otherwise you would still be wandering around aimlessly in the jungle where they found you."

Just then three men came back into Harry's hut and stood inside the doorway.

"I will speak for you," Harry said, "but I can't promise anything."

The three men grabbed me again under the arms and dragged me outside, back across the compound to my hut. Bobdog was not there, and when I tried asking the men carrying me about her, they just turned and walked away. I poked my head outside the hut, looked out across the compound but saw nothing. I crawled to my straw bed and stared up at the bamboo roof, thinking about Tepi and worried for Bobdog. My mind was beginning to play tricks on me. No matter how hard I tried to block out bad images, I always saw Bobdog in pain.

* * *

What I took to be the next morning, I was awakened by the green, tattooed man and another large man poking me with the sharp end of a stick. Again I looked around the hut for Bobdog, but she was still gone. The tattooed man gestured to two other men. They quickly blindfolded me and lashed my hands behind my back. Next thing I knew I was being stood up and led outside by a rope. My legs were wobbly, and I took short tentative steps. When we got to where they wanted me, the blindfold was removed and Bobdog was hanging before me. Her hair had been roughly chopped away in large clumps like Harry's, and her face was painted a bright white. Her ears were tethered like Harry's had been and the side of her face was stained red. I was sick. It was hard to

HUNDRED WATERS

look at her that way. I took several steps toward her, but was immediately restrained, yanked back, then pushed down to the ground. I called out to her several times, and eventually she responded by raising her head, but even that seemed to take every bit of energy she had, and she couldn't hold it up for long.

I couldn't make a fist, but I lunged at the green, tattooed man anyway...screaming at him, but I was quickly pushed down again and held there by the back of my neck. Before I could say anything, I was blindfolded again and dragged some distance from where Bobdog hung and dropped in a hut that smelled heavily of wood smoke and rancid meat. The blindfold was left on, and my hands remained tied behind me. There were several *Cimarrone* voices, some were shouting and others chanting, and then I was pulled back and held down. Suddenly I felt tiny pinpricks over my body. I squirmed against them, not because they hurt, but out of fear of what they might be doing to me. I couldn't see anything. Then somebody pinched my nose; I gasped and suddenly there was liquid in my mouth, and I had to swallow. It was the bitter taste I had tasted before. I was released, and my heart raced again with fear. A cloth was quickly wrapped around my mouth. The voices faded away, and then a loud clear voice was in my ear.

"Eddie...Eddie," I heard Harry say in a hushed voice. "You must listen to me and not fight them."

I tried to talk through the gag, but couldn't.

"Listen, Eddie. Bobdog will not be going back. She must remain, for bringing you out here. That is the only way you leave. You will not remember most of this, but you will know it."

My head started to throb and pulsate like giant fists were pounding their way out from the inside of my skull. My thoughts kept darting away from what Harry was saying.

DAVID GREGOR

"Thank you for being a friend," I heard Harry say. "Goodbye."

I tried to speak, but I lost track of why. I felt something cold hung around my neck...something metallic clanked against my chest. Then my legs began to twitch uncontrollably and so did my arms. My whole body was in one big spasm, slapping wildly, my bound arms and legs flapping and jerking until I felt that I was going to fly apart. I tried to force myself to stop, but I couldn't. All I was aware of was my body bouncing violently, out of my control. Then with no warning, my body stopped jumping. There was murmuring...I couldn't tell whose...followed by a long cold shiver, and then everything went quiet and still and finally dark.

[Tepiyac remembrance. Recorded on a Sony cassette recorder. San Antonio, Texas, December 1998. Transcribed by David Gregor. (Editor's Note: I have taken the following title from a line found in Eddie's journal and employed it here.)]

"The End Where The Beginning Begins"

When I emerged from the Panamanian jungle after four days out, I thought I would never see Eddie again. Four of us had gone into the jungle in search of Harry Miles and only two of us came out. Malique, the young daughter of the policeman in the village of Nombre de Dios who had acted as our guide, saved my life. She led both of us out of the jungle when I thought for sure we were lost. We were both dehydrated, and I know I, at least, was totally disoriented. I had lost my shirt and was barefoot. I had no idea at the time exactly where I was. I just remember the voices I heard echoing inside my head. I can't even remember a word that Malique may have said after the first two or three hours of our return trip. We had left our campsite deep in the jungle in such a hurry that I didn't even grab my gear with our compass and the canteen. There was no time to be concerned about our belongings after we were attacked. I just followed Malique as she ran in the general direction we believed led to the coast. We were only concerned with getting out alive. We had been attacked in the middle of the night by a large group of indigenous Indians and rendered unconscious, for what could have been hours, by something in a rag held over our faces. It was still dark when I woke up and heard Malique crying not far from me. Eddie and his Panamanian girlfriend Bobdog were gone, but their gear was still under their lean-to. I remember going over and comforting Malique. She was crying and shivering, locked in a near fetal position on the ground. She was our only hope of getting out of the jungle, she was our way out. Without Malique's help, I would have been lost in that jungle, so I did everything I could think of to calm her down. After trying in vain to get her to respond to my questions, I gently wrapped my arms around her, pulled her close to me and began reciting nursery rhymes to her in Spanish. She eventually began talking to me. Both of us had been truly terrorized by those who had attacked us in the night, and we were not sure it was over. Part of me believed they were still out there, just out of sight, watching us, waiting for orders to grab us too. That's when Malique and I just got up and started running—when daylight broke—leaving everything of ours under our poncho in the middle of the jungle. Malique took the lead, and I just followed her without knowing for sure if she knew where she was going.

When I woke up two days later, I was alone in a bed on the porch of Malique's house. There were loud voices outside and in the adjoining room, but all I could make out were the words *gringo* and *otro Americano*. I sat up on the edge of the bed and tried to rub some clarity into my head. There was an incense coil burning next to the bed to deter the mosquitos. I heard a blur of women's voices.

When I heard what I thought was Eddie's voice through the din of Spanish, I stepped into the next room and saw a man with a white painted face and chest. His skin was

HUNDRED WATERS

caked with dirt, and he was wearing only a pair of torn pants. He was propped up in a bamboo chair. It was Eddie; he wasn't moving. I thought he was dead and that I had only imagined his voice. But then I saw his eyelids move...then his lips, and I remember falling to the floor.

The next thing I remember, Eddie and I were lying next to each other in a U.S. Army helicopter flying low over the jungle en route to what turned out to be the hospital at Fort Clayton. I recall at the time feeling truly blessed, even though I wasn't sure Eddie was going to live.

* * *

I was kept in the hospital for two days until I was rehydrated and strong enough to go back to work. The first day I came back to see Eddie in the hospital, I was challenged by an MP on duty at the foot of Eddie's bed. I had earlier obtained a clearance from our own S-2 security office so I could see my friend and help with his personal affairs.

Eddie was not a pretty sight. He was secured to his bed with a wide leather belt strapped across his chest, and he was tossing and turning like his bed was a red-hot griddle. He was soaking wet with perspiration and talking incoherently. I remember I went and got a nurse to come look at him, and when we finally got back, Eddie was lying perfectly still, asking the MP questions about something he thought was flying around outside the windows. After the nurse checked Eddie's restraints and the level of his i.v. bottle, she left. Eddie smiled at me and said something like, "The lizard works like this. Cross yourself, Tep, and come closer."

I listened to Eddie talk for fifteen or twenty minutes, mostly about things that made no sense to me. He rambled on about visions of the night, tattooed giants, and potions driven into his soul. Crazy rantings like that. All I could do

DAVID GREGOR

was nod, shake my head and make like I understood. Eddie was clearly not the same guy I had gone into the jungle with. Then the nurse returned to draw some blood, and I had to leave. Eddie motioned me over to him and whispered in my ear: "Bring me paper and pen. I need to remember what these creatures have done to me. Please, don't forget me."

We had less than three months left on our tour of duty, and I wanted to do anything that would help Eddie get better and out of country on schedule. Over the next three weeks, I brought Eddie four to five hundred sheets of paper and took out as much in sealed envelopes he asked me to put in his footlocker. It is in those pages I smuggled out of the hospital past the M.P.s, that Eddie laid out what appear to be his deepest fears and in some cases, his most intense feelings.

[End Tepiyac recording.]

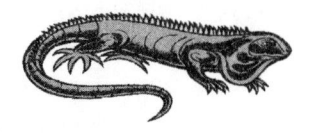

Carr, *JOURNAL*. [Fever Ward. Penthouse. Tomorrow.]

    Sometimes I have the feeling things are happening to me with a design of their own. It is the dry season, and I can smell the mold growing somewhere nearby. The ward is near full, but it is me they come to see. First the doctors, then the nurses, the candy-stripes, the Panamanian orderlies, and finally the boys from S-2. Nothing must get out...no one must know...there must be answers. And I'm their source. It is me Intelligence has come for, it is what I know they are after. My dilemma is knowing the truth. It is near dusk and there are a lot of them circling just above the jungle now. Something has happened out there. Or is it in here? Hard to tell anymore. Something has always happened when they are around. It reminds me of another place.
    Somewhere out there, out in that lush tropical Beyond...just beyond these hospital walls, the Tattooed Lizard chants my name over the open fire. He chants into the eyes of Harry Miles who stares back across the fire...out into the dark with the vacant stare of one who has lost something old. It's so clear, so dark, and I'm so lost until this morning light creases my room...spots the guard, and splashes bright the sky. The black marks return for the nineteenth morning to fill the sky-blue sky as I shake with freezing chills in this tropical Hell only to burn...burn like the Lizard's fire and sweat like a

whore from the inside out and I see flames in the eyes of the Tattooed Lizard and I know he is in me...somewhere ...somehow like he is in the flesh of the dead.

And the black marks circle out there...swelling large, multiplying then shrinking, and I dwell on them...keeping score...giving them names...names of the important—Tepi...Harry...Bobdog. The dreams...and the black marks moving out there overhead are my life...growing, becoming, threatening, shrinking then coming and going like the good days...the days when I cared, days when I wanted more than just another yesterday.

This fever saps you and works on you from the inside like a motive...like fear...no matter what name it travels by...be it yellow jack, American Plague, the unknown virus, miasma, the shakes, putrid fever, Chagres Fever, voodoo...I call it retribution, the penalty for cowardice unbecoming a man. Fear of the unknown. Those black marks in the sky which to ponder are like pondering infinity, because just as you start to get close, something else appears...something beyond...the jungle Beyond...that intoxicating lush Beyond just below the black marks circling, returning, as though Sirens beckoned because everything here comes back to the jungle. There is no escape for me. The jungle is the maker and the breaker. It feeds you or it kills you and the black marks circling overhead keep score. Harry Miles told me that when I last saw him...deep in the jungle, lying next to the night fire across from the Tattooed Lizard. Harry Miles was the truth the way the War was the truth that each of us needed to find inside and God knows I asked for it...I begged for the truth and they gave me this rancid hole that tastes of sweet Jamaican rum, iguana tongue and the sweat beads on Bobdog's neck. Bobdog my savior and my downfall. Bobdog my direction home. God help me and the others!

HUNDRED WATERS

* * *

Carr, MANUSCRIPT. Typewritten. The words: "The Return" are written in ink across the first page.

The point at which I realized I was fully conscious was when I woke up in a hospital bed at Fort Clayton, answering questions from two S-2 officers.

"Before you say anything, Carr," the taller lieutenant said, "let me secure this room."

I had no answers for the S-2 boys in spite of the fact that I knew I had knowledge of so many important things. I just could not straighten out my thoughts or articulate them. I felt like I was a prisoner of my own words, unable to release things inside me that I knew were important. Thoughts that began with the name, Bobdog.

* * *

Carr, *Journal*. Fort Clayton Hospital.

Two officers from S-2 just left. Lt. Woodruff wanted to know about things from the beginning. He said I was being evasive...trying to hide things. I have nothing to hide really. The problem is there are too many beginnings.

I keep looking out my screened window for Tepi. I need a friendly face. I miss Bobdog. It would be good to see Harry again...hear his voice. I can see the jungle just off at the edge of the hospital grounds, and just above the canopy the dark marks moving in the sky. There are a lot of them circling just above the treetops. Something's happened out there. Something's always happened when they're around. It reminds me of a beginning.

* * *

DAVID GREGOR

Carr, MANUSCRIPT.

I remember asking about Tepi, and then I remember calling out Harry's name repeatedly. One moment I could see Harry Miles through the firelight...see his lips moving, then the next thing I knew my wrists and ankles were being secured to the bed frame with heavy leather straps.

My gown was soaking wet, and I was shivering uncontrollably. Through the screened windows I could see the sun shining bright, and still I shivered. There was an M.P. standing at parade rest next to the wall staring at me. I remember trying to speak to him, but I couldn't get the words out of my mouth because my jaw muscles were contracting so violently with spasms that I had no coordination between my mouth and my voice.

Sometime later, Tepi arrived while it was still light outside. He pulled up a chair next to the bed and shook my hand. His hand felt like ice...or maybe it was *my* hand that was cold. I couldn't tell, and I couldn't stop shivering. Tepi pulled a blanket off another bed and draped it over me, tucking in the edges and pulling it high up under my chin.

The shakes continued, and I still couldn't speak. I could feel my mouth move, but there was no sound...no words, just thoughts. But I could hear Tepi speaking to me. At the time I understood each word he spoke, but as soon as I heard the word and tried to remember it, I lost it for the next word. It was as frustrating as when I was first learning Morse code at Fort Devins, consciously focusing on hearing individual words or letters at the expense of the next sound, so that before long I was totally lost in only the sound of the moment.

Tepi left shortly after dark. He waved and smiled at me before slipping away through the curtain around my bed. My arms were still secured with the straps.

HUNDRED WATERS

Later that night the nurses brought more hot water bottles and laid them against my back and legs. They warmed those parts of me for awhile. There was a different M.P. watching me when I finally fell asleep. He did not have the face of someone I wanted to know.

* * *

Carr, *JOURNAL*. March 12, 1969.

The one single question that hangs heavy on my sanity is the question of "ME." Sweat pours from me like a sieve. All day long I get weaker and weaker, and I feel myself getting smaller. I have no inner mass. I'm impotent. I'm disappearing.

* * *

Carr, MANUSCRIPT.

By the next morning the shivering had passed, and I ate a big breakfast. I was exhausted even before the officers from S-2 returned. They had more questions or, I found out later, the same questions just repeated over and over. Tepi sat in a chair near the M.P. at the curtain. It was good to see him. I felt safer when Tepi was in the room.

* * *

Carr, *JOURNAL*. March 13, 1969.

They want to know so much, and I have so little to say. Besides, I've already told them the truth, but they want something else. And they leave that damn guard over there. They're afraid I'll spill the beans on something secret, but— hell—I don't have any secrets. A secret involves something of value. All I had was a desire to find Harry, and I made no secret of that. What the hell else could I know? They don't believe me about Harry. I can tell by all their questions. Hell, I'm not even sure I believe what I know about Harry. I can hear their S-2 whispers, clear and simple: 'Evaporate him! You heard me, disintegrate the son of a bitch.' It could be the fever. So many things are. But either way, I'll try to save myself. I'll confess. Harry's one of them.

* * *

Carr, MANUSCRIPT.

    For the second time since I had woken up in the hospital, I thought of Harry Miles and Bobdog, and my last memories of them made me sad.

S-2:   "Specialist...what can you tell us about Specialist 4th Class Harry Miles?"

"He was a friend of mine."

S-2:   "What about his whereabouts?"

"His whereabouts?"

S-2:   "Correct. Do you know where he is?"

I looked over at Tepi. "Harry Miles is dead, sir."

S-2:   The two young officers from S-2 looked at each other. "You're certain of that?" the shorter lieutenant asked.

"Yes, sir. Harry Miles is dead, and I killed him."

S-2:   "You did what?"

"I killed Harry Miles."

S-2:   "How did you do that, soldier?"

"I went to save him, but I failed."

S-2:   "You know for a fact that Miles is dead?" the taller lieutenant asked. I nodded.

S-2:   "Did you personally see him?"

"Yes sir, I saw him."

S-2:   "Do you have any proof?" the taller lieutenant asked.

HUNDRED WATERS

"Harry Miles is dead."

S-2: "We need verification that he is dead," said the shorter lieutenant.

S-2: "Where was it that you saw Miles, Carr?"

"In the jungle."

S-2: "Can you be more specific?"

"No sir. I don't know where I was. Just *that* I was."

S-2: "Was what, Carr?"

"Was where I was. That's what I know."

S-2: "But you know for a fact that Specialist Miles is dead?"

"Yes sir."

S-2: "We need some kind of proof. Especially for the next of kin."

I looked over at Tepi again, and then I slowly reached inside my hospital gown and pulled out my dog tags. There was a second set of tags...the ones that someone had slipped over my neck that night in the *Cimarrone* village. I held Harry's tags out in front of me. The taller S-2 lieutenant saw the tags and leaned forward. He saw the name and sat back in his chair.

S-2: "We'll need to have that," he said.

S-2: "Could you determine cause of death?" the shorter one asked.

I thought about it for a moment. "Exposure."

S-2: "Exposure...like what?"

"Like the elements. He died from the elements."

S-2: "Elements like water? Did Miles drown?"

I thought immediately of our little trip down the Chagres and how ridiculous it would be for Harry to have drowned in the jungle. I shook my head.

S-2: "Did you ever see him alive?"

"Yes, sir."

S-2: "Did he ever say anything in your presence...give you any information?"

"He was dying, sir."
S-2: "But he did speak to you while he was alive?"
"Yes sir, but he was dying."
S-2: "He said nothing at all? Nothing that would indicate a compromise in security?"
"He was dying, sir. He compromised nothing."

I started shivering again, and before long I was unable speak. The nurse came in shortly after I heard Tepi call out onto the ward for help, and she quickly asked people to leave. I was sorry to see Tepi go. I liked it that he smiled and waved on his way out. Tepi was a good friend.

* * *

Over the next few days, the officers from S-2 returned with more questions about where we had been, what we had seen and what I remembered about those who supposedly abducted me and Bobdog. They wanted precise locations, exact distances, and the names of any nationals we had contacted. But they provided no information concerning my inquiries about Bobdog. Their only response was to state the obvious.

S-2: "Only you and Specialist Tepiyac were evacuated from the village of Nombre de Dios."
"No one else?" I asked.
S-2: "No one."
"Are you certain?" I asked.
S-2: "There was only one other person mentioned in the written report."
"Who?"
S-2: "Seems a boatman from Portobello informed us that two American soldiers still owed him money for a canoe trip."

Later, Tepi told me it was the policeman Señor Huertas who had made the call to U.S. Army authorities in Colon that

HUNDRED WATERS

two Americans were in need of medical attention. He also said I was found alone on the edge of the village in a confused state, two days after Tepi and Malique returned.

* * *

Carr, *JOURNAL*, entry 29. March 27, 1969.

It is now twenty-five days of sweats and the fever fires still burn through my blood. I have very little left. This pencil is beginning to feel like a log. It's all I can do to raise my arm or my leg when the nurse needs to remove my gown. I can still hear the slap my sweat-soaked gown made hitting the floor. The nurse's aim is off. She's having a bad day. I'm having a bad life. Nobody knows what's got me, and that scares me. People die all the time here from things nobody knows about. Yellow fever, malaria, fevers of all kinds. I'm too young to die. Maybe that tattooed Indian really got me. He said he could. The inquisitors from S-2 are due back with more questions. Every session with them is exhausting. They think I have answers, but deep down I don't even have a clue. There is a finality that needs adjustment to save me. Faces and places elude my touch, but I can see before me there is the cold-eyed nude wired for display and she loves me. My God what a word in this heartless place. My shadow is shackled to this breadcrumb genie, Bobdog...my mind tethered to this enchanted circus around me. Hell, I'm not even sure why I bother to write this down. It must be those sounds of a life I hear...echoing back months ago when I was still very much me or what used to be me...no!...what I was becoming...yes!...when I was becoming me! How did all this happen? Why am I being interrogated? How could things get this screwed up? It begins with what was then the end of the end which is the beginning of so much....

DAVID GREGOR

* * *

Carr, MANUSCRIPT.

When I was finally released from the hospital and sent back to work to finish off the last two months of my tour, the operations building was never quite the same. Tepi was transferred to a new position in another room, and Harry Miles was gone. I was at a personal loss without Harry. He was a man of incredible resourcefulness, great conviction and enormous loyalty. He was someone I felt I could still learn many things from. I can say the same about Bobdog. Though they probably never really knew it, Harry and Bobdog were responsible for saving my life...in more ways than one. I have no idea what was ever said or done by them on my behalf out there in the jungle. I only know that to have known both Harry Miles and Bobdog saved my life. And that is enough.

* * *

Two weeks later, on our first day off from work, I talked Tepi into taking the train with me across the isthmus to Colon to act as my interpreter when I went to the address Bobdog had given me for her aunt, that last night in Nombre de Dios.

When our taxi pulled up I remembered the building even though I had only seen it the one time. Tepi told the taxi driver to wait, and we walked across the dirt yard. Bobdog's aunt came to the door, and I asked Tepi to ask her if Señorita Bobadilla was at home. The large woman pinched her lips tightly and shook her head, and I knew without her ever saying anything more what that expression meant. As Tepi explained to the woman that we had also come to see the boy Raul, the woman's eyes swelled up with tears and she began crying.

"Ask her what happened," I said to Tepi. "Ask her why she's crying."

Tepi stepped up closer to the woman and in a quiet, deliberate tone spoke directly to her. He nodded several times and then winced, and I knew something bad had happened.

"Raul is gone," Tepi said.

"Where?"

"She doesn't know. She put him to bed one night and in the morning he was gone."

"When was this?"

"About a month ago. About the time we came out of the jungle."

"Oh Jesus."

"I asked her if she had any idea what had happened or who might have taken the boy, but you saw the look on her face. She's scared."

"No note...no visits from strangers?" I asked.

"Nothing. She put him to bed, and she has not seen him since."

"She knows," I said.

"Sure she knows, but she'll never say. But you can hear it in her voice and see it in her eyes. She knows alright."

"And nothing was done...I mean by the police or the government?"

"You know the answer to that."

I looked at Bobdog's aunt and the devastated expression on her face, and I knew she felt we were responsible for what had happened to Bobdog and Raul. And inside I believed it too, which made it hard for me to stand there and look at her knowing how painful it was for her to no longer have either of them in her life.

I told Tepi to tell her how sorry I was that Bobdog and Raul were gone, but even as he spoke, I could see in her face that it made no difference. Tepi offered his condolences and asked permission to call her before we left Panama, just to see if either Bobdog or Raul ever returned. But she told Tepi not to call or come back. There are those with a thousand eyes, she said, and she had already lost enough. With that, we said goodbye and had the taxi driver take us back to the train station in Colon.

* * *

During the train ride back, neither Tepi nor I said much to each other. Bobdog's aunt had said everything that needed to be said, and it didn't leave either of us feeling like talking much. We knew this one had turned out wrong, and some innocent people had gotten hurt and others had their lives forever changed.

As we made our way over the bridges that span Gatun Lake, the small billowy clouds overhead were reflected on the smooth, mirror-like surface of the canal. I found myself staring at the thick vegetation that came right down to the water's edge. It was like the foliage on the far shore was a door... and the only visible point of entrance back into the heart of the jungle was between the clouds in the sky and those reflected off the water—the real and the imaginary.

I wondered who was watching this train and the ships that made their way across the isthmus. I wondered why I was riding in this train car still alive and free. I thought about Bobdog... how much she wanted to be free...how she chased me naked with a fork because she felt I did not appreciate my freedom...and how much I missed her already. And I missed Harry Miles and all the things I would never hear him say or ever learn from him. I remembered how angry I was when I arrived in Panama, how much I hated being here and how badly I wanted to go to the war so I wouldn't miss out. I remembered the blue crabs coming out of their holes that year by the thousands and moving like lemmings only to be crushed into the dirt like so much neon dust. I thought about the Hitler message I had accidentally stumbled across and tried to put it into a perspective I could make sense of...trying to imagine how it could be true, knowing very well that I had heard it, that I had seen it being formed into words before my very eyes...wondering what it could possibly mean. But I failed. Then tripping over the transmission from one of Che Guevara's lost revolutionaries back in the hills of Bolivia, and months later seeing the letters of his name tattooed on the green neck of a *Cimarrone*.

As we clipped along the clacking rails of the Panama Railway, I stared back into the jungle and tried to imagine Harry Miles, or the man I had once known as Harry Miles, living back there...living the life he believed was important...meaningful...fighting for those with a cause that he honestly believed in. It was not my belief, but then I was not living back there in the darkness of the jungle. It was clear to me that I had a belief of my own to discover, but it did not lessen my sense of loss for two people who had become very important to me.

* * *

Carr, *JOURNAL*. May 17, 1969.

Panama begins and ends in me. There is no boundary—imaginary or real—separating us. We are one now. From day one, my first breath here saw to that. The air is that infectious. I have since found the intoxication that has taken me into the deep corners of this place, and I know I have not experienced enough. Perhaps the only regrettable things are those not spoken...the unexpressed. But I have screamed, vomited and sweated myself hoarse. My only peace rests on saying it all. No wonder I am here. To bring it all to silence...when it will all be over.

* * *

Carr, MANUSCRIPT.

I turned to Tepi across from me on the train and smiled at his large ears.

"What?" Tepi said.

"Nothing. I just wish you were coming to Thailand, Tep. It would be good to spend another year with you."

"Believe me," he said, "I feel the same way."

"If I could trade places with you, you know I would."

"It makes no sense, does it? You want to go to the war, and they send me instead. Angela was counting on me getting stationed stateside, maybe even Texas."

"You'll be fine," I said. "Hell...you encountered the *Cimarrones* and lived to tell about it."

Without thinking, we both turned and checked the empty seats around us, and Tepi crossed himself. "Right," he whispered, "but who's going to believe me?"

"Doesn't really matter," I said. "You know it, and that's got to be better than a pocketful of rabbits' feet. Trust me. The bad guys don't have a chance against you. Besides, you've known Harry Miles."

Tepi smiled when I mentioned Harry's name, and for just a moment, I think a small part of him honestly believed he was blessed. I felt it too. And sometimes that's all it really takes. A part of me wanted to believe that maybe we were all a little better off for having known Harry Miles. Based on what had happened with me out there in that place called Hundred Waters, I have to believe Harry knew that. I knew I was better for having loved Bobdog. And I think Bobdog knew all too well the possible implications of her helping us; perhaps it was her way of gaining a freedom that was not possible in the world in which she had been living. I'm not sure. I would like to think she and her son Raul were okay and that life would be good to them, the way Bobdog had been good to me. It would be a terrible waste...an empty sacrifice...if it were not so.

* * *

Carr. *JOURNAL*. Dated: *Final.* Written in what appears to be orange crayon in an erratic hand.

What I remember about Harry is that he put his hide on the wall...looked into the dark...took a chance to be himself. Last words I remember: "I am like the one who sought the desperate situation and then stared at life and all its little deaths. When death is hungry, I expect no mercy and I regret nothing." Life opened its eyes on Harry...like the yellow gaze of the tattooed one...like a growl heard in the dark. I know what inspires...when it is there...right in front of you. Her name is Bobdog. Alchemy has her own rules...Harry Miles is still here and Bobdog lives.

[End of Journal entry]

DAVID GREGOR

* * *

[Editor's note:]

When I last spoke with Joseph and Thelma Carr in the fall of 1997, they confirmed that Eddie had returned to Panama in the winter of 1971, several months after he was finally discharged from the army. They received several letters and Christmas cards over the next few years postmarked Colon and Panama City, but Eddie has not yet returned to the Northwest. According to his parents, Eddie is still looking for someone or something he lost when he was stationed in the Canal Zone. They hope he will be home soon.